a   novel

The Naomiverse

Book 1

MORE BY J.D. Brown

<u>The Naomiverse</u>

Naomi Shane's The Cabin: Wayward

Naomi Shane's The Cabin: Rancor (*coming soon*)

DEDICATIONS

To James (Dad)

There is nothing I can do to repay you for your help with this trilogy project; they're forever cherished memories! No writer writes by themselves, and I wouldn't change that truth, nor this writing experience, for anything! Thank you for sharing your trilogy with me!

To Sam

As editors go, I was beyond lucky to find you, and your skills give this trilogy the edge it needed! I can't wait to work more with you in the very near future!

TABLE OF CONTENTS

by J. D. Brown

Way·ward (wāwərd) *adjective*

difficult to control or predict because of unusual or perverse behavior

PROLOGUE

My name is Naomi Shane. This Prologue is my story; a prelude to these books, if you will. I honestly don't know how many I'll write, but I'm starting here. As I write this Prologue, today is **June 30th, 2022**.

I am a part of these books, more than I ever thought I was, and definitely more than I should be, but in all, *Wayward* is not my story. However, it is my responsibility to tell it. Though it is not my story, these books are my books, and more than that, they've become my therapy.

I've never written anything before, so please bear with me, and forgive me. (You'll understand my apology later.) I'm telling my story first for several reasons, all of which I'll explain with this Prologue, other Prologues, and all the Epilogues. I'll try to keep them all short.

So, allow me to begin.

I was born in 1996; I'm 26 years old. My upbringing gave me a happy childhood, with a sister, two years older than me, to learn from. Our family was very loving. Our Dad loved technology; our mom loved nature. They both loved to travel. We lived in Montana, and where we lived, we always had a view of Garfield Mountain.

In 2002, when I was 6 years old, we all took a vacation trip with the RV to Utah to visit Arches National Park. I'm not sure what exactly happened to cause our detour, but we got caught in heavy rain and stopped at an RV rest area. I remember it was a humongous stone lot in the shape of a circle. There were many other stranded RVs there.

I was infatuated with the Internet, even at a very young age, and our RV had Wi-Fi, thanks to my dad. I was a tech kid, and my sister was a nature girl. I was Daddy's girl, and my sister and Mom were very alike. When the rain stopped, my mom and sister went to the surrounding woods to explore. I was finding online alternate routes with my dad due to the rain and reports of mudslides. I'm sure he knew what he was doing, but he was probably just humoring me. When they came back, my sister, who was only 8, was badly shaken up.

As I overheard them all talking, I started online searches, using their spoken words, on my tablet. My father took my tablet shortly after and saw the disturbing online results. There were so many [missing persons] reports in the area and surrounding counties, and most of them originated where we were. Needless to say, the discovery didn't help the situation.

Shortly later that day, before the sun went down, I became extremely ill and was put to bed in my RV bunk after some medicine and soup. When I woke up, I was alone, it was night, and it was dark inside the RV. It was raining. My parents and my sister were gone. My stomach hurt, I was hungry, and I was alone. (Do not judge my parents too harshly. I doubt they expected to be gone long.) I don't remember how much longer later, but someone beat on the RV door, screaming to be let in. It was my sister.

She was still in her clothes, soaked from rain, and covered in tree debris and her boots were muddy. I remember her being cold, crying, and shaking so badly. I gave her my blanket and we cuddled in the bunk. I don't remember much about how it happened, but I remember the police came and got us. Our parents were never found, and my sister refused to tell me what happened.

Shortly after, we were placed in separate foster homes back in Montana. We had no aunts or uncles, and no living grandparents. I learned years later that my sister was an obedient foster child. I was not. Our parents were stripped from us, we were separated, and my world was upside down.

From age 6 to my early teens, I was transferred to, removed from, partially abused in, and retaliated against over twenty foster homes, no matter how mean or nice they were. I remember one school and kindergarten; that was it. I made it my intention to intentionally hate every foster home I was in until I was reunited with my sister.

That reunion never happened.

By 13, I had run away well over two dozen times and crossed over nine different counties. I was stealing everything from food to clothes. I even used the Internet to steal money and gain access to rental cars; anything to get away and find my sister. I was never allowed to know where my sister was. Even with my knowledge of retrieving Internet information, her existence was muted. I realized if I couldn't find her, I thought the news reports and broadcasts of my lawbreaking would reach her. Maybe she'd reach out and find me.

That reach-out never happened either.

By 15, I was considered a delinquent in the eyes of the law, a thorn in the face of society, and labeled a lost cause. I had never murdered, killed, maimed, or harmed anyone physically, and the authorities knew our tragedy, but my behavior made Juvenile Hall inevitable.

I was just about to turn 16 and was in light of the threat of juvie. The final time I was caught, the judge ordered one action: a meeting between myself and my sister. My sister was eighteen and a legal adult in the eyes of society.

I was handcuffed in a courtroom when I saw her for the first time in eleven years. Before any verbal greeting, before any emotional bonding, before any terms of endearment were expressed, I got loose from my restraints, removed a Swiss Army knife I saw bulged in a cop's pocket, leapt at and pinned down my sister.

I screamed in her face with the open blade at her throat, "WHAT HAPPENED TO OUR PARENTS!? YOU WERE THERE! *TELL ME!*"

I was immediately detained, but my sister surprisingly denied all charges against me and only wished for me to be committed. No jail or prison time. She spoke not a single word to me.

From ages 15 to 18, I was sentenced and sent to Utah's M.I.M.I.C.: the Mental Institute of Manic Intervention & Control. That was where I went into submission. I gave up and shut the world out. I never heard from anyone I knew or anyone I was remotely related to. Therapy was useless because I refused to speak. I wanted to know nothing: personal or worldly. I was never suicidal; I just simply shut off. To this day, I don't know why I exploded in the courtroom.

Radios and televisions were always playing, but like my voice, I muted them out. The world to me was null. I followed directions from the staff, but never verbally acknowledged anyone. I simply placed myself in a mental solitaire and submitted. I was free to leave, under probation of course, after I turned 18 in 2016, but I didn't leave. I stayed. I was in a walking coma, voluntarily isolated from all outside life.

I stayed confined, detached from the world…until New Year's Day, January 2022, just a few months ago.

A thin, young black man around my age came to visit me specifically, by name. His name was Quinton Cay. I refused any interaction with anyone; M.I.M.I.C. staff and patients alike. All tried, all failed.

Down the hall that day, his voice echoed straight into my ears, and I heard various words that poked my brain like a boney finger of an angry Irish grandmother: 'my mother's name', 'my father's name', 'my sister's name', 'Utah', '2002', 'Wasatch Mountains', 'missing', and 'proof'.

I poked my head out from my door and spoke my first words in eight years, "Let him in."

Every day in January, for two hours a day, Quinton visited me 31 days straight. Quinton knew everything about me, from my birth records to my confinement at M.I.M.I.C., and he had the files to prove it. He even had my kindergarten yearbook at Mastodon Elementary in Montana, during my first foster home stay. It was his yearbook, and we were in the same class. I had no memory of him, the classmates, the teachers; they were all erased mentally.

Over the next few weeks, Quinton showed me more files. They were the [missing persons] cases in Utah near the Wasatch Mountains; my parents included. Then my police reports, foster care files, and disciplinary documents from various county courts. He admitted that it was his life's mission to find me and get my answers. Quinton had not only my records but my sisters' records as well, all the way from elementary school report cards to her most recent dentist appointment x-rays. A frilly little paper mixed in the pile made my heart skip a beat: she and her fiancé were to be married that February, with their twin children.

I'm...an aunt, my smiling heart thought. Quinton quickly informed me there were problems in the marriage, either due to her not re-enlisting in the U.S. Navy or, more realistically, because the twins were his with a woman he was seeing while my sister was fighting in Afghanistan.

"The babies were left on the doorstep of their home for him to raise," Quinton said. "They're three years old now." *So, I'm not an aunt...*I sadly thought.

It was terrifying how much he knew, and yet, I was impressed by his research. But sadly, he didn't have the one thing I needed with all my heart to know: what happened to my parents and why didn't my sister ever tell me. Without realizing it, Quinton became my only friend, my therapist, my counsel, and my re-entry into the world.

On January 31st, 2022, I left M.I.M.I.C. with Quinton Cay and one hundred and fifty thousand dollars in cash of M.I.M.I.C.'s funding. Not only did Quinton have information on me, and my family, but also had information on M.I.M.I.C.'s financial wrongdoings and unethical behavioral practices. He traded his physical evidence and things called 'flash drives' for the cash. Quinton also told them to shred all the documentation they had on me and his documentation on me that he had, then watched them do it before we left.

I was in M.I.M.I.C. from 2014 until 2022; I never saw a thing. Then again, I blocked everything out. Quinton and I left M.I.M.I.C. in a rental car and drove to a small town just over the Utah/Idaho border. During the one-hour drive, Quinton confessed that the trade was the only way to get the money needed to get his life on track and to help restart my life, and he needed me to pull the whole thing off. At the same time, in the same breath, he also said since my disappearance from Mastodon Elementary, he was empty and became obsessed with my disappearance. I learned he had an adopted white sister who looked just like me, but one year younger. She died before school started that year, so when he saw me in school, it was as if she never left his sight. Then I abruptly disappeared, never to be seen in any school ever again. It crushed him.

(Side inquiry: Should Quinton have been in M.I.M.I.C. as a patient? I've often thought about it…)

Quinton paid a flower shop owner cash to rent an apartment over the store. The man did and we had a place. The only thing we had was the cash in a Utah Utes football gym bag and his files on the [missing persons] cases around the Wasatch Mountains, as well as the clothes on our backs. When we left M.I.M.I.C., I wore a pair of gray gym sweatpants, a gray hoodie without tassels, and gray slippers. We talked about clothes shopping and binging on Chinese food while watching something called 'The Office' after we got a place to sleep.

A half-hour later, after getting the apartment over the flower shop, Quinton left on foot to go find the closest Chinese restaurant. He left me with the gym bag of cash and the files. I watched him out the bay window as he exited the building. He looked up at me when he did with a smile of *Hey, we made it*. I think…I fell in love with him right there at that glance. Quinton ran to the intersection corner, hit a button on the pole, and stood waiting for the traffic light to change. The car was just a half block over.

I watched the light turn from green to red. I watched Quinton look both ways before he stepped out onto the street. The three people on the other side of the sidewalk did too. I saw the school bus as it tried to beat the red light. Then, I watched the three people leap back as the school bus struck Quinton. It struck him and drove over his body with just the front passenger-side tire. It all happened in four seconds.

The police came. Ambulances came. The bus driver was arrested for intoxication, I later learned. Quinton was put in a black body bag. Reports were made and two hours later, life in the intersection continued as if nothing happened. I was never asked a thing, nor did I leave the apartment. When all the authorities left, the flower shop owner knocked on the door. I didn't open it; it was locked.

"He had no wallet on him and no I.D. cards. He told me his name was Quinton Cay, but he never signed the lease. I didn't have one printed out; I was going to do that after the shop closed. I'm slipping his money under the door to you. I want you out by seven in the morning. I'm sorry, but I don't want any trouble. You have my condolences on your friend or brother, or whoever he was," was all he said and simply walked away.

I left just before six that next morning, without a sound and didn't see a soul. I left the cash that was under the door, but I took the gym bag of cash, Quinton's files, and stole a parked car outside a bar down the block. The keys were in the ignition, and it was unlocked, so…I drove.

For the next few weeks, I rekindled with my old friend, the Internet, and found it even more addicting, more useful, and more frightening than I ever thought possible. I found practically anything about anyone without even trying; and yet, nothing on my parents or the [missing persons] cases, which were all still unsolved.

It's right here where my story needs to pause, and the Prologue needs to end. Again, *Wayward* is not my story, but it's a story that I'm responsible for telling. This book is called *Wayward,* for good reasons, and is broken into sections: Prologue, Origin, Warning, Outside, Inside, Underground, Everywhere, and the Epilogue.

The Origin section is the official start of these books, not just *Wayward.* It's a tiny sliver of Quinton's research, which I discovered is vital to the entire story. I read Quinton's full research repeatedly and didn't understand why Quinton researched it, but now—

Anyway, you'll soon understand its importance.

One final time: this Prologue is my story. *Wayward* is not my story, but it's a story that needs to be told…because of all of those who only exist on [missing persons] reports.

And, please, again, <u>forgive me</u>…

ORIGIN

1

April. 1846. Spring. **[Quinton's notes, edited.]**

A wagon train of less than twenty members, that would grow substantially in a few months, began its westward journey from Illinois to California along the Oregon Trail. In Wyoming, the wagon train takes an alternative route by leaving the Oregon Trail in hopes of reaching California a month early. It's this change that jeopardizes the entire wagon train.

By early November, seven months later, the wagon train reached the slopes of the Sierra Nevada, only to be grounded by heavy snowfall, nil food and water rations, and the loss of many cattle and wagons. Divisions of the wagon train quickly formed, for various members had conflicting ways and ideas of surviving the winter's harshness. Various groups continued on foot and others found shelters; both situations had disastrous outcomes.

Stationary wagon trainers would cook their animals, boil animal hides into pastes, and even gnaw on leftover bones. Others would end up, in desperation, resulting in the last line of survival: cannibalism. Several died from malnutrition; resorting to eating human flesh was done discreetly by half of the survivors.

Almost a year into the journey, mid-February through late March of 1847, the relief parties rescued the wagon train, with less than half of its greatest number of participants. This historical story is one of the most famous documented historical references to humankind's will to survive the bitterness of the wilderness when all other options were lost.

History will recall this as the Donner-Reed Party wagon train.

Early August. 1846. Summer. **[Quinton's notes, edited.]**

A small division had broken off from the wagon train in the middle of the night. Exhausted from the haul, beaten down by the distrust of the wagon train's leaders, and fearful of not surviving the rest of the journey, the small group of seven made the conscious decision to take their fate into their own hands. With one wagon, one thin ox, and just a handful of perishables that they all collaborated on, the seven escaped the wagon party's fate.

Of the group were three men and four women. The three men were ages 17, 22, and 25. Of the three men, the two men in their twenties were brothers.

The four women, none of which were related by blood, were ages 17, 20, 21, and 53. The four women bonded early in the trail after the men in their families were murdered during a one-night raid one week before joining the wagon train.

The seven disregarded California and staked land east in Utah's Wasatch Mountain region by fifty miles as the Donner-Reed Party continued on through Utah and Nevada. The small group of seven sheltered in an abandoned cabin in the forest patches of the Wasatch Mountains well before the Donner-Reed Party was able to see the Great Salt Lake.

But the darkness of primal survival was not something easily escapable. The group did not escape the bitter harshness of the same surprise blizzard that would trap the Donner-Reed Party in the Sierra Nevada. Nor did it save them from many of the same desperate actions. However, they did know that they had better chances of surviving the winter on their own.

With a coniferous forest biome to protect from the arctic air masses and various wildlife to free roam the countryside, it would seem the landmass would be ideal to settle, but food was scarce, and water was almost non-existent. The eldest of the group, the 53-year-old, laid down her own life to give the rest the chance to survive. Her sacrifice was enough for the remaining six to survive till spring, as well as additional survival tactics, such as game hunting, conservations, and the purest strength of will. The ox was kept alive as best as possible.

All six distinguished their documented names and began new lives as mountain folk under new identities. As the seasons changed into 1847, the group's lives in the mountain forest flourished, as well as the once-weak ox. In July, the summer of 1847, the six agreed to split into two individual families on the same mountain range.

Each of the three men took a wife, as bonding took place over the months. The 17-year-olds both adapted together moreover personal survival traits and skills rather than love and feelings, not to say there wasn't something there to grow on.

The two brothers separated to individually regrow the family.

The 22-year-old brother took the 20-year-old woman as a wife.

The 25-year-old brother took the 21-year-old woman.

The 17-year-olds left with the older brother and his wife, along with the wagon and the ox as a gift. The younger couple in their twenties stayed at the abandoned cabin, claiming it as their own.

Each of the three marriages continued, with family descendants living to this day. The group of seven that took their fate into their own hands prospered greater than ever expected.

(Personal Side Inquiry) Quinton's notes mention, in detail, each of the seven names. Not just the names they changed, but also their original documented names. And yes, the men who were kin to the four women were murdered before joining the Donner-Reed wagon train.

I decided to remove all of the literal, historically documented names for this book, the living and the dead.

3

Late August. 1846. **[Quinton's notes, edited.]**

Three months before the blizzard that would change the fate of the Donner-Reed Party, three individuals were banished by the wagon train's leader. They were falsely accused of stealing rations and supposedly attempting to steal two sick oxen. The three individuals, a woman and two men, were left to die at the bottom of the mountain as their wagon, rations, clothing, and all other goods were taken from them. Abandoned as punishment, these three were never seen, nor heard from again. Later fraudulently documented as 'deceased', their remains and whereabouts were never discovered or recovered. No rescue attempts ever took place.

(Personal Side Inquiry) I seriously do not know how Quinton discovered this specific information about these three individuals. Truthfully, apart from the rescue parties of the time who found the Donner-Reed party, how ANY documentation was recorded, kept, and found accurate is beyond me. Then again, I'm not a historian and I'm not a researcher, but how Quinton obtained this information about these three specific individuals…kind of…scares me.

It forces me to wonder: What *else* did Quinton have about me in those files of his that he gave to M.I.M.I.C. to destroy, and stayed to watch them destroy it…?

WARNING

1

Mid-June. 2022. Summer.

It was a very warm summer afternoon, even in the shade of the trees. The sun seemed to set quickly on the eastern side of Utah's Wasatch Mountains that day.

An 18-year-old son sat beside his middle-aged father in the dark green hunting truck. They drove toward their mountainside home up a stone jeep trail. Knowing the mountain paths like the back of his hand, the father cut the wheel and drove into the forest, directly up a hidden path. The path was all high grass and was only used by the family and some wandering wildlife.

"They're getting smarter, Dad," the son stated as he looked out his door's window.

"They've always been smart; they adapt. That's how they've survived so long," the father answered. The dad took his eyes off the path and quickly glanced at his son. The teenage son was looking out the edge of the window with a hard stare. His elbow was on the door's armrest and his chin rested on two fingers. In frustration, the boy smacked the armrest with a flat hand.

The teenager belted out loudly, "It's June, Dad. June!" and he turned to look at his father. The panic and frustration in his voice were clear to the parent. "The pack has never ventured around the mountain this early! We have traps all over this mountain! How can—"

"—they dodge them all?" the father finished and shook his head slowly. "I don't know."

The truck traveled just under fifteen miles an hour and wove between gaps of trees with only a gap of a foot on each side from hitting the truck. The father drove the truck with ease up the grassy path. Even

17

the most expert offroad driver in the world would only attempt this path at five miles an hour, at best, and would still hit a tree or two. To the father and son, though, it was simply just the way home. The son turned his gaze back out his window.

"The pack—" the young man started to say, then changed to, "Maybe granddad is right."

"Let's hope not, kiddo," the father responded with a concerned exhale. The possibility quickly burrowed deeply into his mind. "Let's hope not."

2

On the lawn of the family's property were a pair of twin 10-year-old daughters. One daughter, wearing jean shorts and a yellow T-shirt, was reading a red, tattered diary as she lay in the high grass on the front lawn. Her younger twin sister, wearing overall jeans and a pink shirt, was collecting pinecones. Their mother was along the left side of the house, folding large bed sheets just removed from the laundry line. Her white shorts and matching tank top kept her comfortable as she did her chores. The day felt pleasant and uneventful, like many other summer Utah days.

"Put that old book away! Come play with me!" the pinecone collector said to her sister.

"I'm reading, and waiting for Dad," the older twin sibling responded sternly, then cockily happily added. "We're leaving today!"

"You've read that thing, like, a gazillion times!" the sister complained stubbornly, then her tone changed to an over-exaggerated glee. "I Love It Here, And I'm Never Leaving!" At 'leaving', she happily tossed her pinecones into the air all at once as if they were glitter.

"God, you're so annoying!" the older twin scowled and rolled her eyes.

"That's enough, you two," the mother said as she appeared around the corner of the house with the laundry basket. Her blonde hair, mixed with several gray strands, waved gently.

The forest around the home was thick. Tiny streams of sunlight pierced through the trees, but on the home itself, a small patch of sky was open to receive the sun's rays. If one were to look into the forest from the porch, even on a blue-sky sunny day, the forest would only show darkness through the trunks. Riddled with various pine and fir trees, the Wasatch Mountains are thick to journey through. Only those who know the mountain and its forests could navigate successfully through it without paths.

Just as the family's grandfather exited the front door of the home, the headlights of the dark green truck appeared shining through the trees. The eldest twin daughter, 'by ten seconds' she liked to remind the younger sister, grew a large smile on her face and excitedly clapped her book shut.

"Finally, we're leaving!" the older twin daughter boasted excitedly while getting up.

The grandfather let the door close behind him, and he stood in the shade of the porch. He looked toward the upcoming truck and then up at the tree line. The elderly man, knocking on eighty-five next Spring, swatted a fly away from his bushy white eyebrows as he looked into the high trees. The look on his face was not the same look his granddaughters expressed. Carrying the basket of folded sheets, the mother walked up the porch and looked at her father-in-law. His faded white wife's beater tank top looked baggy on him, and his pajama pants also looked loose. He wasn't wearing any socks or slippers.

"How was your nap, pop?" she asked after climbing the front steps to the porch. She placed a hand on his shoulder and smiled lovingly. Immediately, she realized his shirt was soaked with sweat. He responded by patting her hand gently with one of his own and kept his attention on the trees. The mother read her father-in-law's facial expression: alarm.

"Daddy!" the pinecone collector shouted as the dark green truck entered the clearing. Knowing not to run toward a moving vehicle, both daughters waited until the truck was parked beside the house. Once the engine cut off and their brother exited the passenger door, the two sisters ran up to greet them. They'd been gone all morning and mid-afternoon.

The wife looked down the porch at her son, who was hugging his pinecone-collecting sister, and saw two things she didn't instantly like. Her son had a worried look, although he smiled at his sister, and the other was an expression on her husband's face: trouble. Son: worry, husband: trouble, father-in-law: alarm.

This wasn't a coincidence; this was a sign.

The father's face did turn to a smile as the older twin daughter rushed up to her daddy and he bent down to hug her as she leapt. Worried or not, the boys were happy to see the twins.

"Dad! When are we leaving?! Soon?" the eager older daughter asked. The husband looked at his wife across the lawn and that look of trouble returned. The daughter's smiling face quickly faded as she looked in the windows of the truck. It was empty inside.

"Ooookay, guys; on the porch. Family meeting," the dad addressed the kids.

"We're not leaving, are we?" the older daughter said in disappointment as her father set her down. He patted her butt to direct her toward the porch as his son carried the other twin on his back. Once the three children reached the stairs, the father addressed everyone from the bottom step.

"What's wrong?" the wife asked, setting down the basket. "Something happened in town?"

"We never made it to town," the husband began. "We noticed two traps on the way and realized they weren't sprung. You know the 'Y-Split' trap and the 'Crossing' traps?"

"They're always snared, Mom," the teenage son added, shaking his head. "Nothing."

"So, we drove to the 'Patch End' trap. Then, the 'Chestnut' trap and even all the way toward 'Donner Lake' and checked over twenty traps." The father exhaled, looked down at the ground and then back up at his wife. "Nothing. All the baits are gone but the traps are still set."

"Keep going…," the wife said as she rotated her index finger and her middle finger together as if to say, 'get on with it.' He wasn't at the bad news yet and she knew it.

"Three blood trails and three carcasses, and one camp thrashed beyond salvaging," the son said. He looked down at his sisters. "The pack. The pack is back, and it's close."

"I hate it here," the eldest twin daughter said, looking down at the planks on the porch steps and plopping her butt down hard to emphasize her point.

"Aaawwooooo…!" the other sister said, mimicking a wolf's howl lightly to tease her sister and her older twin punched her shoulder. The howl turned into a grunt of expressed pain. "...oooow!"

"Enough, you two," the mother quickly scowled, not taking her eyes off her husband. "That's not possible! It's only June!"

"That's what I said!" her teenage son expressed. "And, like I told Dad, Grandpa might be right." The father, the wife, and the son looked at the eldest in the family, who was still looking up at the trees. The open blue sky was in his view, but the edges of the trees were his focus.

"You two youngins," their grandfather spoke. "Listen to me and listen well." His granddaughters looked up at him and awaited his words. It was several seconds before he spoke again, but they waited patiently. "Listen…do you hear it?" The twins listened all around them, as well as everyone else present. Ten seconds went by before someone spoke.

"I don't hear anything, Grandpa," the youngest of the family said. Her grandpa nodded and blinked slowly.

"Nothing," the wife said after a short pause. "There's nothing!"

"Crap, Dad," the son said, now very alarmed and jumpy. "I don't even hear bugs!"

"There were no birds as you drove up the mountain, were there?" the grandfather asked, now finally looking down at his son. A sudden, heavy weight quickly settled on the middle-aged man's face as realization struck him. The entire family was in grave danger, much worse than he assumed. A panic of his own arose within him as his brain scrambled to put actions into words. Right away, he wanted everyone inside but knew he couldn't advertise his panic.

"Okay, everyone. We're out of time. I don't have the answers or the explanations, but I do know it's too late to leave the mountain…," and as the father spoke, he climbed the porch steps toward his oldest daughter, knelt to her eye level, and said reassuringly, "…until tomorrow morning. Then, we'll pack up and leave for town."

"I hate it here," the older twin said in a low mumble as a single tear escaped her left eye.

"But I love it here!" the younger twin whined loudly. "This is our home!"

"Come on, girls," the mother intervened. "We have work to do…now! Playtime is over."

Uncontrollably, the father spoke up, for his own reassurance, "Grandpa, open the gates. Hon, take the girls; you know what to do. We never made it to town, so all the provisions we have left will have to suffice for tonight. We'll be fine, but we have to hurry."

"Mommy, I'm hungry," the youngest child whined as her stomach growled at the word 'provisions'. The mother knew it wasn't a whiny complaint from a spoiled child. They were all hungry, and the trip to town the boys were supposed to take was to cover them for the next month. Part of her was mad at her husband for this, but the news of the pack's return in early Summer? It wasn't possible, but the evidence was confirmation enough, and the pack was too close to their home to flee. Two hours ago, maybe one if they rushed, but now it was not possible.

The father continued, "Son, get the battery out of the truck. I'll set the bear traps. Here, take the keys," and tossed the keys to his son. The father looked at everyone. "The sun is setting with each second we waste. Once we're all in the house, I'll set the bait, and we'll wait out the night." The faces of the adults confirmed they understood. "Let's get our asses in gear before it gets any later."

The oldest twin barked disobediently, clearly angry, "Why!? Why can't we just leave, right now? Just, get in the truck, all of us, and just leave?" The twin had a point, but there was a key detail that her father didn't announce. He didn't want to either, but his hand was now forced.

"Because hon…we're not alone on this mountain," her father said and looked up at his wife. She understood more than the daughter did. "Now, get your book and go inside."

"Should we warn Homer—" the wife started to ask, but was quickly cut off by her husband. There wasn't anger or frustration in his voice; just panic.

"There's no time."

3

Within ten minutes, the family was in their home and the bait was still being set. With the family secured inside, the father opened all the curtains, closed the front door without locking it, hid the truck battery with the truck keys, and locked the trunk containing some of the family's clothing. Surviving the night depended highly on the bait working.

The spouses were alone in the living room while everyone else was down in the cellar. The two embraced in a hug and gave themselves a quiet moment.

"How far away are they?" she asked quietly.

"There was a silver SUV pulling into the RV gravel clearing just as we came up the path. Their vehicle won't make it up, so they'll be on foot, that is, if they decide to go exploring," her husband answered. "At dawn, we'll leave the mountain, and then figure out what to do about the pack before returning home."

They both looked outside the front living room window. It was already getting late. With mixed thoughts and doubts about the coming night, they entered the cellar.

Their home was a cabin.
The cabin was the bait.
The cabin was a trap.

24

OUTSIDE

Keeping a strong eye on the slightly swerving truck in front of him, Thomas Everlast gripped the steering wheel harder, eager to pass the truck once the oncoming traffic was clear. He'd been driving most of the trip for the last few days, and this was the first vehicle they'd come upon that could cause a problem during their vacation.

Thomas glanced to his right and saw Candy Murray sitting on her tailbone with her left leg crossed over the other; her right foot was up on the dash. Candy was facedown, focused on her cell phone. Whatever it was she was watching couldn't have been very interesting because she kept swiping the screen from the bottom to the top rapidly. Thomas's eyes wandered from her phone, down her bare arms, to her short hiking shorts, to her bare hip, and then followed along her shining, well-lotioned bare thighs down to her ankles.

Thomas met Candy three years ago at a college party, before receiving his bachelor's degree in engineering, but she was with another guy at the time. Upon receiving his degree, they ran into one another after the graduation ceremony, and Candy used Thomas as a diversion to 'end the relationship.' That diversion became a real relationship, almost two full years strong. Thomas reached over with his right hand and patted her left thigh twice.

"You might want to sit up a bit. This fuckhole in front of us is either on his phone, falling asleep, or drunk," Thomas warned her. Candy looked up from her phone and readjusted herself, immediately feeling an uncomfortable pressure on her tailbone.

"Turn left off State Route 32 onto State Route 150 in 2.5 miles," the female GPS voice spoke over the rock music coming from the SUV's radio. Thomas felt a body quickly shift in the seat behind him, causing his seat to jerk slightly. It was Jackson Chad, his best friend, and Thomas knew what was about to be expressed.

"No, no, wait, Thomas! We Missed It!" Jay shouted alertly from the back seat. "We were supposed to specifically take Interstate 80 to—"

"I changed it, okay, Jay?!" Thomas cut Jackson off quickly. He wasn't in the mood for a lecture with the questionable truck in front of them. "Chill out! We're getting off your freaky historic nature hike of the Donner Party/Oregon Trail for one damn day, all right?" Thomas heard a thick sigh from Jackson and then a thump of a body hitting the seat.

Jackson started complaining, "I've spent months planning this hike, calculating the exact path, our walking distance, and the amount of time it will take to do it all before we have to be back! Do you know how much research I had to do?! I had to study every mountainside, the exact hilltops, the right curves—"

"Will you shut up and study *these* curves for a minute?!" the woman beside Jackson spoke, cutting Jackson off. She reached over, grabbed Jackson by his flannel shirt with a grip, and pulled him down toward her. Immediately after saying 'minute', she planted her young lips directly against his. In the passenger seat in front of the woman, Candy started hooting, hollering, and cheering on the playful dirtiness of her friend, Kim Michael.

Jackson, or 'Jay' his friends call him, and Kim met during their first-year student orientation almost six years ago. They each kept one another in the 'Friend Zone' since both were so direct at getting their master's degrees in their fields of study without interference before reaching the age of twenty-five. It was because of Candy that Kim and Jackson became a real couple.

Candy watched Kim give Jackson a very deep French kiss, then reached back behind her seat and slapped Kim's bare leg playfully. The tips of Candy's fingers hit Kim's hiking shorts.

"Get'm, girl!" Candy cheered Kim on, then turned back to Thomas. Thomas gave Candy a sly grin, and Candy gave Thomas back a dirtier grin, but it was her eyes that said more. Much more!

"Turn left off State Route 32 onto State Route 150 in 1 mile," the female GPS voice spoke again, and Thomas readjusted his driving position, eager to get out of the SUV to stretch his cramping legs. Kim finally let Jackson sit back up, and she, too, readjusted her posture.

"So, where are we going?" Kim asked the two upfront.

"I have no idea," Candy responded, giving Thomas another look. This look didn't have what the last look had; she truly didn't know.

"Trust me, guys! You're gonna love it!" and Thomas sharply turned the wheel left onto Utah State Route 150. The wavy truck in front of them continued down State Route 32, making Thomas happier.

2

Their distance since leaving State Route 32 toward their destination was very short; much shorter than the other three had expected. They all saw the signs for a small town named Samak, which Jackson immediately Googled. All four were from Utah, and residents of the state all their lives, but their college was the University of Wyoming. Returning to their home state for a celebration amongst themselves was just what they needed, and all four loved the outdoors.

Each of their fields of study focused on the outdoors. Last week, all four received their master's degrees in their respective fields. The trip was their self-reward.

"Let's stop at that Samak town," Jackson started to say while scrolling on his phone. "Says here they ha—"

Thomas cuts the SUV to the left without warning. Kim, Candy, and Jackson all shifted to the right in their seats as a large grin grew on Thomas's face, feeling the SUV slide a bit under some loose gravel on the asphalt road.

"Follow one quarter—" the GPS started to say, but Thomas shut off the stereo, including the music.

"That's enough of that shit, thank you very much!" Thomas boasted at the GPS voice, then said to his companions, "Trust me, we're almost there."

"A little warning next time, huh!?" Candy jarred, trying to sit up in her seat, cupping her eyes over her face. The sunlight shone directly onto the left side of the vehicle and Thomas saw the sun's beam shine straight through Candy's beautiful red hair. For the second, it looked like Candy's hair was a raging fire. He could see each strand in the sun's light. Then, just like that, the sun was gone as trees cut off the light.

"Thank you!" Kim expressed to the shade of the trees from the backseat. A shift in the road made all four of them bounce in their seats, and Candy looked over the engine's hood.

"What happened to the road?" Candy asked, confused.

"We're going off-road," Thomas said, smiling, "and we're going there." Candy watched Thomas point at the upper windshield, and she turned her gaze. The stone road they were on led straight up the side of the mountain with a small field on the left, but on the right were the thickest trees she had ever seen, and she'd been in the forest before.

"We're going into the Wasatch Mountains?!" Jackson asked, almost sounding excited if Thomas had to guess. "I've never been here in the summer! The winters here…? Whew! You want to talk about

COLD!" A second after the exaggerated pronunciation of 'cold', a hand grips his left thigh firmly.

"You've never been in those woods with me in the winter, Jay," Kim whispered in Jackson's ear. He turned to her and smirked.

"It's still cold," Jackson jabbed. "Whether we're naked or not." Kim laughed, bopped his nose with her index finger, and gave him a quick kiss on the cheek.

"Wow!" Thomas said upfront with a small gasp, ignoring the two in the back. "It just goes straight up, doesn't it!" and Thomas pushed the gas pedal down. The SUV shifted in the gravel a bit, which caused Candy to grab the 'Chicken-Grip' handle above her. She saw Thomas's hands grip the steering wheel tighter. "Just a little further…!"

"Are you sure we can make it up this road?" Kim asked, also grabbing the handle above the window, the one she calls the 'Oh Shit' handle. Thomas pressed the gas pedal down further, and this answered her question. The SUV grabbed traction and continued up the stone road.

Just as Thomas's friends thought they were going to get stuck on the slope, the SUV jostled upward, and then the road went perfectly flat. At that, Thomas shifted the vehicle from D-to-P, killed the engine, and unlatched his seatbelt.

"We're on foot from here!" Thomas announced and opened the driver's door. Exiting the car instantly felt good.

3

None of them wanted to admit it, but once they stepped out of the silver SUV and stretched, they felt better almost immediately. None of them realized just how uncomfortable the rental was, and they'd been driving in it for a few days, but not that long a distance to truly notice. The three friends looked around and saw nothing, at first, of real interest.

"It's…a large circle of gravel," Jackson said, unamused as he looked around, turning himself a full three-sixty. Thomas looked around, breathed the aroma of the trees deeply, and tried looking for a specific landmark he saw in the internet's map pictures: a hidden path going into the woods.

Just out of Thomas's peripheral vision, Thomas saw just what he was looking for: a path between tight trees just over a hundred yards away and a truck's taillights going up it. One more second later, and Thomas would have missed it. Right away, Thomas dashed to the back of the silver SUV and opened the back hatch.

"What was this spot?" Kim asked. "I mean, it was a steep stone road up here, and it empties into this huge, circular turnaround." Kim looked at Candy Murray, who only shrugged.

"An old driveway, maybe? To…what? A huge house that no longer exists?" Candy guessed. The sun's rays were hitting the tops of the trees, allowing the beams themselves to be seen.

"Looks like a cul-de-sac, or a resting stop for camping trailers, or something," Kim tipped in as a cold chill went up Candy's spine.

"What time is it?" Candy asked, rubbing her arms with her hands. It wasn't a cold breeze chill as much as a 'Trespassing' chill. Oddly, the SUV now seemed warmer, and safer.

"It's after four o'clock," Thomas said, rummaging through the back hatch, "which doesn't give us too long, but long enough to…," and the three watched Thomas throw on his hiking backpack, "...get up that trail!" Jackson saw Thomas point and turned his head in the direction of Thomas's extended index finger.

"I thought you said we were 'close'! It'll take us a bit just to get over there!" Jackson said, almost on the verge of a full complaint. Behind Thomas, Candy got in Jackson's way and grabbed her bag from the SUV.

"It'll take longer if you keep bitchin' about it," Thomas snarked and threw Jackson's bag carelessly on top of the SUV's luggage rack. Right away, Kim grabbed Jackson's hand, making Jackson jump a bit. He didn't hear her get so close so quickly.

"Come on, Jay," Kim said playfully. "Just one good hike, unexplored by any of your research, and it'll shut him up for the rest of the trip. Okay?" Before Jackson could answer, Kim kissed him, then slid her cheek against his cheek to whisper in his ear. "And besides, this is kinda a turn-on…which only *you* get to benefit from." Kim quickly pulled away, giving Jackson a 'Come On' smile, and dashed excitedly to the back of the SUV.

Jackson took a deep breath in defeat (defeated by Thomas's faux authority and Kim's out-of-character libido), shrugged his shoulders, and walked toward the SUV. Under his boots, Jackson could feel the stones sink into the dirt just a bit, which raised a few red flags that he quickly dismissed.

Thomas belted the straps to his backpack together across his chest and helped Candy with her backpack. The top of her hiking backpack had a rolled sleeping bag on top, which Thomas quickly removed and threw into the back of the SUV.

"We won't be needing that," Thomas told her. "Trust me; we won't be long."

"Then why the detour?" Jackson asked nastily as he pulled his hiking back from the luggage rack. Out of the corner of his eye, Jackson saw Kim giving him a sharp look, telling him to 'stop being a party pooper'.

"When we reach the top of that hill, you'll thank me," Thomas boasted. Thomas slammed the back hatch shut and made the rental beep twice after clicking the key fob lock. "Ready?"

Candy answered quickly with a leap in the air, which Thomas caught, and after Candy wrapped her legs around her man and kissed him, she jumped down and ran for the path. Thomas ran after laughing, excited about the trip's detour.

"Time to live a little," Kim said to Jackson with a leap and a pecked kiss, then jogged quickly to catch up with the others. Jackson sighed again and ran up to Kim, grabbed her hand, spun her around, and planted a very passionate, very apologetic kiss. "Well…that's a start…!" she admitted.

4

As they approached the edge of the circular stone clearing, they could see the path Thomas was talking about more and more clearly, but it was still thin. The trees were very close together, no matter what direction they looked in.

"I hope we see some big game," Thomas said with a huff.

"Getting tired already?" Candy asked, joking at Thomas. "You better get your strength up if you're gonna 'nature these trails' later!" At this, Thomas ran up behind Candy, grabbed her ass with both hands firmly as she squealed playfully.

"This…doesn't feel right," Jackson said oddly, mostly to himself but aloud.

"What's that?" Kim quickly responded, still beside him. She was thinking about Jackson being as playful as Thomas, wishing more than thinking, but Jackson's tone of voice kicked her out of the thought.

"This crazy stone cul-de-sac area…and up here? At the circle's edge?" Jackson explained, pointing ahead past Thomas and Candy, who were ahead of them by forty feet.

"So?" Kim asked, trying to see what her boyfriend saw.

"I think…it's because of the twin tire tracks embedded in the grass," Jackson pointed out. Kim looked ahead with squinting eyes and failed to see what Jackson saw.

"I just see a path in the trees," Kim stated and attempted one last time to be playful. "A path…that could be just what you need, so I can get what I need…!" Jackson looked at Kim and saw her play-biting her lip. Jackson smirked and snuffed comically.

"Will you—" Jackson started, then turned his annoyed tone to a chuckle. "Geez, you're crazy," Jackson joked, but before Kim could respond…

"Let's Get A Move On!" Thomas yelled at the two. "You Slow Pokes Are Holding Us Up!" Jackson and Kim both take one last look at one another, both of them snort a chuckle, and they dash to Thomas and Candy, who were at the stone edge line to the forest.

Kim realized quickly that Thomas and Candy were not as close to the trees as they first looked. It was almost as if the faster they ran, the forest seemed to move back. To Kim, it was the same way staring at a chain-link fence would cause the lawn to zoom in toward you or away from you. Kim didn't mention it, but that was her first bad gut feeling. Nevertheless, Jackson and Kim caught up as Thomas and Candy rested against one of the first trees.

"Okay, then! Let's get started!" Thomas excitedly said after he clapped his hands together, then rubbed them quickly against one other.

"Gonna start a fire with those hands, Daniel Boone?" Kim snarked at Thomas.

"Those hands *DO* start a fire!" Candy fired back comically at Kim, then she slapped Thomas on the ass with a healthy smack. All four, amidst the joking, quickly realized the upward hill was much steeper than they expected. Not thirty feet up, the four felt it in their ankles and calves. The stress of leaning forward with hiking backpacks was already a strain.

"Wow…! You hear that, guys?" Jackson said quietly. None responded right away. The only sound they all heard was the crunching of nature under their boots and the tiniest of zips from gnats that buzzed in their ears. "It's… weird, huh?"

"I didn't see what you were seeing before, and I'm not hearing what you're hearing, Jay," Kim stated, trying not to sound harsh.

"If you're not hearing it, then you *ARE* hearing what I'm hearing! It's quiet, ain't it? No birds singing. No rustling from rabbits…do you guys hear anything?" Jackson asked the three. Right then, the four stopped, almost in perfect unison. The instant the eight feet stopped, they realized the forest was silent as a country road with no traffic.

"Jay, seriously, if you're just trying to get out of this hike, the pickaxe and I—"

"No, Thomas, he isn't," Kim cut in quickly. "He's right. Listen! There's…nothing!" For a few more seconds, the four didn't say a word. They all stretched out their hearing, trying to get a sound of, well, *anything*, and there was nothing. "Almost like…a feeling…of something or someone is watching us."

"And your stupid-ass goddamn pickaxe tattoo isn't going to do shit, Thomas!" Jackson quickly added smartly.

"Have any of you ever been in the woods like this?" Candy asked quietly, almost whispering. "This was fun, until now, and now I'm getting uncomfortable." Candy turned her gaze and looked down the hill they barely climbed. It was very steep indeed. Candy turned around and looked at her three friends. "Do any of you feel the same?"

"All I know is I'm not going back to that cramped car without stretching my legs and seeing what I hope to see with my own two eyes! It was gorgeous on the website, and I want to see it for real, and none of you guys are stopping me!" Thomas barked, getting annoyed with Jackson creeping the girls out. If it was turning into three-verses-one, the 'one' was getting his way, no matter what.

"Jay, it might all seem odd because it's hot out and we don't know the terrain," Kim stated calmly, playing an 'It'll be okay' hand on his shoulder. "But I will say one thing, Thomas, that it's just a little dark in the woods for this time of the year. Can you agree on that?"

"Yeah, but fuck it! Let's keep going!" Thomas coaxed and once again led the way. Candy gave Kim a quick look of worry, then quickly caught up to Thomas.

"Not even a single bird, or bird call," Jackson said in a whisper so low that Thomas didn't hear, but loud enough for Kim to not only hear, but nod in agreement.

5

As the four hiked up the steep path, each one kept looking around, seeing the oddness of the woods. As beautiful and colorful as the Wasatch Mountains were, things seemed weirder. There were no caught furs snagged on tree branches, no burrows, and no animal callings from anything to echo in the air.

There were barely any fallen trees on the ground or heavy tree limbs; just grass, weeds, and forest debris. Kim was paying the closest attention to plants in the woods, carefully avoiding poisonous leaves and potentially toxic bushes that would end their trip very quickly.

There was next to no direct sunlight breaking through the top of the trees to shine down on the forest floor. The summer was bright enough to illuminate the trunks to where they could all see ahead, but direct beams of sunlight were not visible, like a beam breaking through thick clouds on an overcast day.

They hiked for another ten minutes without saying a word, with the occasional huff of breath or strain on muscle. Each of them was in their mid-twenties and in the best shape of their lives, but the trek of the mountain's incline was a toll.

Kim stopped once, slightly pushed Jackson to the left, helping him to avoid a plant that he almost brushed his bare legs up against.

"Stinging Nettle," Kim stated to Jackson before Jackson could ask why she pushed him. Kim stopped and bent down to get a closer look. Without touching the plant, Kim told Jackson, "This grows in moist, shaded woodland areas. Look, its stems and leaves have hairlike structures on the sides. Touching this would cause skin irritation and is quite painful."

"Thanks," Jackson said, both impressively and thankfully. "Anything else to avoid before I get shoved again? I mean, every plant looks the same to me!"

Kim laughed. "That's why you fell in love with me in the first place: I'm smart, sassy, and you're…just…'Jay'!" Kim joked and pushed Jackson away again, but playfully, after standing up. Kim looked around and said, "But since you asked, the usual poison ivy, poison oak…oh, and Myrtle Spurge! Don't get involved with that!"

"M-Mortal Sponge?!" Jackson repeated back incorrectly, curving his face in a questioning expression.

"Myrtle Spurge," Kim corrected. "It's like poison ivy times ten. I'm talking blindness!"

"I'd welcome that," Jackson threw back. "It'd keep me from seeing Thomas's face…!" Kim slapped his shoulder playfully, and they both chuckled. Jackson stepped around the plant that Kim pushed him away from, and they both looked up the hill. Thomas and Candy were very far ahead, so the two double-timed a jog to catch up.

6

Before Jackson and Kim caught up, Thomas and Candy were discussing matters amongst themselves. They knew that Kim and Jackson had fallen back a bit, and this gave Thomas the privacy break he needed.

"Did you tell them yet, or at least Kim?" Thomas asked Candy in a cautious tone. He was keeping his voice low, just in case.

"No, I haven't. I haven't had the opportunity. Jay is always around," Candy answered.

"Yeah, I know. They're not exactly joined-at-the-hip, but they are seriously connected, like two nerds in a Dungeons & Dragons club," Thomas joked. "We need to tell them."

"Thomas, we're all graduated. We're adults; we all have our degrees, and this trip? This is our last hurrah before…well…before we go off to our lives in our fields," Candy explained modestly. "I'm sure they know we're all not going to be everywhere together forever."

39

"I haven't told anyone that I proposed to you, not even my three brothers," Thomas said. To Candy, his words sounded disappointed, and she was right. "I, truthfully, haven't been in contact with them much."

"School does that," Candy said, and she crossed her path to put her arm against his arm. She reached down and grabbed his right hand with both her hands, squeezing tightly. "I said 'Yes' to you, Thomas H. Everlast, and when the time is right, we'll tell everyone, and I'll finally get to meet your three older brothers, officially."

"Be careful what you wish for," Thomas said as he rolled his eyes. He laughed a bit, stopped to give his heels a small break, and turned to face Candy. "We'll tell them all soon." Thomas reached around, grabbed Candy around the waist, and brought her in very close. When their lips met, Candy felt his one hand grip her waist tightly while his other hand went up her shirt and under her bra without hesitation. Candy melted in his embrace.

"Put my initials under your pickaxe tattoo," Candy joked after the kiss. "That'll do it." Thomas immediately laughed.

"Candy, your middle name is 'Urielle'," he reminded her. "I'd rather just tell them than explain why 'C.U.M.' is under my initials!" Candy immediately snickered.

7

Within a minute, Jackson and Kim caught up to Thomas and Candy, who had just broken from an embrace. Jackson commented on the 'horny duo,' and Kim laughed, then mentally said how much she envied Candy. Kim didn't, and had never wanted Thomas, but Kim *did* want the playfulness that Candy and Thomas had. Her actions as of late were not herself, but it was worth a try to get Jackson to 'live a little.'

"Sun's starting to set!" Jackson yelled at the two above them. "There's no wind blowing, but do you two feel…I don't know…a chill? You know, in the air?"

"Not after where that hand's been," Candy snarked easily. Jackson groaned and shook his head as Kim winked at Candy. Candy deviously smiled as she bit her tongue between her teeth.

"Guys, play all you want, but it is getting late. I'm getting a little tired and…," Kim turned around in a full circle, then met eyes with Thomas, "…what the hell are we supposed to be seeing?! Our legs are getting a little sore from all this straight, uphill walking." The three looked at Thomas, expecting a quick answer, but all they got was Thomas looking around, confused.

"I-I don't…I don't want to ruin it. It'll be at the top."

"Should we head back to the car?" Jackson asked, being serious without sounding offensive. Jackson expected an outburst, but to his surprise, he didn't get one. Thomas's tone was nothing but mature and a bit apologetic.

"I don't think we can make it back down this hill and to the SUV before the real heavy dark," Thomas admitted. "Jay, we should keep walking, maybe we can find…something."

"My sleeping gear is in the car, genius," Candy reminded Thomas. Her tone wasn't pleasant compared to the moment they had just had a minute ago.

"I still have the two-man tent," Thomas told Candy. "And so does Jay!"

"No, I don't," Jackson responded. "It's in the car. I didn't think we'd need it the way you were sounding." Both women exhaled disappointing huffs. To avoid eye contact with the opposite sex, Jackson looked up the hill. "This goddamn path is never going to end…and it's getting late."

"It's okay, guys. We're not lost. We'll find it soon, just wait and see," Thomas reassured everyone. "And when you see what I found online, we can sleep there, undisturbed and unbothered, even by nature!" The three looked at Thomas, puzzled. "Tonight is supposed to be clear, and it's high on stilts! Trust me! You're going to love it!"

At this, the four marched upward. One was eager to see the mountain outlook he'd found on the website; the other three were ready to go wherever Thomas led them, just so they could go back to the SUV.

<h1 style="text-align:center">8</h1>

For five more minutes, the four hiked on, surrounded by fir trees, forest debris, and not one sign of a single animal. Not a squirrel, chipmunk, bird, or even a rabbit. There were no deer antler rattles, no moose calls, and thankfully, no sign of mountain cats or bears.

Except for one sign, but there was no way it was done by a panther or a bobcat. The marks were in the wrong direction. *Bear, maybe*, Thomas Everlast thought when he saw it for himself but didn't say a single word verbally. Candy Murray was already getting cranky, and the thrill of Thomas's spontaneousness had worn off. Several trees, one very close, but the other two were very far off in the distance, had carvings of a claw. Three claw gouges in the bark around the trunk, not down the side or along the parallel. *Bears grabbing the trees…has to be,* Thomas thought amongst himself.

"And still no sound in the woods, from anything! I…I don't like this," Jackson Chad added after a short pause. Kim Michael thought the same thing and was glad Jackson spoke up.

"There's that creepy feeling, now more than before," Candy alerted as she hugged herself to rub her hands along her arms.

"I know what you mean, Candice," Kim replied, keeping her pace ahead of Jackson. "I feel it, too." Immediately, Candy spun around and pointed a darting finger at Kim with a scowl on her face.

"Don't Call Me That, *Kim-Ber-Ly!*" Candy angrily snapped. "I Hate That Name!" Kim, only trying to be funny, raised her hands in defense.

"I was just—never mind, sorry…," Kim retracted, and corrected herself. "…Candy."

"Candice…*Ugh!* Fuckin' Christ, I can't stand that goddamn name!" Candy growled in frustration.

"I Said 'Sorry', Okay?!" Kim slightly barked back, then calmed herself. "I-I'm sorry, I—" Kim exhaled deeply, "I just…want out of here."

Thomas cut in, "Yeah, yeah, yeah, I hear you. You're just imagining things—"

"No, Thomas, we ALL feel the same way!" Jackson barked loudly. It caused his voice to echo. "That's it! It's getting dark, and we are heading back now! At least that way, we know where we're going and what's waiting for us!"

"These woods keep getting creepier as we go, baby," Candy said nervously to Thomas.

"Thankfully, there's sky ahead," Jackson said, looking forward. There was a break in the trees, and seeing a yellowish, orangish sky did ease him a bit.

"We're almost there, see?" Thomas pointed up the hill, not looking in the direction of his hand. "Just a few more—" and Thomas turned his head uphill. At once, Thomas saw a wooden peak. "That's It!"

Immediately, Thomas bolted up the hill, instantly rushed with excitement and adrenaline. Right away, the three followed, not wanting to separate.

Thomas was the first to see the whole thing. It was not what he thought it was going to be at the top of the hill. A few seconds later, Candy stopped beside Thomas. Both Kim and Jackson arrived just three seconds after Candy and all four of them stood frozen in their tracks.

What was in front of them was not what Thomas expected. It looked old, and dark, as if it didn't belong there, but looked stable.

There, by itself, on a slight slope in the hill, was a wooden structure, but it wasn't on stilts, and it wasn't what Thomas saw in his internet search. All alone, in a clearing, stood a weather-beaten, but strongly supported, cabin made of logs. Not exactly an old west, cleanly stacked cabin, but it was nonetheless a lone cabin in the woods.

"Oh…Hell-To-The-No!" Candy shouted in protest. "I've seen this fucked-up movie!"

9

In the forest, well behind the cabin, behind a single tree, a head popped up at the sound of a girl's loud voice. Immediately alert, the individual grabbed their rifle and watched with annoyed, but interested eyes. *No one's supposed to be huntin' on this mountain but me,* the individual thought.

10

"This-This is not what I saw online," Thomas choked up the words, confused beyond the rest of them. They were by no means at the top of the mountain, but the steepness was done. "There's supposed to be an overlooked structure here to be as tall as the trees so you can see down the mountain and over the treetops!”

“So…where is it?” Jackson asked mockingly. Thomas spun around in a burst of frustration.

“How The Fuck Should I Know, Jay?!” Thomas roared. “I Didn’t Build The Goddamn Thing!”

“Because You’re The Dumb Fuck Who Took Us Off Our Route And Brought Us Way The Fucking Hell Up Here!” Jackson shouted back. Kim stepped a step closer toward the cabin, completely dismissing the banter between the two men.

Her voice almost sounded dreamy and distant when she spoke. “An old cabin…just left out here?” Kim asked, sounding confused.

“Where else do you expect to see a cabin!? In Antarctica?!” Candy jabbed sarcastically, then added strongly. “And I am NOT going up there!”

“Well, I mean…it’s just…abandoned? That’s crazy!” Kim spoke foggy as she took another step toward the cabin. “Weird, huh?” Thomas and Jackson, no longer throwing words at one another, turned and watched Kim step toward the cabin. Jackson thought Kim looked hypnotized.

“Kim!” Jackson yelled, not angrily, just to get her attention. Kim didn’t respond. Candy took two steps forward and quickly snared Kim’s wrist to stop her from walking any closer. Kim’s body jerked to a halt. Right away, Kim turned in Candy’s direction with a clear expression of ‘What are you doing?’. Candy let go after reading Kim’s stern face.

“Okay, OKAY!” Thomas interrupted. All three looked at Thomas as he spoke. “Sorry, and you’re right, I don’t know what went wrong, or where the tower is, but this…,” Thomas raised both arms and aimed his open hands at the cabin, expressing interest and excitement,

"…just can't go ignored! It just seemed to kinda pop up from nowhere, you know? Just for us?"

Jackson turned his attention back to Kim and asked, "Kim? You good?"

"I'm good," Kim said, no longer foggy or dreamy. "We can at least knock." Kim turned her attention to the cabin and began to step out of the tree line and into the grassy yard. Candy followed directly behind her, still not truly wanting to go near the abrupt cabin.

Jackson took a moment and looked around the property. In a circumference shape, all the trees were cut down around the cabin, exposing sunlight and open sky. The tree trunks of the cut-down trees were gone, except for two, and the grass path that led to the left of the cabin had tire tracks. *Vehicle tracks, but no vehicle,* Jackson thought, then said aloud, "Well…this is where the tire tracks end."

Thomas didn't respond verbally, but he thought, *I knew goddamn well I saw a truck going up that hill! I knew it! Keep it to yourself, Thomas. Don't want to freak anyone out…!*

Together, now over their debacle just a few moments ago, Thomas and Jackson start to walk into the clearing. Kim was ahead of them, leading the four. Candy walked behind Kim, for she felt an ominous feeling, but it was soon overpowered by pure curiosity. Candy walked toward the front of the cabin as Kim seemed to head toward the far-left window.

"CANDY!" Thomas barked cautiously as Candy approached the front of the cabin. What Thomas saw was so well hidden, none of them saw it until a glare from the overhead sky shone right into Thomas's eyes. That glare caused Thomas to wince. Candy turned her head to face Thomas. "Don't take another step forward!" Immediately hearing this, Kim and Jackson looked down at their hiking boots. So did Candy.

"What the hell?" Jackson asked as he looked down. "I don't see anything!"

"Not you, you idiot! Her!" Thomas said as he pointed at Candy. Candy looked down and saw her boots had sunk a bit into the ground, then saw what Thomas was warning her about. As still as a mirror, reflecting the green of the trees, was an enormous water puddle. "Either your boots get wet, or worse."

"Leeches," Jackson said, filling in the 'worse'. At this, Candy took a slow step back, now feeling her skin creep all over her. Goosebumps sprang up all over her exposed skin, despite the warm day. Slowly, Candy started to step sideways and found the edge of the puddle where the ground was harder. She had seen 'stand By Me' as a kid and knew what leeches were.

"Guys, go help her," Kim scuffed, "and enough talking. It's getting late and the sun is already going down. We…we might have to stay here tonight." Kim changed her direction from the window to the thin porch. The cabin was still in full view, and Kim looked at the structure: a few windows on the face, the single-file steps to the door, and on the far right was a stone chimney stack. "Maybe there's a door out back."

"Or maybe we knock on the front door and not just barge in?" Jackson stated smartly. This caused Kim to turn around with a glare of her own. Jackson knew that bodily gesture and tried not to make direct eye contact. Jackson added, "I'm only saying this could be someone's home and we just shouldn't barge in!"

"Why don't you go knock?" Thomas joked at Jackson's expense.

Jackson turned and protested, "I didn't even see the goddamn thing climbing up here, and now you want me to go knock?!"

"ENOUGH!" Candy roared suddenly. The three turned to face Candy. "We walked upon it, we found it, and now, I don't know about you guys, but I'm going inside and taking off this hiking gear!" Candy heaved the backpack up. "Enough of this shit! If someone were here, they would have come out!" As Candy walked around the pond, she started to rub her arms again and Thomas heard her say, "All I can feel is them black bloodsuckers slithering all over me!"

Kim reached the steps first, but in time for Candy to meet up right behind her. Jackson headed over beside Thomas and from the front lawn, the men watched the women walk up the wooden steps and knock loudly on the wooden door.

Thomas whispered to Jackson, "They forgot the Girl Scout cookies." Jackson snickered. The girls knocked again, and both turned to the boys, throwing their hands up, palms up, as if to express 'what now?'. Thomas and Jackson start to walk up to the front entrance, but Thomas got a good look at the left side of the cabin.

Where did the truck go? he thought.

"Screw it. Candy has a point. Just try the doorknob," Jackson insisted as he observed the cabin. "There's no trash, no decorations, no welcome mat, no flower garden." Jackson looked down around his boots. "But there's a small pile of pinecones." Jackson looked back up at Kim directly. "Maybe it's just an abandoned cabin." Deep down, Jackson knew this wasn't completely true. The twin pair of tracks in the grass all the way up the hill to the cabin was his second red flag.

Thomas had run to the steps, grabbed Candy from behind, put his arms around her, and kissed the back of her head against her red hair. Jackson watched Candy almost melt in Thomas's embrace and knew Kim wanted that same feeling, that same attraction. He was going to have to work on it while they were there.

"It's not locked," the three heard Kim say, and when the squeak of metal hinges shrieked out, each one of them had a cold chill jolt down their spines. All of them hid it well.

"Thank God," Candy said, and walked up the single-file steps, pulling Thomas along with her. She wasn't going in without him. Kim opened the door all the way, and Jackson, still in the grass, got the farthest look. Inside the cabin, from Jackson's view, was pure darkness.

11

A moment later, they were all inside, and each one had removed their hiking backpacks.

The ceiling was low, which explained to Jackson why it was so dark, and he also realized that his eyes were adjusted to being outside. The inside of the cabin was still quite dark.

"I can't believe how well-kept it is!" Kim stated, sounding marveled by their discovery. "Maybe it's a hunter's cabin, you know? Like, maybe they only come here when they have vacation time from work or a guy's weekend getaway retreat from the wives!" Jackson listened to Kim, and whatever was going on in her head had put her in a better mood.

Thank God for that! That'll help in more ways than one, Jackson thought to himself.

The outside walls of the cabin were long logs that were filled in where they were stacked. All four sides were structured to withstand the support of the home. The inside walls were flat, but not with drywall, and they weren't painted. Just flat wooden walls. On every wall, there were dozens of small squares covered in dusty white rags and old towels.

49

The ceiling was about seven feet high, but on the outside, it was much higher. Thomas mentioned storage space, or crawl space, which the other three were forced to guess. Kim mentioned bedrooms being above them, but Jackson disagreed.

"There wouldn't be enough room, I think."

"Why's that?" Candy asked, curious.

"No stairs. Nowhere to take up furniture and no headroom," Jackson answered, and right away, Candy laughed playfully. Kim watched Candy grab Thomas's shirt, and she kissed Thomas quickly with a peck on the lips.

"You don't need a lot of room for *head*," Candy joked and kissed Thomas with a second peck on the lips. Kim and Jackson rolled their eyes and shook their heads in unison.

"You should have known that was coming," Kim said to Jackson, and Jackson nodded with an expression 'Yeah, I walked right into that one!'. Thomas accepted the playfulness that Candy expressed eagerly. She sounded like herself again and just in time.

"You know," said Candy singsongy. "This is really…not a bad place." Candy let go of Thomas and began to walk in the middle of the living room. "A small kitchen area toward the front, a fireplace on the far wall, and to the left of the fireplace is an old desk. A writing area, I think." Candy turned around. The fireplace was behind her. "Two doors; one on the left, facing the fireplace, and one on the right. I'm guessing…bedrooms? What do you think?" Kim looked around the small cabin space, shrugged, and nodded her head.

"Yes, it's quaint, kind of cute…but dusty! At least there's furniture in here. Enough room for all four of us: a sofa and a matching chair. No one has to be on the floor," Kim responded.

"I call both women with me on the sofa! Jay, you can have the chair and watch!" Thomas joked, only to receive a hard, disapproving stare from Kim.

"Is that what you and your hand talk about when we're not around?" Kim jarred at Thomas, which made Candy clap and giggle.

"Oooh! Good one, girl!" Candy laughed and high-fived Kim when she approached. Thomas, unamused, didn't respond. Thomas and Jackson watched the two girls laugh, but quickly after, Kim's eyes went right back to the interior of the cabin. Once again, the hypnotic effect seemed to re-grab Kim.

"You would know," Thomas responded confidently with a smartass grin. Candy scuffed.

"Jay, I wonder…how long this has been out here? Who built it? Who owns it? And why leave it abandoned?" Kim didn't give Jackson any time to answer. She was mesmerized by the ambiance of the structure. "I mean, they did a great job! It's solid."

"Well," Thomas announced loudly and clapped one loud clap, clearly bored with the growing conversation. "We have got to find some water to drink. Our water bottles are not going to be enough if we're going to be here all night, and especially if we get that fire going."

"It's, like, eighty degrees out!" Candy burst out. "Unless the windows open, you ain't starting no fires, junior fire marshal!"

"You see any electricity in here? A lamp? A toaster?" Thomas jabbed at Candy.

"The puddle…the pond out front!" Jackson reflected quickly. "It hasn't rained in weeks here, and yet, there's a puddle of water out front." Thomas stared at Jackson, wondering *Where in the hell did that come from!?*

"I don't get it," Kim stated.

"I bet there's a flowing stream nearby and under the cabin, there's probably an underground runoff," Jackson explained. "I'll go and see. I'd like to get back outside a bit before being inside all night. It's kinda…claustrophobic in here." It was the darkness Jackson didn't like and just like that, Jackson walked to the door. The front door to the cabin had a wall immediately to the left when you walked in, but the wall was to the right if you left. Jackson had a quick moment of vertigo, where he couldn't tell which door led outside. *The fewer doors to open in this place, the better.*

"Hang on, Jay," Thomas said. "I'll come with you! Cool?" Jackson waved Thomas off.

"No, dude," Jackson said and waved a hand palm-down. "You stay here with the girls. You three check out the gear and see what we have. We already know what we left in the rental, which would have helped." Thomas, at the last statement, flipped Jackson off. Jackson responded with a mocking smile that said, 'Yeah, that was at you, dipshit,' and turned the handle to leave.

"Okay," Thomas replied. "Just don't let us hear you out there slapping the clown!" Jackson returned the comment with a bird of his own, opened the door, and walked back outside.

Right when the door shut, Kim asked, "Thomas, where's Jay going?"

"S-Seriously?" Thomas asked, bewildered. "Did you just not hear that conversation?" Kim only blankly stared at Thomas. "Jay's going out to see if he can find water. He thinks there's a stream nearby."

"Sorry, I missed that whole conversation, apparently," Kim responded again dreamily. Thomas looked at Kim with a questioning look and thought, *We're all in the same room. How did you not hear any of that?*

As Jackson walked out of the cabin, three miles away, the pack caught his scent as well as the scent of the others. The scent of the four college graduates was the second of the senses that was triggered. The loudness of the four voices on the mountain, echoing through the trees, was the first. It traveled with the wind. Sight will eventually be the third sense. If the third of the three were strong, then taste and touch would be a joy. Anything would be better than the scraps they've collected in the traps set on the mountain.

Even with the thrashed campsite they discovered the night before, their prize was less than satisfactory. The pack have hunted this mountain longer than the last twenty generations of deer, mountain cats, and bears combined. Their senses were exemplarily keen; no prey ever stood a chance, unless the pack ignored it.

For over the past three weeks, the pack rummaged from the northern sides of the Wasatch Mountains and then scavenged through the eastern forests. Now, just back from the southern region, home was to the east. They traveled by night, for their eyesight is keenest in the hush of the midnight starlight, fine-tuned by dusk. But rations, recent earthquakes, and the unsettling of climate change had altered their natural hibernation routine.

The gathering of food and preservation in those warm months had become beyond crucial. Woodland creatures had flocked from the area, in acknowledgment of the pack's existence, more so due to their change in recent behavior. The pack could hunt and travel in sunlight, but the travel was slower and heavily strained their sensitive eyes.

Nevertheless, survival trumped all, and instincts are powerful masters. The pack was relentless and unbiased. To them, survival is life.

Alone and succumbing to the stillness of the wilderness, Jackson casually strolled away from the cabin's clearing and eased into the eastern bordering woods. Completely unbeknownst to Jackson, he missed an open-set bear trap by a single inch in the high grass that surrounded the cabin. In no time, Jackson entered the woods that surrounded the property.

Within twenty feet into the forest, Jackson was swept away by nostalgia: a scene from a beloved childhood movie favorite. Although there are no redwood trees in the Wasatch Mountains, the overwhelming sensation of being a visitor in 'someone else's world' overrode his imagination.

The scene in 'E.T.' when the little alien strolled through the California forest, admiring the steep redwoods, seeped into Jackson and he instantly knew how the tiny, heart-glowing creature felt. The smell of the fir trees, the slight breeze with the summer warmth, and the oddness of literally trespassing into Mother Nature's world without permission were exhilarating.

It was romantic. It was awe-inspiring. It was…freedom.

As Jackson strolled, he watched where he walked, and his guess was correct. Less than a thousand feet from the cabin, Jackson found a small stream of running water. Not big enough for fish, but the crawdads were aplenty.

A quick notion told Jackson to hurry back to the cabin, but Jackson disregarded the instinct to rush back to Thomas's faux leadership, Candy's libido, and Kim's…

"What the hell is going on with Kim anyway?" Jackson spoke aloud to himself as if his head was trying to get answers. Uncontrollably,

Jackson's brain and mouth started having a conversation, which Jackson didn't try to stop. "First, she's acting like Candy, getting all touchy-feely and playful, which she's only like that when we're alone. Then, she completely becomes herself on the hike up the hill while observing the plants, which 'Thank You Very Much, Thomas, for our little uphill, ankle-killing hike', and then…" Jackson's mouth stopped because his mind went racing to where his mouth couldn't keep up.

A new red flag went up in Jackson's head. The hypnotic effect Kim had was too odd to ignore. Kim became enthralled by the cabin twice. First outside of it, then inside, just as he was leaving. *Something's not right…there's something very wrong with that. Kim doesn't do that. She's too focused as a person to let her 'mind wander' aimlessly, let alone twice!*

14

Forty feet away, behind a tree, a lone observer watched the young man with curious eyes as he walked and talked to himself. This observer wasn't armed. Careful not to be seen, the observer stayed behind the tree, hoping for two things: first, the boy wouldn't see them. Second, they hoped the boy would leave the mountain as soon as possible. The second was more important than the first.

Deep in thought, Jackson's eyes stared ahead as he returned to the cabin. His mind pondered about Kim Michael when something poking around a tree slid back. It was fast enough to catch Jackson's attention, but Jackson was too slow to see what, or who, it was. Since parking the car, Jackson had not seen or heard a single animal, minus the crawfish in the stream.

"Who Is That!?" Jackson barked loudly; his voice echoed lightly. Without realizing it, Jackson had stopped walking. "Come On! Come On Out!" Three seconds go by, and nothing. Jackson forced his mind to overpower his feet to resume walking, but his eyes continued to switch back and forth, left to right. *Now I'm making myself paranoid,* Jackson said in his head and began to jog back.

The observer watched Jackson, first as he arrived and now as he left. As Jackson reentered the clearing, Jackson not only missed the bear trap he had almost hit when he left but also missed a second. Its jagged teeth pointed upward, awaiting a fleshy bite.

Also, something else caught Jackson's attention. Something he didn't see when he left the cabin to go find the source of the mountain's water. In the clearing of the cabin, in the backyard amongst the high grass, was a dark green pickup truck that was dirty with dried mud and dust from traveling. A sickening feeling of real trespassing sank straight into Jackson. Right away, Jackson realized he needed Thomas.

16

Jackson returned to the cabin within fifteen minutes and caused Thomas to jump when Jackson pushed the cabin's front door open. There were no restraints on the door, so it slammed against the back wall. Everyone is so used to doors having cylinder stoppers or a wall mount, but the cabin entrance door had three iron hinges and a handle, and that was it.

"Good Fuckin' Goddamn, Jay!" Thomas shouted, clutching his chest. He was in the middle of the living room kissing Candy…again. Kim was nowhere in sight.

"I knew I'd find it," Jackson said, pleased that he got Thomas good, even unintentionally. "I found the stream. It's not far." As the door closed, Jackson started to walk toward Thomas with concern. "Hey, um, Thomas?"

"Hey, um, Jay… you forgot the canteens, numb nuts!" Thomas scorned. "Want to take them down there and fill them?"

"I'll go with you," Candy said, letting go of Thomas. They were chest to chest, her arms around his neck, but she had lowered them. As Candy started to walk toward Jackson, she was jerked back, harshly, but playfully, as Thomas had reached out and grabbed the back of her shorts, pulling her in. Candy giggled as Thomas wrapped his arms around her.

"No, that's okay, Candy, but thanks," Jackson said. Still concerned about his discovery, Jackson started to say, "Hey, Thomas, there's a—" but was cut off by a loud door squelch.

Kim appeared from the door across from the tiny desk. Her hypnosis seemed to be gone again, but she was scanning the interior of the cabin's structure. When her eyes locked on Jackson's, his mind went blank. Something about Kim in that second made him swoon, just like when he saw her for the very first time.

"Glad you made it back safe sand in one piece, nature boy," Kim said, smiling and ran to Jackson. She leaped in the air and Jackson caught her, grasping her firm buttocks for support. Kim's legs wrapped around his waist as Kim whispered in Jackson's ear, "There are two bedrooms, and we're getting the one with the thicker bed." Kim gently bit his ear. "That's a hint...!"

"They both were a little worried about you leaving on your own, but since you're back, we can get settled in for the night," Thomas told Jackson while he hugged Candy from behind. He had both of his arms wrapped around her waist and wasn't letting go.

"You can let me go now," Candy said to Thomas with a laugh, and Thomas did, but not before growling into her neck and hair, kissing all he came into contact with. "This place is small and cute, but you make it creepy!"

"Awe...just like his dick," Jackson added at Thomas's expense. Candy and Kim quickly laughed, and again, Thomas not so much. Jackson, for the moment, completely forgot about the truck behind the cabin. Thomas had no rebuttal, except a downcast stare of disapproval.

17

The eyes that watched Jackson while he walked in the woods now had eyes on the back of the cabin. Still behind a tree, trying not to be seen, right at the property clearing, the observer watched the wooden home carefully. Very carefully. The sun was dropping quickly, and the observer didn't acknowledge it in the slightest. Not only did Jackson not see his observer, but neither did the hunter with the rifle, and both were less than fifteen yards away.

58

18

Less than three miles away, and closing in fast, the pack locked onto the scents of the mountain travelers, and another scent the pack already knew well: exhaust.

19

Even though it was summer in the Rocky Mountain region, dusk came quickly. Late evening sun on the highway had sharp sun rays that blinded most drivers, but in the forest of the mountain, there were no sun rays. Sunsets are not visible amidst the trees, so the heavy shadows of the wooded land cast heavy darkness quite quickly.

But luckily for Thomas's pushing and Kim's help, the four were squared away before the sun fully went down. Candy and Thomas inventoried all the backpacks while Kim and Jackson left to fill the canteens. Before they left the cabin, Jackson found a small empty wooden crate in the kitchen.

Kim and Jackson weren't but twenty feet from the cabin when they heard Thomas's muffed voice groan in ecstasy from inside the cabin. Kim snorted a chuckle and thought about surprising Jackson in the woods with the same gesture, but when she glanced and saw him shaking his head, she dropped her smirk and disregarded the idea. *He's clearly not in the mood, I guess.*

Neither talked as they walked; the silence and company were nice. When Kim and Jackson reached the water stream, Kim gasped at the beauty as Jackson collected as many crawdads as he could grab.

"Hopefully there's a pot in that cabin," both sets of watching eyes heard the young woman say. The entire time Kim and Jackson were

59

outside the cabin and in the woods, two sets of eyes watched from behind different trees. They watched the two hold hands, kneel by the tiny stream, heard the two apologize to one another, and watched the two kiss. The eyes also watched them return, missing four bear traps in the high grass around the cabin.

20

When they returned, Candy and Thomas, who were done with their extra-curricular activities, announced that all their gear was 'sufficient' in the cabin, for they weren't on an actual nature hike.

Aside from a few bags of various snack foods, two flashlights, a change of clothes, and four minor first aid kits, everything else was better left in the backpacks. The girls put their backpacks, along with their men's backpacks, in the bedrooms of their choosing and talked as the two men talked in the living room. The sun was low.

"Sorry, Jay, I haven't ventured around out there. Candy's been… well…playful," Thomas said, hinting at Jackson, trying to be low-key. The girls were in the bedroom. Thomas and Jackson were in the living room. "She wanted something to eat before you guys got back…!"

"Yeah…we heard; thanks for the warning," Jackson joked sarcastically.

"So…um, if you hear us 'trucking along' tonight, try to get Kim to not interrupt, huh?" Thomas hinted. Jackson knew exactly what he meant. Kim was very well known for ending romantic moods when she wasn't getting anything romantic herself.

"Not a problem. We'll probably be 'trucking along' as you…Oh, Shit! Trucking!" Jackson's voice and tone changed mid-sentence. "Son

60

Of A Bitch! I completely forgot, even after going out twice!" Jackson quickly barked at himself. "Damn it…you fucking moron!"

"Dude! Calm down!" Thomas said as Jackson smacked his own forehead repeatedly with the palm of his hand. "What's your problem?"

"Trucking…The Truck!" Jackson harshly said, as if trying to scowl himself as punishment. "Out back, there's a black or dark green pickup truck! I think it's the cabin's owner's truck as if, maybe, someone actually lives here!"

"Lower your voice, will you!? You want to scare the fuck out of the girls?!" Thomas warned through almost clenched teeth. "What do you mean there's a truck out back?"

"I'd show you, but—"

"No, I believe you," Thomas said, cutting Jackson off. "I just— listen, show me later. We'll just act like we have to piss or something. And I don't see any shotguns or hunting gear in the cabin, so if this is someone's place…well…it's like Candy said," Thomas pointed at the closed bedroom door that Candy and Kim occupied. "Maybe this is a weekend thing for them, and we found it on a day when they're not available, huh? Hey, lucky us!"

"Maybe…but the tire tracks—"

"Jay…think about it like this, okay? This is something else! We're on vacation before we're fully injected into our careers, we find this cabin in the middle of the woods on a forest-covered mountainside, and we have warmth, a roof overhead, and our girls! This is beyond great, and mathematically lucky! You have Kim all night long, alone, and no more finals to cram for! The ONLY CRAMMING we're doing tonight…is THEM!"

At 'only cramming', Thomas motioned a gesture that was either 'grabbing hips in a sexual nature' or Thomas pretended to put a large loaf of bread into an invisible oven repeatedly.

Jackson couldn't argue and smirked at Thomas. Thomas was an egotistical perv, but he was right. Jackson looked back at the bedroom door the girls were in and thought of Kim's feelings. *If today is to be special, then I'd better make it special,* Jackson thought.

21

Both Kim and Candy sat on the edge of the bed, which was surprisingly comfortable but smelled old. They spoke to one another in low voices, at first.

"Tonight, you have Jay, in a bedroom, without coeds, all night long and all to yourself," Candy said slyly. "Which means…?"

"Which means you and Thomas don't want to be interrupted," Kim finished with rolled eyes. "You're like a goddamn horny teenager, Candy."

Candy's face came to life. "You goddamn right, Ms. Stick-up-her-ass! We don't want to be interrupted, so don't fuck with us tonight! Okay? Are we good? We have an understanding, yes? I saw how playful you were in the car. Get that back!" Candy drilled into Kim to get her point across. Candy didn't like the sound and the tone of her own voice, but tonight was special.

"I did that ONE TIME to you two, and you will not—"

"Six, Girl! *SIX!*" Candy expressed four fingers on her left hand and two on her right. Her voice grew louder as she continued, "Every time I get some and you don't, you cockblock us!"

"You're Fucking Loud!" Kim exclaimed, matching Candy's volume. "Jay and I will be done, and you two sound like Pornhub.com injected with Red Bull and NyQuil!"

"Thomas has a huge dick, alright?! And he knows how to use it!" Candy expressed with hand gestures, then her hands slapped her legs. "It ain't my fault Jay's a two-pump chump."

"Stop! He's Not!" Kim protested, then blushed. "We're just— he's—we're not loud, like you two freaks! We heard Thomas's *'Uugh'* right when we left and—" At Kim's words, Candy stood off the bed slowly with a large gaping mouth that curved to a smile and surprise.

"You…OOOOHHHHH!" Candy gasped, now understanding everything about Kim and Jackson's sexual relationship as of late. "You WANT him to—"

"Stop!" Kim said directly, raising her index finger. A shy smirk appeared on Kim's face as Candy covered her own mouth with two hands. Candy lowered her voice but didn't stop. "No, Candy! Stop right—"

"You want to be me and Thomas! *You WANT Jay* to thrash you up against the headboard so hard, the nuns in the neighborhood church will need a cigarette, huh?!" Candy smiled and recovered her O-face. Candy giggled as Kim blushed a hard red. Candy slapped two hands on the edge of the bed. "I have JUST the thing…!" At this, Candy bopped backward toward the bedroom wall.

"What are you talking about, Candy?" Kim quickly corrected herself, not wanting to make the same mistake she made earlier. Deep down, Kim hated the name change Candy legally gave herself. *Ugh! 'Candy' sounds so immature! You're a college grad, for fuck'sake!*

"These," Candy said matter-of-factly, and like a model on 'The Price Is Right', Candy expressed two hands, palms up, as if to display a prize. The prize Candy was hand-modeling for hung on the wall. "We've only been here just a little over two hours, and all over the cabin are these hanging picture frames, right?"

"Yeah, each one is covered with a towel, or a cloth, or something," Kim agreed. "Kinda creepy, huh?" Then asked, "So? Clearly, the cabin's owner is protecting them."

"And what do we have behind curtain number one?" Candy joked and pulled the dusty cloth off the picture frame that hung on the wall. The picture frame was just about a foot wide and was longer than taller. Inside the frame behind the glass was an old black and white picture of two boys and four girls standing in front of the very cabin they inhabited.

"What does that—"

"Oops…wrong one," Candy mistook it and covered it back up. The next frame on the wall was wider. Candy quickly uncovered it to display a mirror that was much longer than wide. For a millisecond, Kim saw a transparent face in the glass, and a sharp tingle went up her spine. *It was just a mental reflection from that old black and white picture, you chickenshit*, Kim quickly told herself. Candy threw the cloth that covered the mirror at Kim, which Kim batted away.

"You're sick," Kim said, getting Candy's point. "Mirrors?"

"Just because they're not on the ceiling doesn't mean they can't be fun!" Candy expressed with a large, sarcastic, faux-model smile. "There are at least four in each room, and every single one is a different size, and all are covered up. Might as well put them to use!"

"Creepy," Kim said as she looked around. Candy was right: they were all over.

A minute later, Jackson knocked on the door and asked the girls if they were hungry, to which Candy replied, "Oh, believe me, Jay.

Kim's *hungry!"* Kim threw a pillow at Candy and missed as Candy ducked out of the door. The pillow struck the door and fell to the floor. Kim's eyes drew back to the mirror, and immediately wanted to cover the mirror back up, which she did.

22

No longer behind the trees, the hunter with the rifle, who watched Kim and Jackson, now watched all four of the cabin's inhabitants up close through a window and impatiently waited for them all to leave. They didn't. Instead, the four bunked inside the cabin for the night. All was not lost, but none were safe.

The plans for the night were now drastically skewed, now that the cabin was no longer vacant, but the final result still needed to happen, regardless of the variable. Alert in the front yard, the hunter stood motionless in the high grass and came to a final decision: *They're innocent bystanders who are in the wrong place at the wrong time. FUCKING HELL! Fine…okay…change of plans…!*

Unbeknownst to the hunter, just a foot to their left was a bear trap, teeth open and ready.

23

At the tree line, the observer who watched Jackson and Kim stood solemnly and also wished for the four in the cabin to leave. The observer had their eyes on the one with the rifle, who was looking into the cabin's window, and hoped they too would leave. Sad in thought and lonely with worry, the observer heard a sound and quickly jerked their head in the direction of the front of the cabin. The eyes were no longer curious; they were immediately terrified.

No! Oh, oh, no! Something diabolical caught their attention. Something that the observer hadn't felt in a very, very long time. Their eyes were now wide with the horror of things to come. *Oh, no…the mirrors!*

A new sound, too far away for a regular person to hear, attracted their attention, and the observer in the woods raced around the tree line that surrounded the property. Everything peaceful quickly escalated from bad, to worse, to nightmarishly impossible. *The pack…they're close! Oh, no, the pack is coming back!*

24

Nightfall fell onto the Wasatch Mountains and covered the forest in a hush darkness. The pack traveled faster than ever with the smell of fresh meat in the woods still lingering in the air. Better yet, the smell became thicker as they traveled toward home. Gripping the forest floor with their claws as they ran, the pack trekked on all fours towards home, and their fresh prey.

INSIDE

1

After the fireplace was lit, thanks to a box of blue-tip matches Thomas Everlast found in the kitchen area, the four casually ate from their backpacks and boiled the crawdads in a small pot they found in the kitchen area. It was no gourmet meal, but it kept the hunger edge off until the morning. The four knew that by morning, the hunger pains would be fierce, but the car was at the bottom of the slope, and they'd travel somewhere to eat a full breakfast.

The four friends discussed finishing Jackson Chad's planned trail, which pleased him, and they palavered about their future jobs. Throughout the evening, Candy Murray gave Kim Michael several expressions and eye directions to head to the bedroom multiple times, as if to say 'Go take Jay to the other room', but Kim would instead bring up other topics to talk about. Finally, just after ten-thirty, Candy took off her shirt, revealing her sports bra, and threw her shirt in Thomas's face.

Quickly, Jackson averted his eyes to Kim as he cupped one hand on the side of his face and mentioned going to bed. Playfully, Thomas carried Candy to the bedroom door by the cabin's front door. Jackson glanced at the front door; the locking mechanism was in place.

Kim grabbed Jackson with one hand, helped him to his feet, and led him to the back bedroom. All four left their phones turned on in the main room. Kim and Jackson closed their door as Thomas and Candy's door closed with the sounds of Candy's muffled giggling.

2

Candy and Thomas were not interrupted one time, and Jackson learned quickly that having an exposed mirror in the bedroom was something he and Kim, too, could get very used to. For the first time in their relationship, Jackson let down his uptight guard and gave Kim a night that he hoped would be a challenge to top. The firelit oil lamps in the bedrooms were another detail that all four of them liked. Soon after, both women fell asleep beside their fully satisfied men.

By eleven thirty, all four inhabitants of the cabin were asleep. By eleven thirty, two phones were below twenty percent. By eleven thirty, the pack was less than a mile away. By eleven thirty, every single mirror was uncovered, then quickly recovered, throughout the cabin. By eleven thirty, the cabin's warm summer atmosphere was dropping rapidly in temperature.

3

"…ddddiiiieeee…"

Candy's eyes opened at the sound of a whisper in the bedroom that wasn't Thomas's voice. Immediately frozen in fear, Candy slowly looked about the room as her eyes adjusted to the darkness. The window offered next to no helpful light, although if Candy had looked out the window and looked up, she would have seen stars in the overhead clearing. Candy, still snuggled with Thomas, taps a finger on Thomas's bare chest.

"Thomas…!" Candy whispered urgently. She tapped three times again. "Thomas!"

At her whisper, from the outside of the bedroom, just behind the walls, a low moan bellowed long and wavy, like an old man yawning but unable to catch his breath. Then a second, but from above the ceiling. It wasn't a moan, but a wailing cry, as if a lost person sobbing uncontrollably.

"…wwwwhhhhyyyy…"

"Kim, you better knock it the fuck off, bitch!" Candy yelled enough to be heard, but apparently not loud enough to awaken Thomas. "We talked about this!" Candy snuggled against him, having doubts that Kim would stoop so low. The cabin was creepy enough, but this would be a new low.

The moaning traveled from above the ceiling to under the floor, then behind the wall that separated the bedrooms, as the temperature of the bedroom quickly dropped. Candy looked at the window and saw that the glass had started to crystallize slowly with ice. Candy exhaled her breath and saw it suspended in the air for a moment.

Okay…that's not Kim! Candy thought.

Candy, having no luck with the finger jabs, did the next best thing to wake a sleeping man up. With cat-like quickness, Candy opened her hand, slapped it down directly in the center of Thomas's chest, grabbed a handful of chest hair, and yanked violently. Thomas shot up vertically, screaming in pain.

"WHAT THE HELL!?" Thomas screamed at Candy, and Candy shot up, too. At Thomas's shout, the bedroom door burst open and slammed against the wall without bouncing against the wall, causing the bedroom door to expel a cracking sound and Candy to scream.

"*WHAT THE HELL?!*" Thomas shouted louder as a floating essence rushed into their bedroom. It was too distorted to see clearly, and neither Thomas nor Candy had any intention of sitting around to find out who or what it was. Out of view, another door banged open, and a shout of 'Who In The Hell?!' sprang out. Thomas immediately recognized Jackson's voice.

"JAY! KIM!" Thomas shouted as he grabbed Candy's hand. Thomas ran out of the bedroom, wearing only boxer briefs, with Candy, who was wearing nothing. They both ran through the white apparition as if it were merely fog, and darted out the door.

Expressively vocal in panic, from the other bedroom door, was Kim and Jackson. Jackson was in his loose boxers with the slit in the front. Kim wore panties and Jackson's shirt. The moaning, crying, and wailing increased in content and volume, which traveled throughout the living room and kitchen areas. Thomas saw Kim exit the bedroom first, cupping her hands over her ears. When Kim saw Candy, she saw her bare 34C's, and the professional Brazilian wax that she had bragged about two days ago.

"CANDY!" Kim shouted as she removed Jackson's shirt, revealing her bra. Kim threw Jackson's t-shirt at Candy, which Candy caught and quickly threw on. That was when both bedroom doors slammed shut thunderously at the same time. The moment the doors slammed shut, the cabin went mute.

None spoke for several seconds, until Thomas barked, "What The Fucking Hell Is Going On?" Thomas then looked coldly at Candy. "Why The Fuck Did You Grab My Chest Hair!?"

"To Wake Your Fucking Ass Up, Rip Van Dillhole!" Candy barked back as she slapped his shoulder with a bunted open palm. Kim spoke next.

"I was asleep…and in my dream, someone told me to 'Get out of their house' and that we are 'trespassing on their property' or something like that," Kim continued in a rapid panic. "Then, the blanket on the bed compressed down on both Jay and me, like stretch wrap!"

"We couldn't move, couldn't breathe; then the door sprang open on its own!" Jackson added, then looked directly at Kim. "I don't know if you saw it, but I swear a fucking ghost flew in through the wall!"

"A fucking *what*?!" Thomas asked unbelievingly. "There's—"

"What The Hell Do You Think We Just Literally Ran Through, Thomas?!" Candy shouted, bluntly striking him again, unpainfully. "Jimi Hendrix's Purple-Fucking-Haze?!"

"Okay! OKAY! *FINE!*" Thomas shouted back at Candy. "Fuck, I Just Didn't Want To Admit It!" Thomas shrugged at the other three, then looked at Candy. "*And Stop Hitting Me!*" Thomas ran his hands through his hair and quickly looked around, not knowing what to see or find. "If they had any sense, they would open the door and just tell us to get the hell out of their house."

"Didn't they!?" Kim asked bluntly.

"Are we seriously—" Candy injected, but Jackson cut her off.

"You's right, Thomas, but I think it's something more than that," Jackson started. "If I was the three bears, and I found four Goldilockses in my cabin, I'd scare the shit out of them til they got the fuck out!"

"The phones!" Kim recalled verbally and dropped down to her knees onto the floor. Unable to recall where they placed them before going to bed, Kim began to feel along the floor. Candy quickly dropped down to help Kim. Neither had immediate luck in the dark. It was that second when the four realized just how dark the cabin was.

"What the hell happened to the fire?!" Jackson asked loudly and sprinted to the fireplace. Jackson put his hands out to feel some warmth. The fireplace was dry, cold, and appeared to have never been lit.

"You said 'you think it's something more', Jay," Thomas reminded his friend. "What do you mean?" Jackson turned his attention back to Thomas, who was hard to see in the darkness of the cabin.

"What I meant was—" and before Jackson could finish the sentence, the callings of each specter, ghost, and floating apparition sounded off all at once. The structure of the cabin shook and caused the windows to rattle.

Jackson saw a single amber in the fireplace glow an orange light. Instinctually, and without knowing why he knew, Jackson reached out and hugged Thomas with all his might. Thomas, who was stronger, larger, and more physically muscular in build, was shocked to find out his skinnier, shorter, and lankier friend could not only grab him but also spin him around! Jackson pushed Thomas back to a safer distance before Thomas could react.

The sliver of amber in the fireplace exploded to life, engulfing the entire fireplace in a blaze! Both Candy and Kim screamed and fell backward onto the rug, then quickly stood up. Jackson instantly felt the heat on his back. The roaring of the wailing ghosts, which were not visible at that moment, seemed to use the fireplace to expel their hatred for the fours' presence.

"We need to do something, like weapons or something," Thomas said.

"This isn't 'Ghostbusters', dumbass!" Candy wailed.

"It might as well be," Jackson said, then got a hard look of disapproval from Candy.

Ignoring them both, Thomas yelled at everyone, "Get going! Start looking! Anything!" As the three started looking for whatever they thought would help them, Kim started to once again go into her cabin-admiring trance.

Candy found a hammer in a kitchen drawer, Thomas found a hatchet leaning against the stone chimney stack, and Jackson found the fire poke near the corner writing desk. As all three turned to dash back to the middle of the living room, they saw Kim, standing motionlessly, arms down, with her head cocked to the side.

"K-Kim?" Candy Murray addressed Kim Michael softly as her throat cracked. There was something about Kim's physical position that didn't look…alive, or human. Candy, nearly too terrified to speak, forced out the words, "W-What are—" was as far as Candy got. Kim, who was facing the bedroom doors, turned her head around toward the fireplace where Candy, Thomas, and Jackson stood with their weapons ready. Kim's head turned completely around, but her body didn't. Thomas heard several of her bones crack, specifically in her neck.

Jackson looked at his girlfriend and saw that her eyes were not only rolled back into her head but also seemed to glow hauntingly. Slowly, and softly at first, the three began to hear thumps throughout the cabin. Kim raised both her hands, and the cabin began to come alive: thumps to the floor, pounding on the walls, and the rattling of windowpanes.

There were wood scratching and heavy clawing rips all around as if large metal spikes were carving into the cabin itself. Several of the foundation logs of the cabin began to vibrate as a thunderous growl erupted from what sounded like the roof.

"WHAT IN THE *FUCKING HELL* IS GOING ON?" Thomas shouted angrily.

"I-I-I….I'm not sure, Thomas," Jay answered the best he could. Kim's head raised to face the ceiling and began to laugh with the most horrific, low mechanical laughter that seemed to intensify the shaking of the cabin. Dust particles and splinters of wood fell from the ceiling as the walls and several of the windowpanes cracked.

"TRES-PASS-ERS!" Kim's voice erupted with the echoing voices of dozens of angry spirits all at once. All around the cabin, loose items on walls rattled or fell as loose objects on the floor shook or fell over. All three doors began to slam open and shut repeatedly. The kitchen cabinets repeated the action as well, but none of them in unison. The three adults covered their ears.

Candy shouted to Jackson, "But I think we're going to find out!"

"Kim! STOP THIS!" Jackson shouted as he shielded his eyes from overhead debris.

"TRES-PASS-ERS!" Kim roared again, only stronger and angrier at the sound of Jackson's voice. Every possible loose item in the cabin, from the rugs to desk drawers to the logs in the fire, rose into the air and began to twirl in circles. To Jackson, the cabin had become Carol Anne's bedroom in 'Poltergeist' when the medium finally got her bedroom door to open.

To Thomas, it looked like the world's largest windup before the pitch. At that thought, Thomas grabbed the chair that matched the sofa, which hadn't levitated off the floor yet, and picked it up.

"Thomas! Don't Hit Her!" Jackson shouted and stood corrected as Thomas ran toward the single back window of the cabin instead of running at Kim.

Candy shouted at Thomas, "What Are You Doing!?" as Thomas threw the chair through the window, shattering the four panes on contact. The chair immediately fell to the floor after bouncing off the glass, regardless of the shards. Thomas watched the chair fall back into the cabin, but what it hit caused Thomas's legs to buckle.

What he saw, saw him right back. As Thomas started to scatter backward to his friends, Kim's possessed laughter stopped instantly, causing her head to not just spin back around correctly, but curve to the right to look out the window. Something growled outside and caused Kim's arms to drop limply to her next-to-bare sides. The instant her hands were at her waist, everything that floated in the cabin dropped to the floor like lead.

Jackson grabbed Candy, pulled her down to the floor, and covered her as Thomas curled up into a ball to protect himself from all the falling debris.

"MUTI-LAT-ORS!" Kim growled with hatred, again with the voice of dozens overlapping dozens. In the purest of rage and torment, Kim screamed the scream of every ghost in the cabin, causing her jaw and mouth to stretch down to her stomach, making her teeth look like ancient cave stalactites and stalagmites. All of her exposed skin swam transparently like oil in a lava lamp.

Everything around the cabin flew back into place in an instant. The rugs returned to the floors, the furniture retracted back to their posts, and the broken windowpanes reconnected with the glass perfectly. The frames of each window rebuilt themselves as the burning fire logs retreated to the fireplace. The picture frames on the walls rehung themselves from their nails and every single splinter from every cabin log reattached as if they never came apart.

Before the cabin went silent for the second time, the three heard a sickening thud.

—TH-THUMP!—

5

Slowly, in confusion, fear, and insane curiosity, Thomas quickly rose to his feet as Candy and Jackson slowly rose to theirs. Jackson's eyes looked directly in the direction of the thud and saw Kim lying on her side. Her head faced in the natural direction with her limbs sprawled out in various directions. Jackson dashed away from Candy to Kim without a moment's hesitation.

From outside the cabin, a slow, thunderous growl purred heavily.

Thomas said without checking on Candy, "I-I'm going over to the window and—"

"You're Doing No Such Goddamn Thing!" Candy screamed hoarsely at Thomas. "What Are You Thinking? You're Going To See What's Making All That Horrific Noise? And Do What? Yell At It!?" Still in just her bra and panties, Candy stood up fully and stormed toward Thomas as Jackson reached Kim.

"I-I…I just…," Thomas started to say in comprehension of everything he just witnessed, and that's when he received a heavy slap across the face from Candy. Candy's hand struck Thomas's left cheek so hard, she could feel her pulse in her hand. Thomas made no rebuttal. Candy stormed away from Thomas and knelt beside Kim and Jackson.

Jackson had his right hand on Kim's chest, and his left hand was holding her right wrist.

"Jay?" Candy asked nervously. Jay smiled at her.

"She's alive."

"Thomas?" Jackson asked, with a quiver in his throat. Thomas looked at Jackson with a full blank stare. Jackson read his face easily and sympathized. His face said 'I don't know what to do' and Jackson understood, then turned his attention back to Candy. "Help me put her on the sofa, quickly." With no effort, Jackson and Candy picked up the limp body of Kim and laid her softly on the cabin's couch. Jackson patted one of his hands on Kim's hand and then walked over to Thomas.

"What did you see, Thomas?" Jackson asked. "Everything was insane, and I saw you throw the chair out the window. It hit something, didn't it?" Thomas's mouth dropped open twice as Thomas tried to collect the words, because saying them would be admitting them. Thomas turned to the window and pointed.

"I-I s-saw a large pair of red eyes! T-They looked at me! Sorry…it-it scared me!" Thomas stuttered as he tried to admit the truth, especially to himself. Only one time in Jackson's entire existence as friends with Thomas did he ever hear the young man stutter. This was the second time.

"Okay," said Jackson, and he placed a hand on Thomas's shoulder. "Here, use this," and Jackson gave Candy's hammer to Thomas. "Where there's a hammer, there's bound to be nails. Candy, where did you find this?"

"In the kitchen, in a drawer," Candy answered while sliding her hand over Kim's face gently. Candy didn't look toward Jackson or Thomas.

"W-what is going on here, Jay? This p-place is making me—" Thomas tried to muster the words that he was terrified beyond all rational thought. "H-how are you so…calm?!"

"Dude, I'm worried, frightened, and scared all the goddamn time!" Jackson said in truth, and also in a tone that was supposed to make Thomas feel just a sliver better. It did, but Thomas didn't express it. "I'm used to it."

"I-I'm sorry…w-we never should have come here," Thomas said apologetically. When Thomas spoke, his eyes never lowered, and he didn't slouch. Jackson knew Thomas was not asking for pity and truly regretted ever leaving the highway.

Jackson gave Thomas the hammer and then looked down at Candy. Jackson whistled sharply. It caused Candy and Thomas to look up at him.

"Everything is going to be ok. I'm not going to let anything happen to you or any of us. I promise, alright? I love you guys," Jackson said to them both. "Candy, stay with Kim. Be there when she comes to. Thomas, you and I have work to do before anything more fucked up happens!"

At that second, from outside, a nearby gunshot went off.

6

What In The Fucking Hell Is This Shit!?, the hunter outside the cabin said to themself, once again, back behind the trees. When the entire cabin began to shake by itself, the hunter retreated, not knowing if the cabin was going to fall apart and crumble. *Glad I came prepared!*

The hunter watched nervously behind a pile of brush and a tree trunk as three gangly monsters with long, thin arms and three-clawed hands circled the cabin. Their heads were tiny, and their necks were pencil thin, but their bodies were over eight feet tall, and their legs were just as gnarly as their arms. They looked like the offspring of a gigantic spider and hairless abominable yeti, but with the claws of a vicious sloth!

The hunter had a single one in their sight, and with a sturdy rifle, the hunter took a shot. The creature either howled in pain or roared with anger. The hunter couldn't tell, but regardless, the creature ran off, and so did the other two. *They'll be back…I know it.*

7

Deeper in the woods, the observer watched everything as a single tear trickled down their cheek. *It's all happening again.* For the first time in years, this other watcher in the woods had a swirl of emotions rage through their head, until anger took over. *No, it's not. Not again!*

With one determined step, without making a single sound, the silent watcher headed toward the cabin, ready to do anything possible to make the sun come up faster than it ever had.

8

For fifteen minutes, Thomas and Jackson tried to do everything possible to barricade the cabin. Jackson had moved the writing desk against the front door, and when Thomas found three nails, he nailed one of the rugs off the living room floor to the wall to cover the back window.

When Jackson and Candy weren't looking, Thomas put the writing desk to quick, personal use…just in case.

Coming down off an adrenaline rush, Candy shivered three times and walked away from Kim, who was still motionless on the sofa. Candy had run her hands up and down the sides of Kim's neck and felt no abnormalities. *How are you not dead, sweetie?* Candy asked mentally. She couldn't dare ask out loud. Now, by the fire, Candy felt the heat and was thankful for the fire's light. She just wished she could cover Kim up.

Thomas and Jackson never left Candy's eyesight, and neither asked her how either she or Kim was doing. At the same time, Candy didn't ask Thomas or Jackson if they needed help. Each one was doing what they needed to do to simply keep busy, instead of cowering in pity or defeat.

Jackson and Thomas pillaged the kitchen cabinets and drawers as Candy finally sat comfortably at the fire by Kim. The floor was hard, but the warmth was comforting. Thomas and Jackson constantly talked,

81

asked one another stupid questions, and comprehended rational ideas on what was happening, but to Candy, it was background noise. Almost elevator music, but one thing was said that made Candy respond without thought.

It was Jackson who asked, "Should we attempt to go into the bedrooms? Our clothes—"

"No," Candy addressed firmly. "No, we're fine for now." Both Thomas and Jackson stopped at Candy's response. She looked up at them with an expression of certainty. "I think they want us to. We go in and they'll separate us." Neither Thomas nor Jackson questioned it. It made sense in every way possible. Jackson slammed a drawer shut and looked at Candy.

"I believe you," Jackson said, "And I'm running out of ideas. Anyone got—" and Candy burst into a painful scream.

As Candy's scream cut Jackson off, something gripped her shirt from behind and choked her throat. Candy screamed a second time as something else grabbed her hair and pulled her across the floor away from the fire, right past Kim on the sofa. Jackson and Thomas both watched Candy as she was dragged along the cabin floor by…absolutely nothing!

Jackson dashed around the propped-up sofa as Thomas leaped over the kitchen area counter. Thomas pushed off the counter and landed directly on Candy as if to tackle her, which he did.

"Let Go Of Her, You Bastard!" Thomas screamed at who, or whatever, drug Candy along the floor. Thomas reached up and grabbed her hair also, but pulled it downward to release the hair-pulling tension. Whichever ghost had a hold of Candy released it, and all three heard a cackle of laughter from an older woman's voice.

Thomas looked down at Candy and locked his eyes with hers.

"Are you okay!?" Thomas asked truly and sincerely. Candy nodded and began to sob uncontrollably. The redhead buried her face in Thomas's chest and heaved sobs of tears harder than she had ever cried in her life. Thomas looks down her arms in shock at the scratches on her arm and her back. Small sliver-thin lacerations on her left shoulder blade start to seep blood.

"I…wanna…go home…," Candy sobbed into Thomas's chest, and he kissed her forehead. Thomas looked over Candy's head and locked eyes with Jackson.

"We gotta get outta here, Jay," Thomas said firmly as he shook his head. "Now."

It was here when Kim shot up off the sofa and screamed at the top of her lungs in the purest of nightmarish hysterical fear. Her gasp of air and belted scream sounded as if she had been holding her breath for well over five minutes.

9

"JESUS *FUCKING CHRIST*!" Thomas shouted in shock and terror. He damn near jumped out of his skin, practically shoving Candy off his lap. Jackson quickly looked in Kim's direction but didn't leap four feet off the cabin floor like Thomas did. Instead, Jackson darted to Kim and seized her shoulders, one with each hand.

Kim continued to scream with her eyes closed as Jackson tried to shake her as if to wake her up. After two soft shakes, Jackson squeezed his grip and gave Kim a very strong jolt with a scream of her name. Instantly, Kim's screams stopped, and she looked at Jackson foggily. They were nose to nose. When Kim finally recognized Jackson, the young woman cracked into sobs.

Kim collapsed into Jackson's arms and sobbed harder than Candy cried to Thomas. To Jackson, it didn't feel like he was coddling an adult. It felt like he was calming an eight-year-old child. Kim collapsed into Jackson's arms and buried her face in his bare chest. Jackson turned to look at Thomas, who was still holding Candy.

Jackson saw Thomas's face, and there was no more macho bullshit. He also saw Candy, who was cradled like a child. Candy's bare ass was sticking out of the bottom of Jackson's shirt, but Jackson didn't see more 'revealed curiosity'. He saw painful scratches, raw redness, and bruising from being drug along the cabin's living room floor.

"Yes," Jackson said in full agreement. "Yes, we do."

10

Less than two minutes later, Kim talked as she continued to wipe tears from her face. Candy was out of Thomas's arms and on the other end of the sofa. Jackson was still at Kim's side, kneeling on the floor.

"It was…a violation," Kim explained shakily. "I…I heard every voice, including yours, you guys, and still, I wasn't able to move or think…or even speak. There was—it was a-a another…presence…in me and it took over for a minute. I tried to scream out for you guys, but there was no echo to my voice. Instead, the other voice talked to me."

"What did it say?" Candy asked, deeply concerned.

"I could…hear…its thought as it spoke, like I could read its mind…! It, or they, think we're…trespassers or something. It kept calling you guys something, and then, the thing in me just ejected out so quickly, that I blanked out. Everything went black as if I was punched. Boom! Instant lights out!"

"Well…you, it, *did* call us that, and then Thomas thought about us escaping, so he threw the sofa chair at the window. It hit something. It made the chair fall back in," Jackson explained.

"That's when it left me! I became instantly frozen when it leaped out of me! It's emotion…was—it was terrified! What was outside!?" Kim asked rapidly.

"We don't know, but right after that, the cabin's disaster area picked itself up, rebuilt everything that broke, and then there was gunfire from somewhere outside. Something outside roared. Just before you woke up, Candy was dragged along the floor by her hair by one of your ghosts," Thomas explained, but the last sentence sounded more judgmental than just a review.

"These Aren't *MY* Ghosts, Asshole!" Kim threw back at Thomas.

"Hey, Linda Blair, did you know your head spun all the way around?" Candy asked Kim. Kim only stared at her, squinting with one eye, not exactly understanding the question. Kim didn't have to because Candy illustrated with her hands. "You should be dead, girl."

"H-how can this happen?! I didn't see anyone or anything around you, Candy, and yeah, Kim, your fucking crazy-ass head went a full three-sixty!" Thomas explained unsympathetically. "What the hell is going on around here, anyway?!" He leaned over, kissed Candy on the top of her head, stood, then walked away a step toward the fireplace. Thomas's right hand felt the five o'clock shadow on his face. Thomas quickly spun back around and told the girls, "I'll help you take care of this mess. I'm so sorry you got hurt. I never intended for…ANY Of This! It was just to be a road trip and for all of us to have fun and get out of the city for a while and—" Kim stood up, which cut off Thomas's ranting. She slowly approached Thomas with a sympathetic look.

"I heard you stutter," Kim said calmly. For the first time the whole weekend, Kim hugged Thomas tightly, as if to say, 'It's going to be okay.' Thomas slowly hugged Kim back in appreciation of understanding. Neither Jackson nor Candy protested.

As if someone flipped an insanity switch, a heavy pounding on the front cabin door started again, and the boards of the cabins' floor began to vibrate so violently, two of them actually cracked. All four leaped either onto their feet or off their feet and felt the rattling of the floor. A few seconds later, it stopped. The cracked boards quickly repaired themselves.

"They're like earthquake aftershocks," Thomas said alertly.

"That's It!" Jackson abruptly said, then turned his attention directly to Kim. "Kim, why are we trespassers? What was in 'its' head when it was in your head?"

Just as Kim opened her mouth to speak, a large scrape gouged the outside of the cabin's back wall. All four heard and practically felt the claw rip the back horizontal logs of the outside wall. To hear it was one thing, but to 'feel' it in your goosebumps was entirely another.

"Holy…fucking…shit," Thomas whispered to Jackson with a worried look. "What…the fuck…was that?!"

"Whatever is outside is the reason the ghost let go of its grip on me," Kim whispered as low as Thomas. "They're terrified of it!"

"This is fucking crazy, you guys!" Thomas harshened his whisper. "Fucking ghosts in here shaking up the place and whatever the fuck is out here has claws like Wolverine or Freddy-fucking-Kruger!"

"Where do we go?" Candy asked hopelessly.

"Kim, which is worse…," Jackson asked as he pointed up. "Them?" Jackson changed his pointing direction to the front door. "Or Them?" Another gunshot outside echoed. This time, they all heard it.

"Is there someone outside helping us?!" Kim excitedly asked, but not gleefully excitedly, with a raw-throated voice. This instantly made up Thomas's mind.

"We're going out the front door and making a run for it down the hill," Thomas stated. "No bullshit, no breaks, no stops…no nothing. Pure downhill running, straight to the car!"

"We'd snap our necks, or fall and break a bone, or worse," Jackson rebutted.

"What the fuck could be worse?!" Candy exclaimed, approving Thomas's answer.

"We could find out up close and personal what's out there being shot at!" Kim said factually. "We can't outrun a bear or a mountain cat!"

"I'll take my chances," Thomas said, determinedly. "Forget the backpacks and the gear. I have the keys and that's all we need."

"We're Practically Naked, Thomas!" Candy barked. "Might As Well Be Running Through Razor Wire!"

"Thomas—" Jackson tried to speak, but Thomas's mind was made up.

"You stay, you die. It's your choice!" Thomas barked loudly through his gritted teeth. Thomas then looked at Candy and then at Kim without a word. Thomas stormed towards and reached the door in two seconds. Before fear could grip him to stop him, Thomas opened the cabin's front door and saw one large claw mark across the wood.

It was just under an inch thick. Thomas slowly knelt and touched the carving with his hand. The hundreds of splinters touched his fingers like needles.

"What in the unholy hell made those marks?!" Jackson asked, truthfully not wanting the answer.

"Fuck if I know, Jay," answered Thomas, "but this ain't no cat or bear!"

"I do," Kim said, and the other three looked at her, astonished and odd-faced. "Like I said, before I was interrupted…," Kim reminded them, "I could hear my intruder's thoughts."

11

Kim convinced everyone to go back inside the cabin, and with the distraction at hand, Kim advised them to get their belongings from each bedroom. As a group, all four went into the first bedroom and grabbed Thomas's and Candy's things. Then, again, all four went into the second bedroom where Jackson and Kim grabbed their stuff.

The four quickly dressed in the living room in their jeans, flannels, and hoodies before the next ghostly or beastly interruption stopped them again. There were no jokes, no comments, and no perversion quirks as the four redressed fully in front of one another. Candy, however, did see Thomas's pickaxe tattoo on his back with his initials 'T.H.E.' above it and found herself snickering as she mentally agreed that having her initials 'C.U.M.' would not be a good idea after all. As Thomas zipped up his jeans, he saw Jackson pick up his phone and tap open two apps.

"What are you doing, Jay?" Thomas asked. "Leave it off! Save the battery!"

"I have an idea," Jackson said, ignoring Thomas's advice. "I'm going to try to look up the history of this place…if there's any."

Thomas, now curious, also picked up his phone. It was off. Against his own better judgment, Thomas turned it on.

As it loaded, Thomas turned to Candy. "Is yours on?" he asked.

"I had it on for the alarm," Candy answered and showed him. "And it's at twenty percent." Thomas looked beside her battery life icon and saw there were no signal bars lit. In its place was a tiny 'x'. Thomas looked down at his phone and quickly got excited when he saw his battery was at fifty-five percent, but just like Candy's: it had no signal.

"You have mobile data?!" Thomas asked Jackson shockingly, after seeing Jackson scroll the internet with his peripheral vision.

"No...I-I...I'll be goddamned," Jackson replied, astonished. "I have...Wi-Fi!" Right away, Candy, Kim, and Thomas crowded around Jackson to look at his phone's screen. "There's a...hot spot here!"

"Everyone, turn off your phones," Candy instructed urgently. "Jay, except for you. You find out what the hell this hellhole is. Kim, finish what you were saying about the ghost that possessed you, and what the hell those things are out there!"

"Where did—" Kim started to say, but Candy was adamant.

"I Want To Get The Fuck Out Of Here, So Speak Up!" Candy snapped. Kim did not argue back or make any protest.

"Kim, go ahead. I want to know, but I'm going to search on here, too," Jackson told her. "Don't think I'm ignoring you or anything." Jackson looked up at her, then back down at his phone. "I've got to find something, *anything*, about this place. There's too much going on here for this to be just a regular cabin!"

When Kim started, she knelt, putting her loose items in her backpack. "They're night creatures, like giant spiders but built like skinny bears," Kim started. "At least that's the vision I got from inside its head. Just because I could hear and see what was going on in the mind of the ghost doesn't mean I understand it."

"Keep going," Candy said urgently to get Kim to the point.

"The ghosts, when they were alive, were killed here and then trapped here. Tonight, we set them free," Kim continued. "I saw one when Candy took the cloth off the bedroom mirror, but I thought it was because I was looking at the first picture too long or something, like a negative afterimage."

"They…were trapped in the mirror?" Candy asked, suddenly rushed with guilt.

"Mirrors," Kim emphasized. "We uncovered one in each of our rooms, and then they uncovered the rest, freeing themselves. That's why everything hung on the walls was covered."

"I Didn't Know!" Candy protested, taking quick looks at her three friends as if she were now on trial. "How Was I Supposed To Fuckin' Know!?"

"No one is blaming you, hon," Thomas said sympathetically. "Let her finish." Thomas stretched his legs out, as if ready to go on a run, which he was. Overall, he was getting prepared for the next interruption. It seemed like each time they let their guard down, something started.

"They're tormented spirits," Kim continued. "Not all of them were killed by the creatures outside, which they call…um…Grays, or…Mutilators."

"That's what you said before you collapsed," Candy recalled.

"The ghosts are angry. They were killed here. Murdered. Then trapped…against their will," Kim said.

"By who?" Thomas asked. That was the million-dollar question.

"HA! I got something!" Jackson burst out, interrupting the conversation.

12

"Listen up! It says, 'Since twenty fifteen, over seventeen people have gone missing in the Wasatch Mountains without a trace—'"

"These mountains are huge, Jay! That sounds like any mountain range report," Candy expressed, trying to rationalize the situation.

"I'm not done," Jackson said with a worried but stern voice, and continued, "'...without a trace, in this county alone. With a combination of the eleven counties that occupy the Wasatch Mountains, there are reports of twenty-eight confirmed missing persons. As of twenty-ten, there are reports of thirty-nine missing.' Guys, this list goes back to the nineteen sixties!"

"What's your point?" Thomas asked more sternly than Jackson did when he was interrupted.

"It means there are predators in these mountains," Kim answered correctly. "Probably more than just the wildlife...or abnormal wildlife, to be accurate."

"There's just a bit more. Says here, 'Numerous reports from all eleven counties have searched for all [missing persons] based on their abandoned vehicle registration information. None over the last thirty years has been found. This includes families that were not at reported addresses of living households.' Jesus...!" Jackson finished.

"Are you fucking kidding me?! This can't be true!" Thomas protested.

Candy punched Thomas in the arm. "Look At Us, You Fucking Idiot!" Candy barked at Thomas. "What about what we've been through tonight!?"

"Will you stop HITTING *ME!?*" Thomas shouted in frustration at Candy, directly into her face.

"I think we're in deep shit, Jay," Kim said uncontrollably. Jackson turned off the screen and put his phone in his pocket, then nodded at Kim.

"I agree," Jackson returned, then looked at Thomas. "But we're not lost and we're not missing. We know where we are."

"We have to try to think of a way to get out of here, as fast as possible. The sooner, the better," Candy said, then turned to Thomas. "And without any egotistical, macho man, *bullshit!*"

Thomas looked at Candy coldly. "Then lead the way," Thomas mocked Candy directly and opened his hand, making a 'ladies first' gesture toward the front door. "I insist."

"ENOUGH!" Kim shouted as she turned headfirst to Thomas, then to Candy. "Every Goddamn Time You Two Screw, All You Do Is Fight For Three Days Afterwards! I Am Soooooooo—" and that's when Kim's friends watched Kim rise off the floor with a locked mouth. Kim's voice and jaw stayed in the 'sooooo' position as her eyes rolled in the back of her head. Both her arms and her legs went limp as her head dangled to one side.

As fast as one could blink, Kim's entire body slammed against the ceiling.

—THUD!—

As if Kim were metal and the ceiling was magnetic, Kim hit the ceiling so hard, the sickening thud of her skull to wood would twist the strongest of stomachs. Both of her arms and legs clung to the ceiling as if the ceiling were the floor, but her untucked loose clothing draped.

With her short dark hair dangling down over her face, Kim's head turned to face Candy, Thomas, and Jackson. The three watched Kim's right arm fall from the ceiling and sternly pointed to the cabin's front door. The door slammed open, but it turned out not to be the front door. Instead, the bedroom door that Thomas and Candy occupied opened. It opened so vigorously that it should have cracked in two when it struck the wall. It didn't.

Kim's eyes were still rolled back, exposing the whites, and her mouth was locked open. Without moving her jaw, Kim spoke strongly but softly, and not in her regular voice.

"…Leave…!"

13

"No!" Jackson spoke up assertively and stood up from the sofa. "Not without her!" Kim's head angled to face Jackson directly. "Let Her Go!" Jackson watched the muscles in her face change as if the ghost inside her was showing its former facial characteristics.

"…Noooo…!" the ghost inside Kim said slowly and defiantly. Kim's right arm continued to point at the bedroom door, but the left arm lifted off the ceiling and tapped two fingers on Kim's chest. "…We…keep…her…!"

"Give Her Back, You Bastard!" Candy shouted up at the host in Kim's body.

"…Noooo…T-his…one's…pu-re…!" The voice spoke, referring to Kim. "…Truth…!"

"THAT'S IT!! I'VE—" Thomas started to shout, but was shut up immediately as Jackson extended his arm out and shoved his open hand into Thomas's chest. Thomas looked directly into Jackson's eyes and read Jackson's face clearly: *Don't Do A Damn Thing!* Kim's head turned to Thomas, and the face changed, as well as the voice.

"…The…Ego…!" a ghostly woman's voice from Kim spoke.

93

Kim's head angled toward Candy, and again, the face and voice changed. Candy felt Kim's glare as it said, "…The…Whore…!" in a judgmental old woman's voice. Kim's face was full of wrinkles, but it again changed when Kim's face turned to Jackson.

"…The Cow-ard…!" a harsh, muscular male voice expelled from Kim. After a brief cackling of laughter, Kim's face wrenched and returned to the first face. So did the voice.

"…now…lea-ve…!"

Jackson took two slow steps closer to Kim and lowered the tone of his voice. It was clear they were among many, and the ghosts knew how to read Kim. Which meant they knew what Kim's thoughts and feelings were.

"Your prisoner," Jackson stated, "is important to me. What do you want, so we can have her back?" Candy and Thomas stood motionless, awaiting the ghost in Kim to answer.

"…No…pri-son-er…!" Kim's mouth spoke. The voice was calm and slow, but malicious and angry. It was mentally unbalanced but intelligent, and definitely knew more than all four of them put together. Jackson figured that out all on his own, plus what Kim told them five minutes ago was the real bonus. "…Kim…go-od…!" the voice judged, but then growled. "…Kim…Stay…!"

"Who did this to you?" Jackson asked, hoping sympathy could work over anger. "Kim, she said you were trapped in the mirrors. How? Why?" Instantly, Kim's mouth stretched inhumanly wide, and a carnivorous roar shook the cabin of the purest of raw anger. Kim's body fell off the ceiling and hit the floor with a nightmarish impact of flesh to wood.

—*THUNK!*—

Each cabin room door, cabinet door, furniture drawer, and windowpane flung open and slammed closed in unison over and over and over again as Kim's body began to bend.

Without visual injury to Kim, Kim's body arched its back backward like a crab, with her hands and feet propping her up. Kim's head bent back further than any human could ever do and turned around like a scorpion looking for its target. Kim's face changed multiple times and the roar turned into a growl, then into a deep inhale that sounded like a tight wind tunnel.

When Kim's multiple faces looked at Jackson, Thomas, and Candy, the deafening thudding stopped. Several voices that matched several faces spoke, several overlapping one another. Candy began to cry, seeing her friend in such a twisted position. Thomas grabbed Candy and drew her close to him. Jackson spread his arms out, keeping Thomas and Candy behind him.

"…Out-side…is…death…!"

"…Mon-sters…!"

"…Creat-ures…!"

"…Dev-ils…!"

"…Under…ground…slo-wer…death…!"

"…De ceiv ers…!"

"…Be-tray-ers…!"

"…Kill-ers…!"

Jackson shouted, interrupting the various voices that expelled from Kim, "WE DON'T UNDERSTAND!" At that, the voices stopped. Every door, drawer, and closable object in the cabin closed one final time, all slamming shut in unison. The fireplace burped a burst of air.

Thomas, Candy, and Jackson watched Kim's body relax as it descended slowly to the cabin's wooden floor. She looked like a Macy's Day parade float losing its air.

"Look!" Candy gasped and pointed at Kim. "I-I think they're leaving her!"

All around them, invisible to the naked eye, the ghosts hovered as they left Kim's body. Jackson ran to Kim's side and held her more eloquently than he had ever before, as if Kim were made of easily breakable glass. She was unconscious, and her eyes were gently closed. Her facial features had returned to her natural, young face.

"Kim? Kim!" Jackson spoke to Kim up close. His voice cracked. He truly didn't know if she was alive, regardless of her controlled breathing. At the sound of her name from Jackson, Kim's eyelids began to flicker to life. Slowly, her eyes opened. Jackson saw her eyes were wet and shiny, and the ring of green inside told him she was alive, and physically unharmed.

Kim, unlike before, slowly opened her eyes and smiled weakly. "I'm okay," Kim whispered, and Jackson burst into tears with a thankful smile.

14

Jackson was kneeling on the floor as he held Kim in his arms. Thomas and Candy had walked over and knelt beside them. All four friends were nestled together, each one of them comfortingly lost, but united more than ever before.

All of the bickering, the animosity, the brashness; it was all gone.

Kim began to explain everything to them, how she talked to each one of the ghosts that inhabited her, how each one talked back, and how each one had a story of their death. Kim told them how each one was either a lost hiker, or simple travelers, or a mountain enthusiast who was tricked or betrayed by the owners of the cabin.

Kim said that several ghosts were over a hundred years old, and some had only died three years ago. Some were old men and women, others were children, but regardless of their ages, each one was vengeful, angry, and full of bloodlust against the living.

"Everyone alive is their enemy. They can't tell the difference between those who are just passing by, or visiting, like us, and those who really killed them," Kim told her friends.

"But you?" Candy asked. "What makes you so different from everyone else?"

"She doesn't lie," Jackson answered, not taking his eyes off Kim's eyes. "She never lies."

"Pure," Thomas retracted. "Truth."

"They trust me, and I can see them," Kim said as she looked at the ceiling. When she looked back down at Jackson, she chuckled. "Can't you see them, you coward?" Jackson couldn't help but snicker back at the joke.

"For being ghosts, they're a good judge of character," Thomas joked, to which all of them got a chuckle.

"We need to free them," Kim said. "I promised them."

"How Can You Promise That?" Candy burst out. "We don't even know how we're gonna get out of here, let alone help them!"

"Jackson," Kim said, "Let me up." As asked, Jackson and Thomas, too, helped Kim to her feet. She placed her hand on the wall of the cabin to steady herself, but insisted she was okay. "They said they don't want us outside, because of the creatures. The…Grays."

"Yeah, they're not happy about whatever is out there," Jackson agreed.

"So, what do we do? How do we get out of here?" Candy asked. At the 'here' of Candy's question, the bedroom door reopened on its own. Jackson and Thomas looked at Kim.

"Follow the old woman, guys," Kim said, and Kim started to walk to the door. None of her friends moved. As Kim got to the door, Kim turned her gaze, put her hand to her stomach, and bowed slightly. Then Kim entered the bedroom out of their sight. The instant the three tried to walk in, they all thinned themselves against the doorframe and walked sideways, so as not to walk through the invisible ghost. Kim saw this and chuckled as they entered the bedroom.

"We start here," Kim said calmly. "Start looking for…I-I really have no idea. Maybe something out of the ordinary?" Without hesitation, the four started to look around the mid-sized bedroom for anything odd to them. Kim looked under the mattress, and Thomas looked along the window. Jackson pushed against the walls, looking for a secret compartment of some kind, as Candy clumsily tripped on the woven bedroom rug.

"Fuck! Candy!" Thomas exclaimed as he bent down to help her. "Are you okay!?"

"Goddamn rug," Candy grouched. "I could've—" and Candy froze. Just off the edge of the rug, Candy saw something attached to the cabin floor. It was black, metal, and had two screws. The attachment was flat, black, and rectangular. "Son…of a…bitch…!"

"What is it?" Kim asked, instantly interested.

Candy crawled off the rug on all fours and grabbed the rug with both hands. She yanked it hard and exposed just what they were looking for.

”W-What The Hell?! A Door!?” Thomas shouted, completely astonished. “There was a door under our bed the whole time?!” Candy took two steps back, instantly appalled by the thought that someone could be down there while they were having sex. Thomas thought the same thing, and again, without saying a word, his mind went to the truck both he and Jackson saw. Controlling it, Thomas began to grow extremely angry at himself and his idea to leave the road.

“It’s a root cellar door,” Jackson said after he knelt to look at it closely. “It’s…crazy but it’s not surprising! It’s actually a good hiding place—”

“Oh, Fuck You, JAY!” Candy protested loudly. “You Weren’t Fucking In Here With This Under You!” Candy’s index finger pointed accusingly at the flat door.

“What I’m saying, Candy,” Jackson tried to explain, “is that this isn’t surprising. Most houses have a crawl space or a basement for storing food or a storm shelter.” Jackson looked up at Kim, but Kim wasn’t interested in the root cellar entrance. She was looking at the upright bedroom door.

Thomas and Candy looked at Kim and noticed she wasn’t paying attention, so Thomas burst out, “Kim!” Kim didn’t jump. Instead, she turned her head calmly.

“They want us to go down there,” Kim said.

“This is their dilemma! Why don’t they?!” Candy snapped back, clearly not wanting to go adventuring under a haunted cabin.

“Because we’re alive, and they’re not,” Jackson answered. “Right?” Jackson asked Kim.

"You first, coward," Kim said, smirking at her boyfriend. Jackson, not caring for the joke anymore, grabbed the circular metal ring and pulled the floor-level hatch up.

15

Kim left the room for a few seconds and returned with two flashlights from their travel backpacks. Kim gave one to Thomas and the other to Jackson. They agreed that one man would enter first, then the two women would enter, and then the last man with the second flashlight would be the caboose. The first thing Thomas did was shine his flashlight straight down the hole.

"At least there are steps," Thomas snarked. "Careful, they look steep."

"I hate you guys for this…," Candy said coldly to everyone who could hear. No one responded to her statement. None took it personally.

It took another good minute for all four to muster the courage to travel down the stairs into the darkness of the cellar but they managed. Jackson, who was the tail of the group, told them that he would leave the root cellar door open, and they all had plenty to say.

Candy: "You better leave that fucker open!"

Kim: "No shit, Sherlock!"

Thomas: "Touch that door, and I'll break your skull!"

When a spider's web touched Thomas's five-o'clock shadow, he whipped his hands at it, but when the web came back to hit him again, Thomas struck it with an open palm. Upon striking it, Thomas realized it wasn't a spider's web, but a strand of something, like a shoelace. He shone his flashlight onto it, followed it to the ceiling, and found a bulb.

100

"Son of a fuck…!" Thomas whispered and pulled the cord. Hesitant at first, the bulb's wire inside glowed bright and the root cellar was lit dimly, but bright enough for all to see.

"Now we're talkin'!" Jackson boasted. "Let's see what we got here—"

"WHOA! Wait!" Candy shouted, spreading her hands out palms down. Everyone stopped and looked at Candy, who looked like she had heard something. "What's wrong with this picture?!" It was a good few seconds before someone answered. Thomas looked at the answer dead in front of him, and even he didn't see it. Luckily, Kim did.

"Electricity," Kim stated. "None of this cabin has electricity, just the oil lamps and fireplace!" Thomas, who was looking at the bulb, felt like a complete idiot.

"I'll be a—How Did I Not See That!?" Thomas yelled at himself.

"Your 'ego' got in the way," Jackson joked, but no one laughed. Kim gave Jackson a hard look of disapproval. "What?! You keep calling me 'coward'!"

"You don't take it personally," Kim said with a stern face.

"No," Thomas said, correcting them all. "He's right…and so is whoever said it."

"I Am *NOT* A Whore!" Candy exploded outwardly. The three stared at her in surprise and disbelief, as if to ask, 'Where did that come from?!'.

"Every single one of you agrees with the titles the ghosts called us! Just now, Thomas admitted his 'ego' is who he is! Well, listen here, my so-called friends: I Am NOT—"

"Candy! Easy!" Kim calmly said and rushed to Candy and hugged her hard. Candy tried pushing Kim away, but Kim took control of the situation quickly. "Guys, Candy and I are going back upstairs, just to the bedroom okay?" Jackson and Thomas both nodded. With Candy leading the way, both girls went back upstairs into the bedroom within seconds. Everything went quiet.

"Whew…," Thomas whispered. The hatch door was still open. "She's gonna be a real joy to be around after we get out of this."

"IF we get out of this," Jackson corrected. Thomas raised his eyebrows and nodded. "Let's get at it. Let's see what's so special about down here."

16

For a summer night, there was a slight chill in the air. Maybe it was the creatures, maybe it was the entire cabin shaking a few times, or maybe it was just the simple fact of being alone at night in the woods. Regardless of what it was, it produced goosebumps on the hunter's arms. What it was, was simple: the adrenaline rush was over.

They're going to come back, the hunter said to themself. *It's just a matter of time, and once they're gone, I can burn that cabin to the ground!* The hunter watched the back of the cabin while hunkered in their hiding spot. The individual looked at their watch and groaned wearily. It was going to be sun-up soon, and they'd miss the opportunity!

The hunter, as quietly as possible, pulled the pin back from their rifle to double-check that the next round was loaded and ready. In the moonlight, the shell had a dull shine on it. The individual nodded in acknowledgment of the bullet's presence and reloaded the round.

Alright, you motherfuckers out here: come back out so I can finish you…and to you motherfuckers inside the cabin: you're seriously fucking up my night!

Deeper in the trees, the observer, the one without the rifle, had not only come to a decision but had already acted on it. Through the trees, past the bear traps, out of the hunter's rifle's field of view, and now beside the cabin, the observer waited. *Everything is too quiet…!*

18

Deep in the cellar, under Candy and Thomas's borrowed bedroom, Thomas and Jackson scrounge around the small rectangular room. The walls of the potential underground pantry were of the same wood as the sides of the cabin. The room was stuffier than one would think.

"I thought it'd be cooler," Jackson told Thomas, and Thomas acknowledged the phrase with a simple 'hmph'.

Amongst the dimly lit room were solid wooden shelving along one wall, three large wooden barrels, two washtubs, and three fifty-pound burlap sacks. Other than long-term storage, there was nothing of special interest in the basement, at least nothing that they found to 'be' of special interest.

That is, until Thomas stood in front of the wooden shelving unit. Something brushed his face gently. That 'something' caught his attention. It made him glad the girls were upstairs.

"What did you find?" Jackson asked after seeing Thomas stop motionless and stare at the wooden shelving.

"It's what I didn't find that made me discover what I did find," Thomas cryptically answered. Jackson shrugged his shoulders, unable to see…whatever Thomas found. Thomas looked at Jackson, partially rolled his eyes, then reached out and grabbed Jackson's right wrist with his left arm. Instantly, Jackson tried to pull away, but Thomas's grip was far stronger.

Balled in a fist, Jackson tried a second time to pull away, but Thomas, again, kept his strength solid and held onto Jackson's wrist firmly. It took Jackson one more attempt to pull away and several seconds of facial stares before Jackson finally spoke.

"Will you let go of my fucking arm!?" Jackson demanded.

"What do you FEEL, idiot!?" Thomas asked harshly, trying to emphasize his point without letting Jackson's arm go.

"I feel your death grip on my—" Jackson said, before getting interrupted.

"What ELSE!?" Thomas barked, loud enough for the girls to hear. At that, realization struck Jackson, and both his mouth and his eyes widened.

"A…breeze!" Jackson said in shock, now feeling a gentle breeze traveling through and over the hairs on his arm and fingers. Thomas let go of Jackson's arm slowly. Right away, Jackson felt his pulse rate throb around his right wrist.

"A breeze," Thomas repeated confidently, relieved that Jackson had finally acknowledged it.

"We need to get the girls," Jackson said, and Thomas agreed. "Candy isn't going to like this…you know that, right?"

"We don't have a choice," Thomas fired back. "And thanks to Kim's stupid promise, neither does Candy."

When Candy and Kim exited the underground room and reentered the bedroom from the doorway on the floor, both of them felt significantly better at an instant. Neither one of them wanted to go back down into the cellar. Without saying it, Kim knew Candy was not going to sleep in this exact room ever again, and Kim knew she wasn't going to either. But sleep and the cellar were not on Candy's mind.

"What was all that about?" Kim asked just after emerging from the floor. "Of course, you're not a whore! None of us—"

"Your little ghost friend—It…it read you! It read *us* as it possessed your ass!" Candy shouted. "It, or you, called Jay 'a coward' and said Thomas was 'all ego'. It said you are all 'truthful' and shit!"

"Candy, I—"

"Oh, don't go all defending all the dead bastards floating all around us now, just because you've become all 'Ghost-Whisperer' and shit! Some old lady bitch cut my arms and back with scalpel-thin cuts, grabbed my hair painfully, and dragged my ass along the fucking floor!" Candy ranted loudly, growing more and more angry. "Then both Thomas and Jay start agreeing with them, saying they are what they were called, well one of them called me a whore, and I AM NOT—"

"*CANDY!*" Kim barked. Candy stopped and continued to breathe heavily. "Why would it say that?" Kim calmly asked. Candy turned and looked at Kim with a gaping mouth and cold eyes. It took a few seconds for Kim to reiterate, "I'm not judging or anything, I'm just asking!"

"I…passed…EVERY…CLASS…on…my…OWN!" Candy spoke her answer very strongly and defensively, the last words were behind tears. Kim had wondered how Candy passed her last three exams when she wasn't on campus, and none of the exams were online.

"Candy—" Kim tried to speak sympathetically.

"OH, I JUST WANT TO GET *THE FUCK OUT OF HERE!*" Candy screamed at the top of her lungs just as Jackson Chad popped his head up from the floor door.

What Jackson said next did not help Candy's situation: "We found something! Better come down!" Jackson saw Candy's face and immediately wanted to withdraw his words, for on the way up, he heard Candy shout. Before Candy could explode at Jackson and before Kim could reiterate, another gunshot rang outside. It sounded so close, Kim and Candy bent their knees and ducked down as if it came from the next room.

Thomas barked from the cellar, "What Was That?!"

20

Jackson and Thomas both came up from the cellar, and one of each stood on both sides of the window, trying to see out. The oil lamp cast its reflection on the window's glass, making it too hard to see outside clearly. They didn't want to see someone aiming a gun at them, nor did they want to see just what whoever was shooting at.

"They're back, aren't they?" Candy asked with a shrill in her voice. The strong, confident, and angry college graduate with a master's degree in Outdoor Education now sounded like a terrified, frightened-beyond-rational-thought, witless teenager.

"Think it's the thing that stopped the chair from going out the window?" Jackson asked Thomas, not showing any acknowledgment to Candy in the slightest. He heard her stance on the entire situation and knew anything he'd say to her would result poorly. Thomas didn't answer right away because he wasn't sure how to answer. Jackson and

Kim looked at Thomas carefully, for they didn't know if he was lost in thought or still mentally accepting the situation.

"Thomas…?" Kim asked from the bed, afraid to finish the question.

After a few seconds of looking out the bedroom window, Thomas finally stated, "Alright, no more bullshit," and turned to look at his two friends and his girlfriend. Thomas nudged Jackson away from the window and closed the inner shutters, then went to the floor door and closed it before pulling the rug over it. "We're getting out of here."

"Outside—" Candy spoke as Thomas barged back in.

"Outside, there is a person. A person with a gun and they're shooting at something. What? I don't know, but whatever it is, our floating companions are terrified of it. The hunter out there hasn't tried coming in here once for help, assistance, or even to ask how we are. And downstairs?! What Jay and I found is a seriously fucked up discovery! The last place I want to go is downstairs…!"

"Okay, then…," Kim said, getting to her feet. "What's first?"

"LEAVING!" Candy burst out.

"We're leaving. Now!" Thomas sternly agreed. "We're going out the door and down the hill, just the way we came in! The backpacks, the gear; leave the shit behind. All of it! We're taking the flashlights and the keys, that's it. Kim, I'm sorry," Thomas looked up at the ceiling and all around, "but fuck your ghost, fuck their dilemmas, and for the most part: fuck this cabin!"

"The phones—" Candy spoke as she remembered them. Signal or no, they would be smart to take.

"Leave Them!" Thomas barked heavily and, after a pause, "We're Leaving! Right Now!"

The bedroom door was still open, and it did not close on its own. Thomas walked through the door as if he owned the cabin, and there was no rebuttal from the living nor the dead. By the time Thomas had grabbed the handle to the cabin's front door, Candy and Jackson were behind him. Kim pulled up the rear.

Kim looked toward the living room and saw the fireplace was dim. The room was dimly lit, but Kim could still see the faces of each ghost as they stood along the back wall of the cabin. The ghosts were visible as wispy figures in streamed cigarette smoke. Their presence hovered like a thin satin dress underwater as it descended into an abyss. Each face showed expressions of sorrow, pity, anguish, suffering, and a longing to no longer be dead. Kim returned to them an apologetic expression and a look of vindication. They were lost and miserable.

Their faces also had other looks: warning, caution, and some threatening stares. Kim didn't have to put apples-to-apples together to read their faces: *If you go outside, you will die.* None of the ghosts spoke as the cabin door opened, and none of them moved as the four travelers dashed outside. Kim closed the door, causing it to click shut.

21

Thomas left the cabin the way a person would leave a house angrily: without a care in the world and a thought of self. Thomas was beyond frustrated and was on the brink of snapping at anyone who would tell him to change his mind. In his head, once the four were down the steps of the entrance to the cabin, he was going to run to the SUV, downhill, and nothing was going to stop him. Thomas had one of the two flashlights and when he turned it on, its illumination showed Candy's face up close.

Candy, who was behind Thomas, was nowhere near Thomas's level of awareness, consciousness, and determination. Since being woken up by real-life ghosts, little by little, Candy's mental status on a grip of reality had slipped drastically. Being physically assaulted by ghosts, watching her friend be violated by ghosts, being insulted by ghosts, and lastly, getting forced to enter a dark, musty cellar that had a hidden door under the bed she was sleeping in; this was not the trip she signed up for. Now, here she was, about to run like a maniac in the dark of night through a forest downhill to escape her nightmare.

Third in the row was Jackson, who, to be frank, was collected on the situation, and that was only due to his girlfriend's state of mind. For someone who was calculated, detailed, and thorough about his surroundings, Jackson was the most gathered and rational. Not once had he seriously argued with anyone since being forced awake by ghosts, for the only thing on his mind was leaving with his life and Kim. Both times when Kim's body cracked or sounded mutilated by the ghost's bodily devastations, Jackson thought her injuries killed her. Both times, Kim recovered the instant the ghosts left her body. The science of it all was impossible, and yet, here they were. The four of them are alive, ready to face death and danger in the face, and then promptly leave.

The last person to leave the cabin was Kim, with the second flashlight. Thomas was going to light the way in front, as Kim would light the way for Jackson and Candy. Kim, the most violated of the four, was the only one truly calm and levelheaded. Her mind was not only able to wrap everything they've learned into a rational bow, but also understood everything, from past to present.

Kim figured, *Well…when you're possessed by over fifty different ghosts, each with their own personalities, emotions, and tantrums, you accept the smallest of things quickly.*

Outside, they heard the stomping, the clawing, and the grunting of something very large without a full view of whatever a Gray was. Also, they heard numerous rifle shots, which meant a fifth person, or persons, were there as well. Whoever they were, they were also not seen.

Then again, in the darkest of night and only the stars to light the way, it was almost impossible to see your hand in front of your face. *Good thing for the flashlights*, each one thought without saying it aloud.

Once Kim's feet touched the ground below the bottom step, Thomas pointed his flashlight down the front yard, right where they arrived, grabbed the front of the flashlight, and adjusted the beam to focus sharply on their exit. The wide view grew smaller as the light shone brighter.

"I'm running. I'm not stopping. If I hit a tree or fall, you keep going. If you hit a tree or fall, I'm not stopping," Thomas whispered deeply and strongly. Even Candy knew from the raw emotion of his eyes, he was not exaggerating or joking. "Ready?" The other three nodded.

22

As warned, Thomas turned around and in a mad dash, took off for about two steps. In a second, Thomas's dash to escape the cabin's fuckery came to a sudden stop as Thomas, then Candy, both slammed flat into the massive puddle of water in the middle of the cabin's front yard. If the sudden splash of water wasn't enough to grab the attention of anyone, or anything, around them, Candy's high-pitched screams of hysterics did.

"LEECHES! *THE LEECHES!*" Candy screamed insanely as she splashed all around, attempting to reach her feet. "GET THEM OFF! *GET THEM OFF!*"

Kim quickly aimed the flashlight on Candy and Thomas so Jackson could get to them. Kim watched Thomas first as he slowly stood to maintain his balance. Thomas looked deeply annoyed, agitated, and embarrassed. Jackson instantly went to the end of the water and extended a hand to Candy, who was closer, but Candy was not looking for a hand. Instead, Candy frantically screamed and flapped her arms and hands across her body, trying everything to get the three-inch long, black bloodsuckers off her body.

Thomas walked out of the knee-high puddle like a quarterback who had just been sacked and tried to keep his dignity. When he reached his hysterical girlfriend, Thomas grabbed her arms and put his face nose-to-nose with hers.

Thomas shook her slightly and screamed, "THERE AREN'T ANY!" at the top of his lungs. Candy's hair was flat against her face, her yellow sleeveless hoodie dripped with water, and her mindset was a thin sheet of ice riddled with several cracks, barely held together. Candy stared at Thomas and uncontrollably began to sob. The shoulders, the arms, the chest, and her chin all shook in unison to the sound of her sobs. Thomas, still shin-deep in the front yard puddle, brought Candy in and hugged her.

Kim and Jackson didn't say a word. Jackson stood watching the two as Kim aimed the flashlight at them. Thomas reached down, picked Candy up, cupped her two legs over one forearm, and carried his crying girlfriend out of the water puddle toward the tree line, where they arrived. Kim lowered the flashlight and started to walk around the puddle. Jackson walked directly into the puddle to recover Thomas's dropped flashlight. It still shone in the water.

That was when all four heard...

—*T'CHOMP!*—

23

"What The Hell Was That?!" Jackson shouted when something metal snapped. Without an immediate answer, Thomas slowly released his hold of Candy.

"Do…not…move!" Thomas said to Candy very slowly and very directly. "Got it!?" Candy's head nodded quickly as boots touched the ground. Thomas heard Jackson and Kim Michael approach from behind him and instinctively stretched his arms out widely. "NO! Both Of You! STOP!" At that, Thomas heard both Kim's and Jackson's feet stop shuffling. "Nobody moves! If there's one, there's another somewhere close by!"

"What was it?" Kim asked as she shone her flashlight at Thomas. Jackson had Thomas's recovered flashlight and pointed it at Thomas, then down at Thomas's feet. In seconds, all four saw the tip of Thomas's boot caught in the triangular teeth of the metal device. "A bear trap…!"

"The hunter!" Jackson recalled quickly. "The one shooting! You think it's theirs?" Jackson quickly looked around the yard, hoping to see anything else for rationality or answers. Jackson was five yards from Thomas; Kim was ten feet away from Jackson.

"It's rusty. No way this is a local hunter's bear trap. This thing looks ancient and weather-worn," Thomas said sternly, but shakily, as he looked down at the trap.

"How did we not step in it when we arrived?" Kim asked nervously.

"Dumb fucking luck," Thomas answered as he attempted to pull the boot from the trap.

"Want me to help—" Jackson tried to ask, but Thomas was adamant.

"NO! DON'T MO—" Thomas burst out, but couldn't finish. Something slammed into Thomas, pushing Candy to the ground face-first in an instant. Thomas hit the ground second, but on his back. Jackson heard the —*Oomph!*— from Thomas and Candy's impact and it caused him to frantically aim his flashlight in all directions. Kim saw the impact but all she saw that did it was a large black shadow.

After a hurtful scream of agony, Candy screamed, "My Arm!" Thomas, now ironically free of his trapped shoe, rolled over to Candy and found her cradled in the fetal position on her side in the grass. Candy cradled her arm as if something had injured it.

Then, it happened again. Something dark and large dashed past Jackson, knocking the flashlight from his hands. Jackson was hit so hard that he half-flipped in the air. Kim watched Jackson's aerial spiral in the flashlight's beam, then watched him hit the ground.

For the second time, Kim didn't see what it was, but all four heard the same thing.

Behind them, fifteen yards back, to the left of the cabin, something growled low. Before Kim could collect her wits and aim the flashlight, Jackson, who was on the ground, grabbed his flashlight and aimed the high beam in the growling direction. For a mere split second, two of the four friends saw the most disfigured creature they had ever seen, or even processed the thought of its existence.

The creature stood on two legs and had a long torso with two horrifically long arms. The head was almost to the bottom of the edge of the roof. The body had no hair that they could see. It was slimy, shiny, hairless, and more muscular than an Amazon gorilla. It was cut to the core in muscular display, but the nightmarish creature was lanky, gnarly, and thin. It was tall enough to potentially reach up and touch the top of the roof, if it stood fully stretched, but they didn't see toes. On each foot and hand, all they saw were three talon-like claws.

At the shine of Thomas's flashlight, the creature roared and instantly disappeared, as if it was faster than the fastest superhero from any comic book.

"B-Back Into The Cabin! NOW!" Kim screamed at Jackson directly. Jackson then ignored Thomas's warning: 'don't move'. Jackson got up and ran at his friends. First, he grabbed Thomas with one hand and yanked him upright as hard as he could. Second, Jackson bent down, and both he and Thomas picked up Candy. Both of them carried her back up the yard toward the cabin.

Around them, two more rifle shots rang out. One so close, Jackson heard the zip of the bullet as if it missed his head by an inch. Thomas saw the muzzle flash from the tree line in his peripheral vision. Neither Jackson nor Thomas watched Kim, who had already reached the front porch stairs of the cabin.

Kim aimed the flashlight at the door and immediately came to a stop, clutching a scream. Standing at the front door, Kim caught sight of a smiling young girl with long brown hair, in a summer dress and small red Mary Jane shoes. The moment Kim and the young girl made eye contact, the young girl vanished instantly, and the cabin's front door opened casually on its own.

Without time to rationalize, Kim frantically spun.

"Get Inside! Come On, Move It! Go!" Kim shouted and pressed herself against the wall of the cabin's entryway, allowing Thomas and Jackson to reenter first while carrying Candy. Thomas shoved his half of Candy at Jackson after quickly seeing they could only go in one at a time. Jackson took Candy, cupped her legs under his left arm, and dashed back into the cabin.

"Go! Get Inside!" Thomas shouted at Kim, who was trying to turn off the flashlight. With only one boot on, Thomas and Kim were both at the door side-by-side when something at the bottom of the front stairs reached out and grabbed Thomas's bootless leg. Kim watched Thomas get dragged down to the porch floor, where Thomas instinctively grabbed the railing of the cabin's porch. Kim saw Thomas's muscles bulge as his body lifted off the wooden structure. Whatever was pulling Thomas was extremely strong.

"THOMAS!" Kim shouted. "JACKSON! IT'S THOMAS!" Jackson had just set Candy down on the sofa when Kim screamed out. Without hesitation, Jackson ran to the door.

24

When Jackson arrived, he pointed the flashlight out into the darkness and saw the same gray, hairless creature pulling at Thomas's leg. Thomas clung to the cabin's railing. Kim had dropped her flashlight, and the beam was shining directly off the steps. Jackson looked directly at the face of the monstrosity and saw a true living demon: two red eyes, misshapen spiked teeth, massive upper and lower jaws, and eye sockets deeper than a hollowed-out skull. While trying to pull Thomas, the creature also tried blocking the light.

The snarling chomps from the monster's mouth clamped like a vicious wolf's mouth. One of its three-clawed hands clung to the soil for support in the cabin's lawn while the other had a hold of Thomas's leg by the knee. One strong yank and Thomas's was done for. Luckily, Kim was there for additional leverage. Thomas had lost one grip on the railing and now had Kim, who was using two hands to hold one of Thomas's arms.

When Jackson exited the door fully, he saw Kim struggle. Jackson dropped the flashlight and grabbed the same arm Kim had. That was when both Kim and Jackson heard the ripping of Thomas's pants and the violent howling of pain erupt from Thomas's mouth.

Kim looked down to get her footing; she was losing her grip. At a fast second glance, Kim saw it wasn't just the pants that ripped. Dangling from Thomas's leg was shredded skin and loose flesh. The creature was losing the Tug-of-War and its claws dug in when it slipped.

"PULL, JAY! *PULL!*" Kim shouted as she placed a foot on the railing for leverage. Another shot from the gun in the woods erupted and Jackson heard the bullet strike the creature. It finally let go and fled the yard momentarily. Thomas, with screams of agony, fell directly onto the wooden steps. The heart-ripping wails of Thomas echoed throughout the night's darkness.

"Grab His Arms!" Jackson shouted, and both Kim and Jackson pulled Thomas backward into the cabin. The moment they got Thomas's feet into the cabin, the cabin door shut on its own. Just before it closed, Kim saw the little girl again, standing just outside the door.

"MY LEG! *MY LEG!*" Thomas shouted as he looked down. Bright red blood pumped out of the torn wounds in squirts. The entire floor of the cabin's entrance was soaked in drag marks of fresh seeping blood.

"Kim! First-Aid Bag! QUICK!" Jackson instructed, but Kim was already ahead of the situation. Jackson watched Thomas's fingers disappear into the ooze of blood and flesh.

"We Don't Have Anything For This!" Kim shouted back, frantic but collected. Kim looked around to find the one thing that would help and saw just what was needed. Kim looked at Jackson, and Jackson saw her expression: *Thomas is not going to like this…!* Kim said sternly and with a heavy exhale, she ordered, "Jackson, hold him down."

At that, Kim ran to the sofa and placed her mouth directly next to Candy's ear. Candy was still lying on the sofa, cradling her arm. For a second, Kim thought Candy had passed out. "Don't look, don't peek, and Candy, trust me…plug your ears..!" Kim kissed Candy's head and ran to the fireplace.

Jackson knew exactly what Kim was going to do, and she was right: 'Hold him down'. Jackson removed his sleeveless flannel and began to spin it like a towel. Once it was in a twist, Jackson grabbed the thinnest end with two hands and brought it to Thomas's face.

"What are you do—" Thomas tried to ask with confused and wide eyes but was muffled by Jackson's flannel when Jackson shoved it in his mouth. Thomas looked at Jackson and then saw Kim back in view. In her hand was a smoking log from the fire with an ambered end.

"Thomas? Bite Down Hard!" Kim said as strongly as she could. Thomas, now fully aware of the extremities, quickly nodded his head and prepared himself for the worst pain he knew he would ever experience. Jackson looked at Kim, nodded, and then looked at Thomas.

"I'm going to hold your ankle, okay? Your bad leg ankle," Jackson said. Thomas nodded. "This is going to hurt like hell, bro! I'm sorry!" Quickly, Jackson dashed across the room, grabbed a canteen, and ran back to Kim.

"Pour the water anywhere you think is a gash. The moment I see it, I'm striking," Kim instructed Jackson, and Jackson nodded. Jackson did exactly as he was told.

With a muffled voice and two tears, Thomas screamed, "DO IT! *DOOO IIIIT!*"

Thomas, with closed eyes, felt the stinging cold water hit his gash, which caused him to grunt heavily, but the sound Thomas made from the burning log being pressed against the clawed tear was a sound Jackson would never get out of his head for the rest of his life.

25

It was crazy, and thankful, for how quickly the training the hunter once received came back. In the silence of the night, the hunter and their rifle were unstoppable. Every single time one of the creatures would arrive back at the cabin, they'd flee after being shot, but the lone hunter outside the cabin had convinced themselves enough that these gangly monsters were either immune to pain or their hides were bulletproof.

Sure, they'd screech, growl, or squeal when a round would hit them, but the shooter didn't speak their language, nor did they even know what the hell the goddamn things were even called! Or that matter, where they come from…or fuck, what they even *were*! But they were one thing, and that was unmistakable: they were in the way.

Luckily, the hunter had their favorite rifle with them, and thus far, the hunter was eleven-for-eleven. *I don't have a U.S. Navy Marksmanship Medal and ribbon for nothing,* the hunter said in their head proudly.

When the cabin's four inhabitants came outside, the hunter heard a splash of water and knew they were in trouble. Against their better judgment, the hunter moved their position from the back of the cabin to along its side. Just in time, too, for one of the four dumbasses snared a bear trap, which seriously changed the entire situation. Using the advantage of the night's darkness, the shooter was completely hidden and had yet to be discovered by the monsters. *May fortune favor the foolish...*

And now, with a bear trap being sprung, that told the hunter that where there's one, there is more, and like the hunter, the traps also took advantage of the darkness. The hunter never saw a single one the entire time they were on the mountain, even in the daylight. Now, for all the hunter knew, *They could be littered anywhere!* Miraculously, the one who sprung the trap was uninjured, but another one near them was either injured or terrified because they hit the ground like a sack of rocks.

The hunter watched the three on their feet flee back to the cabin, two of whom were carrying the fourth. One of the monsters rushed them at the stairs and grabbed one of the four by a leg. When the hunter shot their rifle for the twelfth time, they were now twelve-for-twelve. Just before firing, the hunter heard a tearing of fabric, which they assumed was cloth, but the scream that came said otherwise. That tearing sound was more than just clothing. When the bullet hit the monstrosity at the bottom of the cabin's front stairs, it yelped like an injured dog and ran off faster than a terrified rabbit.

Two minutes later, outside the cabin, hunkered down behind a pile of discarded mossy rotted logs, the hunter listened to a sound from inside the cabin that would haunt them for months. A muffled scream of agony roared louder than any sound in the woods, and worse, the scream happened two more times, with repeated cries of pain and torment. *Please don't tell me they're cutting off a leg in there...!* Then, for the next fifteen minutes, alone in the woods, there was complete and unemotional silence.

No monsters, no growls, no gunshots, no screams; nothing. Silent as a grave.

26

The observer, the little girl in the summer dress, felt it was right to help the four. Limited on helpful options, to open the door to the cabin against the will of the ghosts inside was her first act. Every single loose ghost inside that wooden nightmare used its supernatural fury to seal the front door shut. Keeping the Gray's outside was always their first priority.

She knew if any of the four had tried to open it, it wouldn't have budged. When she saw two of the four carry the one to the steps, the little girl knew what to do.

Unlike the emotional imbalance of the ravaging spirits and angry poltergeists inside, the observer had all of their feelings well under control and intact. For being the ghostly reminder of what used to be a happy, adventurous, and observant little girl, who has been dead for almost sixty years, keeping emotions under control was more impossible than winning the lottery.

Using her supernatural ability to open the door was easy, and closing it was just as important. It not only kept the monsters from getting inside, but it told the spirits inside that someone else had power over them. One of the inside ghosts was growing angrier than the rest.

The observer, the ghost girl who watched Jackson and Kim by the water and who shuddered when the ghosts were free, had become as much a part of the night as the four alive inside were, as the fifty or more spirits inside the cabin were, and whoever the rifle-carrying person was, too. The little ghost girl also learned something that only took a minute to clarify: of the four alive, the girl with the short dark hair could see her. They had seen one another as the door closed, and although the situation was gruesome, that connection made the ghost girl smile.

She thought about entering inside, but the four people were together and the poltergeists inside would not do them harm. *They also won't help them,* the ghost girl thought. Instead, until the time came, the ghost girl decided the hunter needed help next.

The haunting observer glided silently to the hunter, who was behind the pile of discarded logs, and learned the person couldn't see her. She also learned a giddy surprise: the hunter was a girl, too! The ghost girl stood in front of the hunter and waited, not for the hunter to see her, but for the return of the monsters. *There was blood on the stairs from that man with a bad leg. They're going to come back meaner than ever, like sharks in the ocean.*

Outside the cabin, a live girl and a dead girl waited silently in the darkness.

27

When Kim cauterized Thomas's first leg gash, Thomas screamed so horrifically, Kim's stomach turned, and it hurt her heart to hear the muffled screams of a man in pure agony. Jackson poured more cold creek water on Thomas's injured leg and found a second gash. With another log from the fireplace, Kim made Thomas scream a second time. The second scream was not as loud as the first but was far more painful to hear, because Thomas was ready for it. Thomas mustered the courage and allowed the second to happen.

Thomas's scream made Jackson momentarily reflect on the movie scene from 'Full Metal Jacket' when the platoon gave Private Leonard Lorance, a.k.a. Private Pyle, a blanket party. Jackson always thought the scene was overdramatic, but now learned that it was by far underdone. Thomas was gagged almost the same way the actor was in the scene, and Thomas's cries of torment and misery, mixed with raging tears and heaving breaths, told Jackson he personally would never have made it as a medical professional or a soldier.

Jackson did find a third gash in Thomas's leg after using the last of the water from his canteen. This was the worst wound of all, for it was in Thomas's inner thigh near the top, but below the groin. Jackson did not need to be told that the location of the gash was near or directly on the femoral artery.

Kim came back with the third log, and Jackson saw that Kim had tears in her eyes. Jackson told Kim that he'd do it since she went through the misery of administering the medical punishment of torturing Thomas to save him. Kim, instead, told Jackson to console his best friend. With her suggestion, it was exactly what his heart told him to do.

Jackson wrapped his right arm around Thomas's head in a manly hold and whispered in Thomas's ear, "I love you, and I'm sorry! It'll be over soon!" Jackson felt Thomas nod and felt Thomas's head push against Jackson's neck. When the burning log pressed against the final wound on Thomas's upper thigh, Thomas shrieked in agony as Jackson hugged him harder in sorrow. Quickly, Thomas passed out from the pain.

Kim ran to her canteen, grabbed it, returned, and poured her water all over Thomas's leg. The smell of burnt flesh and burnt blood curdled her stomach fiercely. She was thankful that there was next to nothing in her system. If there was any real, solid food in her belly, it would have already been vomited up and splattered on the cabin floor.

Kim and Jackson stopped Thomas's bleeding. On the sofa, still curled up in the fetal position, Candy never moved. The angry ghosts against the wall did not interfere.

Jackson's watch beeped abruptly: two o'clock in the morning.

28

Kim and Jackson gave themselves a minute to mentally and physically recover in the silence of the cabin. Neither spoke. The rest was short, but necessary.

Kim eventually walked over to the sofa and pulled on Candy's arm. It was like pulling on a small log stuck under a large pile of heavy logs, or like pulling on a child's arm that was clinging to their favorite toy. Candy didn't budge and didn't speak. Kim lowered down to meet Candy's face up close and saw that Candy's eyes were wide open, her wet hair was a matted mess, and Candy was breathing, but slowly, through her nose.

"She's catatonic," Kim revealed, even if it was just for her own ears to hear. Kim turned around and saw that Jackson was staring at Thomas with tears. If Kim had just walked into the room, unaware of what had just happened, she would have sworn that Jackson was crying over a dead man. Slowly, Kim walked away from Candy toward Jackson, knelt, and softly rubbed his back with her hand. Jackson sobbed but relaxed at the feel of her hand.

"What—What are we gonna do?" Jackson asked with a muffled voice. It was heartfelt for Kim to see Jackson showing his raw affection for Thomas and his suffering.

What is Jackson going to be like if Thomas didn't make it out of here? Kim's brain asked inappropriately. Kim shut the thought out immediately, not wanting the answer. "I don't know," Kim said solemnly. "But we're not just going to sit here." Kim looked at the ghosts along the back wall, looking like a police lineup. None moved or even acknowledged the misery the four were in. Kim's patience was thin, and she shouted, "And Fuck You All, Too!" No response.

Jackson sat up and wiped his tear-streaked face, looked at Kim, and asked, "Feel better?"

"I'd feel better if all of them motherfuckers would just disappear or something, instead of looking down at us all judgmentally and shit!" Kim answered, giving the haunting lineup a direct, hateful look.

A third voice, raspy and harsh, spoke low and angrily. "We…to-ld… you-to…leave," the voice said. It came from the sofa.

"Oh no," Kim whispered. "Candy…!"

"Out-side…is…death," Candy's mouth spoke, without her body moving. Candy's mouth wasn't muffled like Thomas's was, but it was cupped in her position, which pressed her voice.

I hope I didn't sound like that, Kim said in her head.

"Now…you…lea-ve!" At this, the front bedroom door opened a second time on its own.

"They want us downstairs," Jackson said, standing up alongside Kim, who was already on her feet. "Again."

"Get the fuck out of my friend," Kim growled through her teeth, inhaled deeply, exhaled even deeper, and finished with, "And…we'll leave."

"All…of…you!" Candy's mouth growled, and Kim watched Candy's body go limp. Kim looked at the wall, and a figure reappeared. Kim instantly felt hatred fester deep inside her.

"Do that again, and I swear, I will find your bones, and after I piss on each one of them, so help me God, I'll grind EACH FUCKING BONE TO DUST *WITH MY OWN TWO HANDS!*" Kim roared at the ghosts along the wall. Jackson saw nothing standing at the back wall but knew Kim could.

At that, Candy rolled off the sofa and hit the floor with a lifeless thump.

Jackson and Kim dashed to Candy's limp body, picked her up, and attempted to put her back on the sofa when the sofa slid across the room. It slammed heavily against the back wall with a hard thud. Behind Kim and Jackson, the bedroom door with the floor door rapidly slammed open and closed. Open and close. Open and close.

"Alright, We Get The Point!" Jackson shouted, and the door stopped. It was open. "Alright…alright! We're gone!" Jackson looked at the wall. "I'm taking the blanket. You can keep the couch," Jackson said and walked toward the sofa. It didn't move. Jackson grabbed the blanket off the back of the sofa and threw it at Kim.

"What's this for?" Kim asked.

"Put Candy on it and drag her into the bedroom. I'll use the rug for Thomas," Jackson instructed. "We'll get them downstairs together, but for now, I'd like to get as far away from these no-longer-living-bastards as fast as possible."

Kim nodded.

The ghosts watched Kim and Jackson pull their friends along the cabin floor and into the bedroom. The moment the four living people entered the bedroom, the door slammed shut with a heavy wooden thud.

29

"Over here," Jackson instructed as he pulled the rug with his unconscious friend on it. When Kim set down the blanket with her catatonic friend, Candy, on it, Kim looked over and saw Jackson had pulled the rug away from the bed. Jackson and Kim pulled their friends along the floor by the end of their feet. Kim had said that keeping their feet elevated meant more blood to the heart and brain. Jackson mentioned 'They weren't having heart attacks', but he didn't argue.

Jackson set down Thomas's legs and stood up, stretching his back, then pointed to the bedroom door.

"We're sealed off that way," Kim responded, knowing Jackson was about to ask about opening the door. "I don't think they want us back there. They did warn us, and now, I think, they just want us gone."

"Now I have no problem with the 'gone' part, but these two?" Jackson pointed at Candy and Thomas, "They're kinda the problem and now, we only have two ways out of here."

"Two?"

Jackson pointed at the window, still covered by the inner shutters, and then the doorway on the floor. Kim voicelessly pointed to the hidden floor door, with a clear expression on her face. Jackson understood her expression immediately and returned her gesture with a heavy sigh.

"You're not going to like what Thomas and I found down there," Jackson replied.

"Not like I have a choice," Kim returned and bent down to grab the blanket under Candy.

"No," Jackson stated quickly. "Not yet. Just you and I first. You need to see what we're dealing with before we carry them down there." As Kim stood up, Jackson shouted, "OH, FUCKING HELL!"

"What?!" Kim burst out in surprise. "What's the matter!?"

"We—Awe, God…DAMN IT!" Jackson ripped at himself in anger and pounded a fist on the bedroom wall. "WE NEED—" Jackson shouted, stopped, took a deep breath, and exhaled deeply to calm himself. "We…need the goddamn flashlights! They're still—" and at that moment, the bedroom door opened as if summoned.

Through the foot-wide door opening, their two flashlights rolled into the bedroom along the floor. One spun and gently hit the wall, the other rolled and hit a dresser leg. As the door closed, Kim caught a millisecond peek of the little ghost girl who opened the cabin door for them when the guys carried Candy. Jackson watched in shock as Kim calmly collected the flashlights.

Kim walked over to the bedroom door, placed a gentle open hand on the wood, and softly said, "Thank you."

Jackson shook his head lightly. "I hate it here…!"

30

Moments later, Jackson walked down the cellar after moving the rug and opening the floor door. Both had a flashlight, which Kim had given him. Jackson didn't ask about the flashlight and didn't ask Kim who she thanked. As far as Jackson was concerned, the less he knew, the better. Kim followed Jackson down the stairs, and he took her straight to his and Thomas Everlast's discovery. Jackson led Kim to the shelves of canned goods and questionable glass jars.

"A shelf unit?" Kim asked, unamused. "A shelf unit, full of…," and Kim looked closer at the glass Mason jars. She didn't shine her flashlight directly into one. "…I don't want to know what's in these, Jay."

Jackson didn't respond to her comments but only grabbed the shelf unit itself. When he pulled on the shelf unit, Kim jumped back a foot, not expecting the shelf unit to slide along the floor at her. Kim watched Jackson pull the shelf unit away from the wall with ease. Every single one of the five shelves was mostly full.

Kim saw the back of the shelf unit and realized it was attached to the wall, but this wall had a secret door. Kim took a second step back before shining her flashlight through the doorway opening. Immediately, her light illuminated a natural stone wall.

"A secret door to a secret passage," Jackson stated. When Jackson turned on his flashlight, it caused Kim's eyes to focus elsewhere because Jackson's light wasn't shining where hers was. It was lower and aimed far back down the doorway a bit.

The entryway displayed a tunnel system with solid stone walls and a floor made of mountain rock and loose dirt. The tunnel was wide enough for two people to walk side-by-side tightly. The ceiling was too dark to tell if it was braced with wood or stone. There was a slight breeze coming into the wooden shelter that was the cabin's storage space.

"What is this?" Kim asked slowly, not completely sure she wanted the answer.

"Look," Jackson directed, and in her sense of shock, Kim saw what Jackson wanted her to see: a folded-out cot with two dusty folded wool blankets on it. "Our guess: this is a hiding shelter, probably for storms or—"

"The authorities," Kim interrupted. "Think the cabin's owner was, or is, a poacher?" Kim showed her light on the cot and guessed it had been there for quite some time, giving the layer of dust and dirt on the blankets. "Looks like no one has been under here for quite a while." The metal railings of the cot's structure had the same amount of dust and dirt as the blankets.

"We should put Candy and Thomas down here to keep them safe. Candy on the cot, Thomas on the ground. We'll use the blanket and two rugs as padding for Thomas," Jackson suggested.

"This is creepy as fuck," Kim whispered loudly.

"Oh, and being possessed by ghosts isn't creepy? Being twisted and folded like Emily Rose isn't creepy?! Talking to my girlfriend whose head was on backwards isn't creepy!?" Jackson had a whole list to mention and like verbal diarrhea, he couldn't stop. "Or how about doors that just open on their own? Or the—"

"Alright, Jay! I Get The Point!" Kim barked, but not loudly. Just enough to shut him up.

"Thank you," Jackson huffed repentantly. "I'm…rambling, and I just—"

"I know," Kim said apologetically, and she grabbed his hand tenderly. "We're getting out of here." Kim smiled at Jackson. *A kiss would feel inappropriate under the circumstances.* "Let's get them down here, then we can go back upstairs and figure out what the hell we're gonna do."

"They're safer down here, I think," Jackson guessed. "There's no creatures down here and no gho—wait, do you see any ghosts?" Jackson asked Kim, to which she did not verbally answer. Kim simply shook her head side-to-side and blinked slowly. "Good."

"I haven't heard any gunshots outside either," Kim stated. Jackson spent five seconds debating her comment and didn't know if it was a good thing or a bad thing. The good thing would be that the hunter shot and killed the creatures, then left without any introduction. The bad thing would be that the hunter missed and was killed instead. Either way, outside was not the best place to be.

"Five hours til sun-up for this side of the mountain," Jackson said. "We'd better go and get them down here."

31

Kim and Jackson carried Candy first since she was lighter. If one were to watch, Candy was carried in the blanket like a hammock, which made Kim and Jackson the poles that supported the human hammock.

129

When Jackson picked Candy off the blanket, a huff came from her mouth. Candy's eyes were wide open as if she was frozen in space or locked in time. It was far beyond creepy to see, so as fast as he could, and without Kim knowing it, Jackson quickly remembered what Candy looked like in just her bra and panties to mask the mental image of her catatonic eyes wide open. The trick worked.

Carrying Thomas was far more difficult, for the rug didn't fold around Thomas like a cocoon like the blanket did for Candy. Thomas was carried more like a large chalupa taco shell than like a human hammock. The rug was thick, which made Thomas far heavier, but Kim and Jackson were successful in carrying down both Candy and Thomas without additional injury to their friends or themselves.

In the wooden-framed cellar part of the underground, Jackson found six candles and a box of blue-tip matches. Jackson and Kim staged the candles in the stone passage along the floor. Thomas was on the floor tucked partly under the cot while Candy remained unconsciously (or consciously; Jackson couldn't tell) on the cot. Given it was summer, the underground was quite cool in temperature. The candles were for when either woke up, whenever that would be, so they could see.

Kim and Jackson left the shelf door open and the electric light on in the wooden-walled portion of the cellar, as well as the floor door to the bedroom. With their friends below, Kim and Jackson sat on the floor in the bedroom with the dim room lit by the oil lamp. In the dimness, on the floor, they sat and listed their options on what to do, for there were several to choose from. As they talked, exhaustion crept up quickly.

Kim: "We can run to the car, just us two, and return for them."

Jackson: "We'd have to break the bedroom window, which the ghosts will repair and not let us back in."

Kim: "Hmm…"

Jackson: "We can find the shooter…and get help."

Kim: "And when Candy and Thomas wake up alone, what do we explain to them that doesn't sound like abandonment?"

Jackson: "Good point…"

Kim: "We can walk the tunnel below…and see where it leads."

Jackson: "I don't know how long the flashlights will last…and we have no map. If it's an abandoned mine tunnel, we'd…definitely get lost."

Kim: "Yeah…"

Jackson: "We can call someone, like 9-1-1…or something."

Kim: "Ghosts won't open the door. They've dominated the living room."

Jackson: "We got the flashlights, didn't we?"

Kim: "Not from them. They…came from—"

Jackson: "Sorry…I don't want to know. I've had enough…of things that aren't supposed…to exist."

Kim: "Me, too…"

Jackson: "We could…just…"

Kim & Jackson: "…sleep…"

Both yawned at the same time and in mere seconds of one another, both fell asleep on the bedroom floor. They were propped up against the side of the bed as they talked, both staring at the bedroom door to the living room. Kim's head rested on Jackson's shoulder as Jackson's head rested on the top of Kim's head. Exhaustion had won.

32

Outside, the hunter stayed hunkered for a considerable amount of time, just short of an hour. The monsters hadn't returned, no sounds emanated from inside the cabin, and it seemed the entire world was in silent mode. The silence of the woods was unbelievably unnerving. *No crickets chirping, no owls, no scattering of wildlife along the ground. Nothing.*

The hunter looked at their watch and then pulled a cell phone out of their inner vest pocket and tapped a button on the side, which brightened up the screen. *No bars? Go figure.* A notification of a Wi-Fi Hotspot did pop up in the notifications, but the hunter not only didn't want the Wi-Fi to be used.

The hunter double-checked to make sure the GPS and Locations on the phone were off. The only good part was the time. *Three o'clock...no time like the present.* It was time to set out and do what they were here to do in the first place. *You four in there...I hope you got out.*

33

The little ghost girl had left the hunter just long enough to give the nice girl the flashlights they had lost. Controlling the front door and overpowering the ghosts was easy. Emotional stability was the ticket, and those ghosts inside were raging mad, furiously angry, and completely monumentally unbalanced, which made them easy to manipulate, but handling electronics was the problem.

When a ghost puts out enough emotion, they can disrupt the natural flows of the powers of the world: water stability, electrical currents, and even gravity. That is why poltergeists have such ease with moving objects and disrupting electronics. Inside the cabin, the ghosts were petrified poltergeists: ghosts that function with rage and raw emotion that have next to rationality or concept of understanding.

The little ghost girl was just a benevolent spirit with a full consciousness and mental stability that even living people had a hard time possessing. To carry powered electronics a distance was the equivalent of a living human being carrying red-hot coals in their hands without gloves.

What was more painful was being around the other ghosts, for the little ghost girl could hear them. Every single one was full of rage and anger at everything: the living, their existence, their deaths; it was endless, with no signs of ever ending. Just a non-living torment of hate.

Sadly, the ghost girl knew two of them, and neither one of them acknowledged their own daughter's presence.

To keep from dwelling on the heartache, the little ghost girl returned to the woman hunter outside the cabin and watched her from just two feet away. Time meant nothing to the ghost girl, for she had an abundance of it. When the lady with the long gun looked at her watch, then looked at something bright and small from her vest, the hunter got up and ran silently to the back of the cabin and through the tree line.

Curious, the ghost girl followed until the person stopped running at a small camping spot. How the hunter saw so well in the dark was a very curious thought. For only a second, the hunter turned on a lantern that was on the ground by a tent. The lantern had two white sticks inside it that were extremely bright.

The last time the ghost girl saw a lantern, it had to be lit with a long match. This one was far brighter, much smaller, and for the first time, in the glow of the lantern, the ghost girl saw the hunter's face.

The hunter quickly grabbed a black box with a handle on top of it, turned off the lantern, and ran back to the cabin. The ghost girl was amazed at how quiet the long gun owner was. Just before the tree line, the ghost girl stopped her pursuit, allowing the living hunter to run ahead. A sound in the distance caught the ghost girl's attention.

The monsters…they're coming back!

34

Jackson heard the scream first, but it sounded muffled and distant. The sound was far away and wavy as if he were underwater. Jackson was exhausted and didn't want to open his eyes. Kim heard the sound too, but it was in her dream. Kim dreamt she was driving the silver SUV, and someone was trying to scream in the back seat, but something was covering their mouth. It must have been Candy and Thomas in the back seat. In her dream, Kim was laughing playfully and trying not to look in the mirror.

Then, to Jackson, the screaming became louder, clearer, and more hysterical. Still feeling head heavy, Jackson tried ignoring the sound, knowing it was just subconscious noise. Jackson wasn't dreaming, nor was he hallucinating; he was just exhausted. To Kim, the playful screaming in the backseat became screams of pain and terror, rather than playful, and was louder. Much louder.

That's when a heavily loud —*BANG!*— from underneath them jolted both Kim and Jackson out of their slumber, followed by more hysterical screaming. With numb legs, Jackson and Kim scrambled to their feet after realizing the screams had come from Candy down in the cellar, and both fell on the bedroom floor.

Kim and Jackson both failed to maintain balance as their legs began to tingle back to life. They both struggled but managed to get to the cellar stairs. Holding the door's frame for support, Jackson and Kim both found coming up the stairs at them was indeed Candy screaming, but with a hand to the side of her head and blood pouring down her wrist, between her fingers, and down the side of her neck. Candy's screaming didn't stop.

At the sight of Jackson and Kim all of a sudden, Candy freaked out on the stairs, which caused Candy to lose her balance and fall back down the stairs on her side. Candy pulled her hands away from her head to balance herself, exposing a surprising amount of blood on the side of her face. Kim reached the cellar floor first and was on the floor beside Candy before Jackson.

"Candy! Candy, It's Us!" Kim shouted, trying to cut through Candy's hysteria. Right away, Kim saw where the blood was pouring from, despite the tangling of hair and dirt from the stone tunnel. Candy was shaking her head side-to-side in fear and defense, which caused Kim to grab both of Candy's arms. "CANDY!"

"SOMETHING BIT ME!" Candy screamed, not wanting to make eye contact with Kim. "*SOMETHING BIT MY EAR!*" Kim held her and drew Candy in close as both lay at the bottom of the wooden staircase and the cellar floor. Neither was on their feet. "Something…laughed," Candy started, then corrected, "No—giggled," Candy sniffed shakily, "then I felt hands on me and…and something bit my ear with sharp teeth!"

"Jay, get something—anything! She's still bleeding profusely!" Kim begged.

Just before running off, Jackson asked, "Is Thomas awake?" Candy turned her head and looked up at Jackson. Her face was worn out, her skin a mangling of blood, dirt, and hair. Candy's eyes were on the verge of a total mental lockdown. Jackson saw Candy's eyes directly.

"I—I woke up, alone, in a dark hall, with hands on me and Something Biting My FUCKING EAR, JAY! *HOW WOULD I FUCKING KNOW WHERE THOMAS IS!?*"

"Candy," Kim locked eyes with Candy and tried to explain, "W-We placed you and Thomas down here. We placed you on the cot. You were catatonic, and Thomas—honey, Thomas is in bad shape!" Candy stared at Kim's face for a few seconds, trying to comprehend what Kim was saying. "Candy, he's under the cot we put you on. We—"

"Kim!?" Jackson barked, and Kim looked up at Jackson, but Jackson had walked toward the shelf door. Jackson stood at the secret passage to the stone tunnel. "All the candles are out!"

"I was on the hard floor. I was attacked, alone, in the dark, and…," Candy whimpered. "Why would you…leave me…down here, Kim?" Candy sobbed and slowly collapsed into Kim's huddle like a child being comforted by a parent. Kim lifted her arm and allowed Candy to cradle into her lap. At once, warm blood dripped from Candy's ear onto Kim's pant leg.

Kim turned her head and watched Jackson walk two steps into the stone passageway, and when Jackson turned on his flashlight, Kim saw the cot. It was empty on top and empty on the bottom. Kim thought the same thing that Jackson verbally said next.

"Thomas…is gone…," Jackson said solemnly and in confusion. Jackson illuminated the floor of the stone tunnel and knelt. "Candy's blood and Thomas's drag marks are in the dirt."

"Jay, come back in here!" Kim shouted, but not in a panic. Within seconds, Jackson was back in the wooden-walled cellar. "Shine the light here," Kim directed, pointing a finger at Candy's head. What Candy had described was horrifically accurate.

Bright red blood drained out of her left ear from ripped flesh and torn cartilage. The size of the bite was not of a large animal or a tiny mouse. A full-size New York City rat, maybe, but here, underground, in Utah, there were no such creatures and no animal tracks. *Plenty of shoe prints though,* Jackson thought to himself.

"We have to treat her ear, Jay," Kim said in alarm. "I don't think she'll bleed out, but—"

"There's no way we can do what we did for Thomas to Candy down here," Jackson stated. "I—I'm out of ideas on this one!" Jackson stood up and looked about the cellar. "Whatever attacked Candy and Thomas is—"

"Do you think Thomas—" Kim started to ask, but Jackson stopped her from finishing.

"NO!" Jackson barked. "No! No! And No! Attacked her and ran off!? There's not a single cell in his body that would make him do such a thing! And besides…Thomas running? Just running, *period,* is not possible!"

"Okay, Okay!" Kim threw back. If she could have put two hands up, like she had to do for Candy when Kim pissed her off about her old name joke, she would have. "I'm just thinking all altern—"

"No, and that's final!" Jackson barked. Kim kept quiet, for the moment. Kim knew Jackson was right, but if that meant Jackson was right, there was something else down there with them. "Listen," Jackson said, turning his tone apologetically. "Take Candy upstairs and get her bandaged up. Try to stop the bleeding, okay? I'm gonna—"

"Oh, The Fuck You Are!" Kim barked back. It was her turn to claim the orders. "All three of us are going upstairs…Now!" At that, Kim slowly stood up, and Candy did too, along with her. As Kim and

Candy climbed the cellar steps up to the bedroom, Jackson closed the shelving door that led to the stone tunnel hallway.

Right after it closed, Jackson ran up the stairs like a child dashing up their basement stairs before a monster's hand could grab him from the dark. Candy murmured something incoherent, but the girls were too far away to hear clearly. Jackson's flashlight was still in his hand, and before he questioned it, Kim took hers out of her pocket.

—BAM!—

Just as Jackson stepped up into the bedroom, the floor door to the cellar behind him slammed shut, missing Jackson's ankle by an inch! Hard!

UNDERGROUND

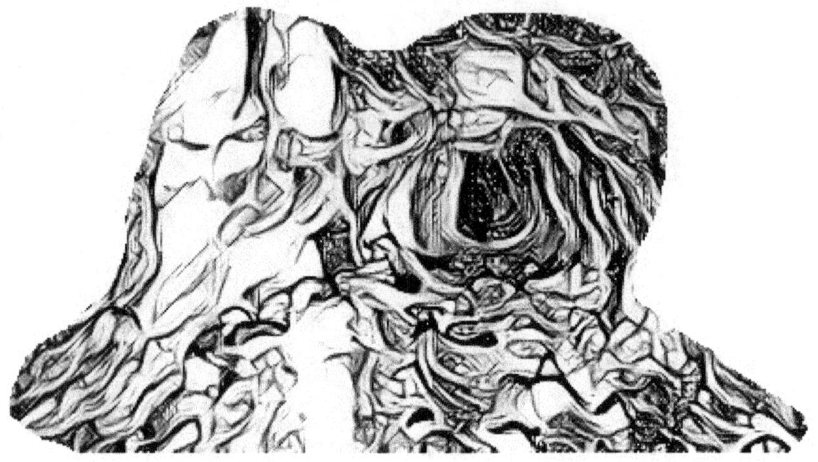

1

When the door slammed shut, the floor door was to their backs. Instinctively, Jackson Chad spun around, dropped down to his hands and knees, and tried to find the iron handle. It took two seconds, but when Jackson grabbed it and pulled it, it was as if the door was now locked. It didn't even bob loose each time Jackson pulled as hard as he could.

"Someone Was Down There With Us!" Kim Michael screamed in both terror and anger. "It Closed Right After You Came Out!" Kim was looking directly at Jackson, who displayed expressions of shock, disgust, and awareness all at the same time. Everything Kim said in those two sentences made a disturbing sense. Jackson had fled up the stairs as if something was behind him, ready to grab him, and he was right.

If it wanted you, Jackson, it would have, Jackson's conscience told himself. Rationality had its moments, but this detail was failing. Jackson had to tell himself, *Bullshit, I got away!*

"I…Can't…Open…It!" Jackson grunted as he pulled on the iron handle.

"No! NO!" Candy Murray screamed. "Thomas! We Have To Go After Thomas!"

"Candy, No!" Kim said strongly to Candy. "We don't know where Thomas is, and now that you're awake, we have us three."

"No! Thomas! WE NEED TO *GET THOMAS!*" Candy shouted to the point of hysterics. Blood from her ear whipped about and dripped off her dangled hair as Candy shook angrily. Neither Kim nor Jackson stopped her ranting. Both thought the same thing about Candy as they looked at one another: *At least she was conscious enough to know what was going on!* Jackson let go of the iron handle, feeling his throbbing pulse in his hands.

Under the bedroom, a smaller —*thud!*— thumped the floor.

Mouthing the words without a sound, Kim spoke to Jackson slowly and directly to the point, "Someone…is…still…down…there!" Kim directed her eyes at the door.

"No…Shit!" Jackson mouthed verbally but voicelessly.

"What…Do…We…Do?" Kim mouthed back. Jackson raised his hands, palms up, out in front of him. His mouth was wide open as he tried to answer, but Jackson couldn't articulate the right words. This facial expression said, 'I have no idea'. Candy saw none of this, for she was looking down at the floor.

Candy whimpered low, "…my ear…hurts…," and collapsed onto the bedroom floor right out of Kim's grip. Kim and Jackson quickly dashed to the floor to adjust Candy's bodily position. Once again, another one of their friends was unconscious, and it was back to just them two, even worse than under an hour ago.

2

Jackson and Kim spent the next ten minutes in silence as they both nursed Candy's ear as best they could. Jackson took off one of Candy's long knee-high socks and wrapped it around her head after Kim used one of her socks to pad the mangled ear. The sock was not going to stop the bleeding, but at least the wound would clot.

Kim was about to gently slap-tap Candy's face to wake her when Jackson waved a hand to stop her. The conversation between Jackson and Kim was no more than a whisper.

Jackson: "Not yet! Don't wake her just yet."

Kim: "Why not? We have to get her, and us, out of here!"

Jackson: "And Go Where?!"

Kim: "…"

Jackson: "I can't believe I'm going to say this, or even suggest this…"

Kim: "What?"

Jackson: (Sigh) "We…we need help."

Kim: "From Who?!"

Hesitatingly, Jackson pointed at the bedroom door and said, "From…your friends in there." Quickly, Jackson received a very hardcore 'Fuck You' look from Kim with a headshake of 'No! I Don't Think So!' that made her hair sway in her face. Jackson put up both hands in defense, then up with palms up, expressing 'I don't know what else to do.' to Kim.

Kim's eyes darted over as if the answer just struck her. Quickly, Kim began tapping her right index finger and her middle finger on her left wrist. Jackson made a circle in the air and put up three fingers to say, 'Around three in the morning.'

Instantly, from under the bedroom, a violently loud but heavily muffled, blood-curdling scream erupted. Very loud cries of terror and agonizing screams escaped through the wood planks of the bedroom floor, but the sounds were emanating from somewhere deep below. The horror of the screaming was so intense, it emotionally stabbed their hearts. They knew the screams of torture and agony had come from a full-grown man.

Without hesitation, Jackson and Kim bolted for the cellar door in the floor. Jackson grabbed the metal ring handle and again tried to pull it up, only this time, it budged loose but closed back rapidly as if someone grabbed the door handle inside. Further away, deep under them, a secondary scream erupted.

"Christ, Jay! That's Thomas!" Kim shrieked from the back of her throat. "It's Thomas!"

"JESUS, FUCK! OPEN…YOU…FUCKING DOOR!" Jackson swore in frustration as he pulled on the door handle with all his might. The pressure pain in his fingers was excruciating, but he knew Kim was right. It was Thomas screaming in pain.

"Jay! Get It Open!" Kim began to scream in panic. "Open It, Jay!"

Instead of screaming at Kim that he was giving it all he had, Jackson roared with all his might, mixed with pain, frustration, and the purest of raw anger. Suddenly, the door gave way and caused Jackson to fall back and slam hard against the wall, and then the floor.

Thomas screamed one last time, not louder, but still very distant. It was the horrific kind of scream that caused the blood of the listener to turn to ice. Kim barked something to Jackson, but Jackson was out of his thoughts after the impact with the wall, and then the floor.

Kim whipped the door open. "Someone Was Holding The Door! There They Go!" and at that, Kim instinctively ran down the cellar stairs into the darkness. Jackson saw that the lightbulb in the cellar was off. "Get Back Here!" Kim shouted at the dark, fleeing figure.

"KIM!" Jackson tried to shout, but Candy's scream mixed with Jackson's shout. Jackson looked up and saw that Candy had already come to and was scrambling to her feet. Jackson raced to his own feet and met Candy at the stairs. Before Kim's head disappeared into the floor, a second —*THUD!*— came from the cellar. *The shelf door just closed again!*

"KIM! WAIT!" Jackson screamed as Candy's feet hit the stairs. Once again, Jackson was the caboose. For Candy to come to just as chaos ensued was not the best of timing.

"KIM!" Candy shouted, then shouted louder, "Thomas! Thomas! We're Coming, Baby! We're Coming!" Kim was on the cellar floor and pulled the shelf door open by the time Jackson had hit the bottom of the stairs. Jackson shone the flashlight just as Kim stepped through the secret door, which caused Candy to take two steps back.

Realization hit Candy as she remembered frantically running back through there, but not knowing where she was. The darkness of the stone tunnel caused Candy to self-reflect in her head for just a second.

Oh, my fuck! I...I came from inside there and never thought about Thomas once!

Candy teetered her mindset for just a second, and without any other thought, she dashed into the stone tunnel after Kim.

"WAIT, GODDAMNIT!" Jackson shouted, hoping both would stop. Neither did, so Jackson forced himself to run in after them, thankfully with his flashlight.

3

Kim, Candy, and Jackson didn't travel far.

"What in the hell...?" Kim asked rhetorically in the air. Candy didn't ask anything when she saw what Kim saw and when Jackson trailed up in the back, his own feet came to a stop before his brain told them to. In front of Kim was a wooden wall, constructed into the stone hallway, with a wooden door in the middle of the structure. The wood used to make the wall was solid, but weathered and dark. The wooden door, which looked like a simple bedroom door, did not match the wood, or grain type of the structure. Neither Jackson nor Candy wanted to open it, even though the floor showed drag marks and shoe prints in the dust and dirt.

"I don't thi—" Jackson started to say as Kim reached out and opened the door. Right away, as it opened, the three were hit by a backdraft of wind. The wind was warm but had a strong odor that pinched all their sinuses, like the smell of uncooked fish in a microwave. Before they had time to question the smell, they entered the passage.

On the opposite side, there were more natural stone walls to the tunnel and a second cot, just like the one outside the cellar. There were two folded blankets on it, covered with a layer of dust. No sign of Thomas, just drag marks on the ground. The three continued on voicelessly until the inevitable arrived, something that Jackson suspected would happen. When they reached it, all three stopped in their tracks.

"Great…it splits to a 'Y'," Jackson huffed and looked straight at Kim as he raised his flashlight directly at her. "We're NOT splitting up!" Kim didn't turn around.

"There's no need to," Kim responded low and shakily. Her flashlight was aimed down the underground hallway to the left of the 'Y'. Candy slowly crept up behind Kim and peered over her shoulder through her matted hair. Jackson approached both women and aimed his flashlight down the right hallway first to get a quick look, just in case. All three of them knew they were not alone, but what the women looked at blanked out their rational thoughts.

Jackson, satisfied with not seeing anything down to the right, turned his flashlight to the left hallway and like the girls, his mind instantly forgot about who they were chasing. On the floor, at the end of the dirt drag marks, was an enormous puddle of splattered blood. In the puddle were handprints, shoe prints, and more drag marks. Whatever was there was butchered and then dragged away, leaving a trail of blood and dirt. Whatever was butchered thirty feet ahead of them not only died there but was no longer physically there. Due to the shine of the flashlight, Jackson saw a splatter on the stone wall of the hall that dripped to the ground floor.

It took several seconds for the silence to break. It broke when the realization struck Candy. Candy screamed so hard and so sharp that her throat cracked, causing her scream of devastation to pitch a squeal. Candy's legs collapsed from underneath her, and she tumbled to the floor of the underground tunnel. Her hands struck the ground with a slap.

Jackson and Kim couldn't turn their eyes away from the puddle. They were both frozen in position, knowing that the puddle of blood was Thomas's final living place on Earth.

They couldn't move or acknowledge Candy, who cried out repeatedly, "THOMAS! THOMAS! Oh No, Thomas…!"

Seeing the blood was a trance that both Kim and Jackson couldn't easily snap out of. Amongst the repeated screams of Thomas's name from Candy, Kim finally pulled herself out of her mindlock and knelt to Candy, still not able to take her eyes off the puddle. Candy immediately clung to Kim's arm and Kim grabbed Candy's shoulder.

"C-Come on, Candy," Kim said tonelessly. "We—we need to go." Kim's voice had no life or personality to it. It was purely mechanical, the way a person staring at a vicious dog would speak before the snarling dog would lunge. "Jay?" Kim asked instinctively. "Jay?"

"Y-yeah," Jackson responded, also mechanical, almost hypnotical. "I…I—"

"NO, No, Thomas!" Candy continued screaming, then, "No, KIM! No! We have to—" Candy began to snarl and growl her words. "Get Off Of Me! Let Me Go! No, We Need To Go That Way! Thomas Is That Way! Let Go—" Kim ignored all of Candy's words as Kim began to pull Candy and retreat into the tunnel the way they came.

Jackson saw Candy fight and pull at Kim, which caused him to snap out of staring at what was left of Thomas. Kim was walking backward and pulling Candy along like a parent pulling a stubborn child having a temper tantrum in a store. Jackson walked over, grabbed the other side of Candy, and both Kim and Jackson pulled Candy back down the hall. Each one had an arm and they kept pulling until they reached the 'Y' of the hall again.

"Right leads us back to the first cot," Kim said with a tone back in her voice.

"Left could take us anywhere," Jackson explained.

"I WANT MY THOMAS!" Candy barked out, weary from fighting her losing fight. Like a woman who finally snapped, Kim whipped herself angrily toward Candy, grabbed Candy, shoved her against the hard wall, reared back with a right open palm, and —*SLAP!*—

"THOMAS IS DEAD, *CANDICE*! GET IT THROUGH YOUR *FUCKING HEAD!*" Kim roared angrily. The realization caused Candy to collapse to the floor. Kim fell with her, hugged her friend, and both women sobbed together. Candy cried in defeat, and Kim cried in sorrow for Candy's feelings and the loss of Thomas.

Jackson slowly leaned against the wall and felt two tears uncontrollably fall down his face. Jackson's bottom lip began to quiver as the waves of failure began to flow through him. For the first time since leaving the SUV, Jackson truly did not know what to do.

4

Outside, the ghost girl followed the hunter completely around the cabin. Every single time the hunter would get close to the corners of the cabin, she would slap a handful of putty into a foundation connection log. There was a handful stuck to each log connection at the base of the cabin on all four corners, on both sides of the railing to the porch, and a large glob was stuck to the chimney stack.

The weirdest part, according to the ghost girl, was when the hunter climbed under the dark truck that was parked in the backyard. She placed a handful of that gray putty underneath it inside the gears. The ghost girl watched the woman in the dark plug a black stick into the handful of putty. That was when the monsters returned.

The three creatures circled the tree line repeatedly and, for some reason, were not attacking the hunter or the cabin itself. The ghost girl did not understand what they were doing and to be honest with herself, didn't exactly understand what the hunter was doing either.

Before the hunter woman climbed out from under the truck, the ghost girl watched her pull a gun out of an inside pocket of her vest. The hunter fired several gunshots into the trees surrounding the cabin. That part made sense to the ghost girl. *The creatures are trying to make their attack, which I don't want to watch.* Whether or not the shots hit them, both the outdoor girls heard the creature's clawed hands pound the ground in retreat due east.

Quickly, the hunter woman dashed out from under the truck and circled the cabin a second time, this time in the opposite direction she originally traveled. The ghost girl watched the hunter plug in more small black sticks into each glob of putty until each gray blob had one.

The hunter retreated up the driveway and out the backyard to the northern tree line, right where the hunter had hidden very well right after the sun had gone down. The ghost girl followed closely. The ghost girl watched the woman suddenly collapse to the ground, where she screamed in horrible pain.

On the hunter's right foot was a large metal bear trap that had snapped on her shin. The metal teeth punctured the lower right leg and her ankle. The hunter grabbed the trap with both hands and not only screamed in tremendous pain, but also cried out in frustration.

There was nothing the ghost girl could do, no matter how much she wanted. The ghost girl tried to open it the same way she opened the cabin's door, but this was somehow different. When the hunter woman hit the ground, something else happened that the ghost girl could not explain, at first. The screaming hunter woman completely vanished two seconds later right before her undead eyes! The only thing that remained was the long gun with the wooden handle in the high grass. The small gun she used while under the truck was gone, too.

The ghost girl looked around in confusion, then startled, as she not only saw, but heard, the creatures returning, once again ready to attack the cabin in vengeful frustration.

5

***

6

It took an immeasurable amount of time for Kim and Candy to emotionally and physically collect one another to where both could reach their feet. Jackson was against the stone wall, waiting for the universe to tell him what to do next. A deliberate sign, a cosmic clue, or even an order from Kim would have sufficed.

Candy asked between cries and catching her breath from the hard sobs, "W-we're not…going a-after…Thomas, are we?"

"I—I don't know…! I don't know if he's anywhere to be found down here, Candy," Jackson tried to logically answer. "I-I'm sorry."

"No, y-you're right," Candy said in a stuttering sob and sniffed heavily. "He just disappeared and…and—

Kim interrupted Candy and looked at Jackson twistedly and angrily, "You're So…Fuckin…Fulla'shit!"

Instantly, Jackson grew angry. "Wh-What the fuck did I do!?" Jackson asked harshly as he pushed himself off of the wall and stood. "He was gone when we found Candy bleeding. Then, when we brought her upstairs to hcal her ear, someone—something—closed the cellar door and wouldn't let us back in! *Then,* when we *DID* get the door open, all three of us ran down here and gave chase! Then, we found—" Jackson stopped himself; he couldn't finish.

"I-I don't know! I'm so lost and confused, like you two, but," Candy sniffed strongly, "you're all I have left. The two of you," Candy sniffed again and coughed, but finished with, "you two can bet—I'm going to get the hell outta here!"

"There's no way in hell Thomas just vanished into thin air, Kim," Jackson said, almost completely ignoring Candy's self-motivational speech. "Don't You Fuckin' Blame Me For Any Of This Shit!" Kim and Jackson didn't take their eyes off one another. Both their eyes darted at one another. For some uncontrollable reason, Kim's anger with Jackson's lack of direction rubbed her the wrong way and Jackson's quick anger with Kim's judgment did not help.

"I-I'm going this way," Candy said and walked past Kim, heading toward the left path of the 'Y', which showed Jackson nothing when he shined his flashlight down it before they found the puddle of blood. Kim stared at Jackson for two more seconds, then followed

Candy. When Kim turned away, Jackson instantly realized that Kim wasn't truly *Kim,* and he was right.

"No-you…are…not," Kim almost growled at Candy with a deep voice. "You-are… com-ing…with-me. The…both-of…you," and at that, Kim began to head straight back to the cellar. Kim scowled at Jackson when she walked past, and when the flashlight shone on Kim's face, Jackson instantly saw what he assumed: Kim's face wasn't hers. Kim wasn't 'Kim'.

Those Goddamn Ghosts Have Her Again! Jackson screamed in frustration in his head.

7

In mere minutes, the three passed back through the wooden wall with the wrong wooden door, exited the shelf door into the wooden-walled cellar, and climbed the staircase back into the bedroom. Kim, under possession for the third time, casually led Jackson and Candy through the bedroom door, which was now open, and into the living room, where Kim finally stopped in front of a smoldered fireplace. Several coals still glowed a burnt orange.

Kim never ran, never tripped, and never turned her head to see where she was going. When Candy and Jackson entered the living room, it was so cold, they could see their breath. Kim's breath did not appear. There was a power to the room that neither Jackson nor Candy had felt before. The atmosphere of the living room was fury. Kim's eyes stared at the dying fire and turned around to face her friends. Kim displayed white eyes with no pupils and a violent scowl.

Kim: "You-re…fri-end…is…de-ad."

Jackson: "That's not Kim…!"

Candy: (whisper) "I-It's…Thomas!"

Kim: "But-ch-ered…he…is. Ear…to…ear."

Jackson: "Why? How do you know!?"

Kim: "We…told…you-to…lea-ve! Told…you…de-ath…is…out—"

Jackson: (shouting) "GET TO THE FUCKING POINT! We Can't Leave! There's Fucking Monsters Outside, There's You Fuckers In Here, And There's Something Down In Those Tunnels!"

Kim: "The-re…is-no…po-int."

Candy: "W-what do—"

Kim: (growling) "You-are…all…gon-na…dddiiiiiiieeeeee!"

As Kim's vocalization of 'die' echoed on, Kim's body lifelessly dropped hard to the floor as if shoved. Jackson and Candy ran to Kim's aid as the feeling of fueled anger lifted from the living room. It was as if the living room were a sauna, and the heat quickly escaped. Candy started to pat Kim's face, trying to get Kim to wake up, but Kim didn't immediately respond.

Outside the front door of the cabin, heavy clawing scratched at the wood, just like it did just after sundown. For a second, and only a second, Jackson thought the ghost that inhabited Kim was a fortune teller and it told them a simple, but hard-to-swallow, truth. *Is Candy right? W-Was that really Thomas in Kim?!*

8

(Five minutes of silence passed.)

Son: "Are…are they gone?"

Father: "For now, I think so."

Mother: "What were you thinking!? You could've—"

Younger Twin Daughter: "I'm sorry! I'm sorry! I-I couldn't help it! I'm hungry!"

Mother: "We Have Food Down Here! We Only Resort To— What Were You Thinking of Running Off Like That!?"

Father: "Go to your cot until your mother or I come and get you."

Younger Twin Daughter: (sobbed and ran away as told)

Son: "Mom, we found her, and we lost them! She's okay. Dad's plan worked."

Father: "Barely! That was too close."

Mother: "What plan?"

Father: "We had to…throw them off guard. They almost caught us at the second door."

Older Twin Daughter: "You should have let them."

Father: "That's enough out of you! You were supposed to be watching your sister!"

Grandfather: "Enough, All Of You!" (deep exhale) "Boy, is the second door locked?"

Son: "Yes, granddad."

Grandfather: "Were you or your little sister seen?"

Son: "Not in the light, no. I held the hatch closed tight so Dad could grab the guy under the cot. He never came to. The guy with the two girls was not that strong."

Grandfather: "Son, where is the body you collected?"

Father: "North tunnel, by the creek."

Mother: "Dad, what's wrong?"

(silence)

Grandfather: (deep exhale) "Boy, you check the barriers, make sure all the doors are locked."

Son: "I'm on it." (ran off)

Grandfather: "Dear, attend to your daughters. Your daughters are not each other's babysitters. One harnesses this place, the other loathes it. Attend to them; they need you right now. The pack is here, outside, and I think the girls know it."

Mother: "Come on, come with me, hon. Granddad is right. You and I and your sister (exhales) have a lot to talk about."

Older Twin Daughter: "I hate it here…! We should have just left! You should have—"

Mother: "Enough! Go!"

(silence)

Grandfather: "Son, is the body you found dead?"

Dad: "He's dead, and he's on the table in the north tunnel."

Grandfather: "Was blood spilled in the tunnels?"

Dad: (exhales) "We had no choice, but it worked. The body spewed more blood than anticipated. I cut his throat too deeply in panic. We stood in the turn before the second barrier door in silence as they approached. They followed us, stopped, and froze when they saw the puddle."

Grandfather: "How many?"

Dad: "Three. Two girls and a boy, all in their early twenties. The one under the cot was the largest and strongest."

Grandfather: (exhales) "So be it. What's done is done. There be no changin' that."

Son: (returned, out of breath) "Doors are…secure…and I hate…to say this…but—"

Dad: "Out with it, son!"

Son: (out of breath) "The…ghosts…are free…I think!"

Dad: "Oh…Fuck! Not again! Just what we need!"

Grandfather: "They're not the problem, boy. The pack is. Blood spilled in the tunnel. They're going to smell that. They're already on the hunt. They're starvin'. Food on the mountain is scarce."

Dad: "I Didn't Have A Choice!"

Grandfather: "It's okay, son. We just need a diversion to keep them from comin' down here. Take me to the body. We'll fix two problems with one stone."

Son: "What do I do?"

Dad: "You've done enough already, and I'm proud of you for it. You got your sister out of there and bought me time to allow us to get away."

Grandfather: (deep exhales disapprovingly)

Dad: "Attend to your mother. She'll need your help with your sisters."

Grandfather: "Lock all the barrier doors in all the tunnels, except for the north tunnels. Then attend to your mother, boy. Your father and I have work to do."

Son: "You need help?"

Dad: "Go! We'll be all right."

Son: (nodded and ran off)

(silence)

Dad: "What are you not telling me?"

(silence)

Dad: "Dad?"

Grandfather: (groan of disappointment) "What you already know: we're in deep shit." (exhales) "Get yer knife, son, and let's go."

9

"Oh shit…not this shit again!" Jackson burst out after he heard the clawing at the cabin's front door.

"Kim! Come on, Kim! Wake up!" Candy repeated as she gently slapped Kim's left cheek with her left hand. Jackson began to pace back and forth, conflicted on what to do next. *Thomas, I swear when I find you, I'm gonna kick your fucking ass! I'm gonna—* Jackson stopped pacing and clenched his two fists. *Jesus…fuck! I'm losing it! Get your shit together, Jay. You're not done yet.* Jackson inhaled deeply and exhaled slowly. *I…I know you're not with us anymore, Thomas. I-I'm sorry. I…I don't blame you.*

"Alice…," Kim whispers abruptly in her own voice.

"Kim! Kim! Wake Up!" Candy started to shout louder, acknowledging Kim's whisper. "Come on, girl! Get Up!" That was when Jackson chose brashness over intelligence.

Somehow, Jackson just understood Thomas's decision-making skills: as erratic as they were, they were direct and without debate.

"Candy, stay here," Jackson ordered strongly. "Do Not Leave This Room! Do you understand?" Jackson stared at the cabin's front door when he spoke, not at the girls.

"What?" Candy asked in shock, turning her head. "What are—"

"Take the fire poker and poke the fire. Get it going again. Put Kim on the sofa and watch her, like she watched you. I'm going outside. Sun-up is in two hours at best. Watch her and take care of her, in case I don't come back," Jackson stated. Candy tried to get a word in, but Jackson kept talking. "For all Kim has done and has been through, you can do this for her."

"And Just What The Fuck Are You Going To Do?" Candy shouted, not fully comprehending what Jackson had said or meant. "Go Out There And Get Yourself Killed?!"

"I hope not," Jackson said not-so-confidently and walked to the door. When he reached the door, Jackson stopped and turned to look at Candy. "Take care of her and—," Jackson sighed apologetically. "Candy…I-I'm sorry…about Thomas."

Candy nodded that she understood and watched Jackson walk out the front door. Jackson closed it behind him so quietly that Candy didn't hear the click. Candy covered her eyes and began to cry as the overwhelming sorrow of Thomas's being dead flooded her broken heart once again.

10

Surrounded in darkness, Kim knew she was unconscious. She was warm and in control, but not conscious. Far away, as if from a mountaintop, Kim could hear Candy voice echo, "Wake up, Kim! Come on! Get up!" Kim knew shouting back would be pointless.

"I'm…asleep, or…in a coma, I think," Kim said, and her natural voice echoed. Kim looked around, shrouded in the purest of darkness she had ever known, and discovered she was flat on her side. Kim placed her hands down to push herself up and felt the ground, but couldn't see it. Everywhere up, down, and out was all solid ebony, and yet, Kim was still in her clothes.

Kim slowly stood up on her feet and tried stomping her foot on the ground. The ground was there, but the sensation of hitting a hard floor under her boot was not.

"I'm not in a coma…," Kim realized. "I'm ejected…out of my body!"

Kim started to walk and found quickly that there was nowhere to walk or run to. As if she were in a bubble, Kim knew moving was pointless. Shouting was pointless. Stomping was pointless. Everything that meant something to a living person was now pointless.

"I'm not dead, I'm not dead, I'm no—"

"Don't worry, you're not," a voice behind Kim said kindly. Kim quickly spun around and found herself in front of another woman. The woman was easily ten years older than Kim, but just about the same height and Caucasian. The woman's hair and her clothing, which looked nice and tidy, were decades out of style, but still fashionably cute.

The woman wore flat black shoes without laces and a pair of flared polyester pants with an untucked floral shirt that matched. With a small Scottish beanie hat off to the side, Kim recognized the woman's black hairstyle as the infamous Jackie O. look.

"Yes, I know," the woman said with a smile. "I'm…a little out of date." Kim felt her face flush with a rush of embarrassment. For all Kim knew, she was staring inappropriately, probably with a gape-mouthed expression. Kim straightened up immediately.

"No, ma'am, I—awe, shit, I'm so sorry, I didn't mean to—"

"It's okay, dear," the woman said with a chuckle. Her gentle voice was pleasant, but Kim kept guard. "You're quite alright."

"Are…are you Jackie—" Kim tried asking, and before she could finish, the woman burst into laughter, as if Kim had asked the funniest question she had ever heard.

"No, no, dear girl," the woman laughed, clearly embarrassed. "I'm not the First Lady, no, but to dress like her is to be like her. That, my dear, I'm certainly guilty of. My name is—"

"First Lady…?"" Kim whispered, wrapping the words around her mind. Then Kim quickly gasped uncontrollably and politely covered her mouth. "Oh…you're—Oh, I'm—" Kim felt a second rush of blood to her face, making her redder than she had ever been. "I'm sorry, um, Jacqueline Kennedy…is no longer the First Lady," Kim tried to say apologetically.

"S-She isn't?" the woman asked questioningly. "Is she no longer married to President Ken—" the woman tried to ask, but stopped herself when she saw Kim's expression of shock and sorrow. The young girl knew something the woman didn't.

"Former First Lady Jacqueline Kennedy Onassis died in nineteen ninety-four, before I was even born. She—" Kim tried answering, but the woman erupted once again into laughter.

"My dear, I'm joking with you," the woman said between laughs. "I'm aware of the year, but this," the woman expressed her fashion with her hands, "is how I looked when…when I was killed here." Kim's eyes widened at the woman's words. "Therefore, I'll forever be in this look, which I may add isn't all that bad!" The woman laughed at her own comment. "Oh, my dear, to laugh again! Oh, it's been ages…! I mean, could you picture Jackie O wearing cigarette pants like these?" Kim chuckled at that.

"Maybe not in public," Kim joked, and the woman chuckled. The woman pointed at Kim as if to say, 'You got that right.'

"Oh…oh, how I've missed laughing," the woman said happily with a weary sigh.

A memory flashed before Kim's eyes of when the ghosts in the living room were lined up silently against the back wall. Within the glimpse, Kim remembered seeing this exact woman. The woman wasn't as cheerful or composite as she was now. Then, she was crestfallen and defeated. Now, she was free-spirited, as where before she was dispirited.

"What's wrong with me?" Kim asked in hopes the woman knew. "Why am I here?"

"The problem is: you're not here, and to be quite frank, neither am I," the woman answered straight. "To be honest, honey, the moment you arrived, we were attracted to you. You were a gravitational force to us. You drew us to you."

"But I didn't know—We just found this place, by accident," Kim stated in confusion. "I didn't know anything about you or the cabin. It just…popped up!"

"Oh, the cabin…," the woman said, and Kim saw something happen that she thought was a figment of her imagination. The woman's presence glitched like an old television. Just a millisecond, the woman's appearance appeared as she did along the back wall, then turned back into the vibrant young woman. "It was a paradise when we arrived. Like a heavenly gift from nature." The woman seemed to drift into memory, then glitched again. This time, Kim knew it was a figment. Kim didn't know what exactly it was, but it was definitely emotionally triggered.

"You—You said I'm not here," Kim reminded the woman, who was mentally gliding off-topic. "And neither are you, is that right?"

"You're a medium, dear," the woman said. Kim scoffed in disbelief, but the woman's facial expression didn't change. Kim's face dropped as she thought about it. "I remember when I first came to the cabin, and how mesmerized I was by its beauty," the woman reminisced. "I was taken away immediately. We were on vacation—"

"You! It…It Was You!" Kim said with wide eyes and pointed at the woman. "When I first walked up to the cabin, I felt like I was in—"

"Heaven," the woman finished for Kim. "Yes, it was me, but not the whole me, you see. You see, all of us trapped in the covered mirrors, we all could…smell you, or *sense* you, but couldn't connect with you completely. After we were freed, every one of us connected through you, entered you, controlled you, and manipulated you." The woman's presence glitched twice as she talked. "Everyone of us was trying to get you to listen to us, but you blocked us out, and for good reason. You were terrified!" the woman exclaimed, but remained pleasant.

The woman glitched again, three times in a second. Kim stepped back a small step. The woman's tone deepened as she said, "The strongest of us…he's the one who took you over three times." Kim looked down and all around as she tried to remember.

"Jay was right," Kim whispered aloud to herself. "Thomas said that, too."

"The one who physically abused you and talked through you to your friends? He's a hellacious monster of a soul. If vengeance had a true form, it's him. He's brutal, mean, and powerful, and he always keeps us all near him," the woman warned. "We made him powerful and were powerless against him."

"Then how are we talking?" Kim asked. The woman glitched again, and it reminded Kim of her grandmother's old black and white television set with the wire hanger attached to the back. The woman answered Kim's question, but her tone began to change.

"He forced you out so hard, you're having an out-of-body experience, as they used to call it. I'm here because a tiny, tiny sliver of me lodged in your mind when we were all in your head. You don't remember talking to us, do you?" the woman asked, deeply concerned.

"I'm afraid not," Kim said, embarrassed.

"We connected quickly, you and me. We're almost the same age," the woman explained. "Only I was a mother of two by twenty-nine, a boy and a girl, and happily married to a good man. This, the me you're talking to now, is just a wisp of me, but it's enough."

Kim wanted to get to the point and asked, "How do I get back? My friends—"

"Are in horrific trouble, and you are, too. Especially the boy!" the woman warned, glitched, then her tone changed back to a dreamy state. "Oh, my dear, how he loves you!"

"Jackson? What's wrong with Jackson?!" Kim asked in haste. "Tell me, please!" Again, the woman glitched and her tone grew dark.

"You see, dear, the longer you're a ghost, or spirit if you will, the more bitter, the angrier you become. You become…unstable," the woman droned. "Manic depressant. Fierce. Unbalanced." Kim understood because her patience made her the same way. "Unhinged. Violent." The woman's voice and tone turn darker and more menacing. "Savage! Brutal!" Then roared viciously, "GIVE ME BACK MY—"

"MA'AM!" Kim shouted as she reached out to grab the woman. Kim fell straight through her, and the woman glitched once again. Her stature and tone returned to what would be normal.

"Oh, Lord, I'm fading," the woman warned. "It's happening."

"What's Happening?!" Kim shouted, hoping the woman wouldn't change or glitch again.

"My control to stay sane and rational," the woman answered. "Because of your open-mindedness and kind heart, I'm able to talk to you from my human personality and persona, but I'm dead, and the toll my soul took when I died, as well as the misery of the burden I carry, is turning me vexed."

"I'm sorry for my rudeness and for all you've lost," Kim stated urgently, "but please! Tell me what is happening to Jackson, and what does all of this mean?! How Do I Get Back?"

"I had a daughter," the woman said, "and like me and her father, she died here at the cabin." The woman in sixties clothes lowered her head, glitched, and raised her head quickly. "The boy who loves you with his whole heart needs to find her. She's…not like me, or the rest of us. Her soul is…true and saved from torment."

"The ghost girl at the door!" Kim gasped. "I've Seen Her! She wears a sundress that goes down to her ankles, and she wears red buckled shoes with two ribbons in her hair!" Immediately, the woman began to sob, but to Kim, it was a happy sadness.

"My little Alice…!" the woman moaned, as if she had forgotten what Alice looked like, but now could suddenly remember. "She's still here!" Kim watched a gleeful and hopeful smile stretch on the woman's face. "Oh, my beautiful little Alice!"

"I'll make sure Jackson finds her, but," Kim continued hastily, "how do I get back so I can tell him?" The woman glitched four rapid times, turning her pleasant face into a scowl.

"You can't," the woman said, "and you won't!" Another glitch. "YES! Yes, You Can! Christ, I'm slipping fast!" The woman shook her head as if trying to clear her consciousness. "Listen and listen well! I don't know how much time I have left!"

Kim listened to every single detail the woman from the sixties told her, which wasn't a whole lot, but the glitches were getting faster, worse, and more unstable by the second. Kim took mental notes of each step the woman told her and did everything possible to keep the woman focused. Jackson truly was on his own, but she was told how Alice and Jackson would find one another, which was crucial to Jackson's survival.

But, for them to meet, Kim had to take care of some personal business with the most violent ghost in the cabin. Worse yet, for Kim to get back, Kim would need a massive psychological jarring, according to the woman. Sadly, Kim knew how to get that…and she wasn't looking forward to it.

"You need to stop glitching back and forth, don't you?" Kim asked the woman. "You need to turn this pleasant sliver of yourself into your current ghost persona and unstable despair."

"I need to want to kill you, and attack you, so you can snap back into your body, yes," the woman answered, "But I love the old me and I miss it so! I miss laughing and thinking about my Alice, and the joy the cabin brought us when we first arrived," the woman began to go into a memory trance of pure happiness, clinging to it as if it were her last breath of life. Kim swallowed hard and knew what she had to do. It hurt her heart thinking about it, and the key was the one single detail the woman had barely mentioned.

"Ma'am…?" Kim asked kindly, and the woman looked at her, happily lost in thought. *The moment of truth,* Kim thought, then asked the ultimate question that would destroy the poor woman. "Where is your son?" Like a lightbulb that was about to burn out, the woman glitched rapidly like an old static signal on a very old television during a violent thunderstorm.

"THAT…SONOFABITCH…STOLE…MY…SON!" the woman shouted, so hard her voice echoed throughout the darkness of the mental void. "GIVE…ME…BACK…MY…SON!"

"Where Is Your Son?!" Kim shouted louder, even though it was breaking the last of the woman's human spirit.

"HE…KIDNAPPED…HIM…AND…KILLED…MY…HUSBA ND!" the woman shouted angrily, glitching madly. "THE…MAN…

KILLED…HIM!" More glitches. "I…WATCHED…HIS…WIFE…!" The glitching flickered so quickly, she almost became invisible. "SHE… TOOK…MY…SON…AWAY!" The glitches tripled.

"Where IS *YOUR SON?!*" Kim shouted at the top of her lungs and could barely hear herself. The woman roared with the most violent human roar and leaped at Kim with the fury of a predatory tiger attacking its unsuspecting prey. The sixties woman's human spirit finally snapped.

The moment Kim and the woman collided, Kim sat up consciously in the living room, breaking the trance.

11

Kim opened her eyes, but before she could speak or think, the woman's voice was in the back of her mind. It was kind, gentle, and soft, but was fading away, just like the echoes.

"He was…only three…when we died. My son…is still alive, and lives here at the cabin, with my…grandchildren: twin daughters…and a son. That's…why…I…can't…leave!"

12

Grandfather: "There. Good enough. That'll do it."

Dad: "It'll have to." (Puts metal object down.)

Grandfather: "Go west, quickly. The tree line; hang it there."

Dad: "We'll dispose of the rest later."

Grandfather: "I'm not concerned about 'later'. I'm concerned about this family, right here, right now! You caused a problem, and that'll fix it…until sun-up."

Dad: "Keep the gate open. I won't be long."

Grandfather: "If the pack closes in, barricade yourself in the truck. It'll be your only chance. You won't make it back here on foot."

Dad: "Damn traps better do something. There's enough of them littered about the yard."

Grandfather: "You know where they are. The pack and the ones above don't. Now, son, get a move on! Go! Hang that up and get'cho ass back here or hide in the truck."

Dad: "What a mess…Okay, open the gate now!" (Ran out the gate.)

13

Jackson stood just outside the cabin's door and stared motionlessly out into the darkness as his eyes adjusted. The last time he was outside, the creatures attacked them. Jackson knew they were still out there, but they weren't who he was looking for. He adjusted his eyes to the darkness to find the owner of the rifle he had repeatedly heard. *If that hunter is still out here, we're going to need their help one more time, or we're not going to make it to sunrise.*

Jackson tried to step off the porch and found his legs were locked as if they were covered in dried cement. Jackson also discovered his heartbeat was erratic. It wanted to burst from his chest. Even the blood flow in his temples pulsated so hard, he could feel it.

Move your ass, Jay! Jackson yelled at himself in his head, and with that, Jackson didn't just walk off the porch, he ran! The moment Jackson's boots touched the grass, he turned to the right to dodge the huge water puddle and ran along the front of the cabin. *That fucking thing better still be there!* Jackson reached the end of the cabin, made another right turn, and ran up the side of the house where he saw a clothesline of white rope hanging just over his head.

The truck! Where is the truck!? Jackson ran as if a swarm of giant hornets chased him, and before he knew it, Jackson was at the next corner of the cabin. The last turn to the right was all Jackson needed to find the truck. *I can't see a—*

—WHAM!—

Jackson collapsed on the ground and gasped for breath, inhaling knife-edged stings of pain. The parked truck was still in the backyard, blended in with the darkness of the night, only it was much closer than Jackson remembered it. Jackson ran straight into the passenger headlight so hard, it not only knocked the wind out of him but also potentially cracked a rib. Amongst the high grass, Jackson clutched his chest and breathed in painfully, but slowly.

That was when Jackson heard something in the tree line at the edge of the backyard.

Immediately, Jackson slowed his breath, despite the pain, and listened as clearly as he could. Something walked along the tree line, but it didn't stomp heavily, nor did it exhale loudly. Jackson stared straight up at the sky, seeing millions of stars, and praying to God that he wasn't seen nor heard. The rusting started directly behind the cabin in the tree line and followed toward the side, right where Jackson had traveled when he looked for the creek water stream. *Thomas, I swear, if that's you as a ghost and you're fucking with me, I'm going to kick your ass when I die! I swear to fucking God!* Quickly thereafter, the rustling stopped.

After what felt like minutes, Jackson had slowed his breathing to the point of almost passing out. The sharp pains from running directly into the truck were excruciating, but being ripped apart by devilish creatures with razor claws and diabolical jaws sounded far worse than sharp breathing pains! Then, something happened that told Jackson the monsters were not the ones making the rustling in the tree line.

Whatever moved along in the darkness began to retreat the way it came and huffed as it ran. The biggest clue was the sound of loose keys or muffled change that jingled in a pocket. *That's not one of the monsters that attacked Thomas and Candy, and that's absolutely not the hunter who saved our asses! But…that is definitely a person.*

Jackson stayed flat on the ground for a guess of five minutes after all the sound had left the night. Just when Jackson was about to move, the familiar sound of claws-to-wood hit his ears. *Oh, Fuck-Me-Running! No, Not Here! Not Now!* Emerging over the cabin's peak, Jackson first heard it, and then watched it stalk as it climbed over the cabin's roof!

Jackson closed his eyes as hard as he could, illogically thinking the starry night sky would reflect on his glistening eyeballs and give away his position on the ground. Unbeknownst to himself, Jackson was already holding his breath again. When the malicious beast leaped off the cabin, it landed directly beside the truck. On the opposite side, Jackson lay paralyzed in fear.

Each time the hands, claws, or paws of the creature struck the ground, Jackson could hear it grip the soil, trying to mute its movement. The monstrosity huffed in steady rhythms, like the panting of a dog, only it sounded like whispers instead of pants. The creature also sniffed and chopped its mouth the way a newborn puppy would when roughhousing.

Deep, deep in the woods, something chirped awkwardly, and like a bullet, the creature bolted from the backyard's high grass and disappeared into the forest. Far off, but close enough to tell, two more monsters ran in the same direction. *T-They're like…wolves. They hunt…!*

GET THE FUCK UP! NOW! GET UP! Jackson screamed at himself and surprisingly did. Realizing coming outside was a very stupid idea because the mystery hunter was nowhere to be found, Jackson decided to retreat to the cabin and wait for sun-up with Kim and Candy. Jackson, as calmly and quietly as he could, rolled over, rose to his feet, and began to step—

—CLUNK!— —SNAP!—

It only took a second, but Jackson knew what he kicked and what clanged together. *Jesus, another goddamn trap!* Jackson stood in the yard, four feet from the parked truck, and awaited anything to arrive that heard the trap snap. Jackson stood, waiting for his heart to explode. In the hellish silence that followed, nothing returned, and Jackson stepped around the trap to begin his retreat. Now terrified to step anywhere, Jackson thought, *Whoever walked the tree line didn't set off any traps, but Thomas did find one in the high grass...which means...there's more in the grass all around the property!*

On pure adrenaline juice, Jackson sprinted a straight line for the edge of the yard, finding the exact area where he left to find the water, and didn't step on another trap, but missed the same two he missed hours ago, again by inches. When Jackson entered the tree line, he found something far worse than stepping into a rusty metal trap.

At first, Jackson thought he had run into a wet blanket. He saw the clothesline ropes when he ran past the side of the house, so another line out here shouldn't surprise him. It was his goal to hide either behind a tree or in a tree until it was clear to run back to the cabin. Jackson put a handout, unable to see the blanket, but wanted to know where it was so he could steer clear of it. When his hand touched it—*That is not a blanket! Blankets aren't cold...or clammy!*

Against his better judgment, Jackson did the unthinkable and turned on his flashlight. What Jackson saw was oddly shaped but mostly rectangular. It was stretched out, connected on all four corners to the tree's branches by small metal hooks. The fabric was flesh-colored, except for the bloody edges…and what was imprinted on the upper left-hand side ripped Jackson's heart right out of his chest: a tattoo of a pickaxe with the letters 'T.H.E.' above it.

"Jesus Ch—" and Jackson's throat closed. *It's…Thomas! It's…his…skin!*

Jackson clicked off the flashlight and knew that image would never leave his brain for the rest of his life. Jackson's legs wanted to collapse from under him, but his knees were locked. More than ever before, Jackson couldn't move, knowing Thomas had been skinned recently. The smell hit Jackson late, but it hit him regardless and curdled his stomach. That's when it struck him: *Whoever took Thomas from under the cot…dragged him away, killed him, and they're using Thomas's flesh to divert the monsters…which means—*

Without any more thought, Jackson retreated to the cabin physically unharmed, except for the pain in his ribs from running into the parked truck. Just before Jackson reached the clothesline ropes, part of the ground gave way under his feet, causing Jackson to wobble to the side the same way a woman would stumble in high heels. Jackson dropped to one knee, collected his balance, and instinctively looked to see what he had almost stepped in.

"Holy fucking hell; a fucking hole!" Jackson whispered in shock and surprise.

Despite the use of the flashlight, Jackson's eyes had adjusted to the darkness of the night and could see things much better, although he still didn't see the hole in the yard.

Ready to finish the dash to the cabin, on the side of his hand, Jackson felt something metal and cold. *Jesus…another Fucking Trap!* Jackson stopped cold and allowed his eyes to focus. Jackson cautiously, with the back of his hand, felt the metal. It was smooth, not rusty, and something else told Jackson that it wasn't a bear trap: the metal was cylinder-shaped. He stretched out his hand slowly. gripped the thin metal cylinder tightly and picked it up. *A Rifle!*

Without another moment to spare, Jackson collected the rifle in both hands and ran to the cabin's front door, without finding another bear trap. Jackson grabbed the door, expecting it to be sealed by the ghosts, but it opened easily, which made two women inside shriek in shock.

Jackson entered the cabin and saw both Kim Michael and Candy Murray on their feet. This instantly told Jackson he was going to be faced with two upcoming emotional hurdles. The first hurdle would be Kim, who was back on her feet and conscious. This was a happy sight for newly sore eyes. The second hurdle was going to be a nightmare of its own. *How am I going to tell them what I saw attached to the trees?!*

14

The monsters…! They're…afraid of me!

Alice, the ghost girl, stood where the hunter woman with the rifle disappeared for a moment, wondering where the woman vanished to and how far away the monsters were. They were close, but they were on the other side of the house. The ghost girl had the idea that the creatures were afraid of her, so she put it to the test. Floating gently along the high grass of the side yard, Alice traveled past the parked truck and journeyed around the backyard. Like chasing a squirrel around a tree trunk, one of the monsters trekked along the front of the house.

The ghost girl quickened her pace to get a better look, and just as she turned the side corner on the opposite side of the house, Alice caught the hind end and back legs of the monster as it climbed up the front of the cabin toward the roof. She stood near the chimney, and that was when the cabin's front door opened. *The man by the water!*

Alice quickly floated to the young man and stayed a few feet from him, hoping her presence would keep the beast on the roof at bay. So far, it worked. Unaware of what the man was doing outside, Alice followed him as he ran around the cabin to the backyard in the dark. Alice tried to shout, *"The Truck!"* but the man didn't see or hear her.

The man ran directly into the truck's left headlight. As he fell to the ground, Alice saw something that she had seen before: another bear trap, just like the one the hunter woman stepped on. With all her will, the ghost girl moved it slightly so the man wouldn't notice or step on it.

Then, from above, the creature clawed down the roof and circled both Alice and the man. The ghost girl looked down at him, who had his eyes closed, and she could feel the fear emanating from him. Alice stood her ground, protecting the man in any way possible, and an idea struck her. *I'll be right back. I promise!* The ghost girl vanished instantly.

Far off into the woods, Alice re-emerged and sought just what she hoped to find: an owl. The ghost girl fused into the woodland bird and forced the owl to call out with an inhuman-sounding chirp screech call. Alice then instantly ejected from the bird and sensed the sounds of the approaching monsters. *It worked!*

Alice flashed back to the cabin just to see the young man on the ground get up. She couldn't talk to him, nor get his attention, but she could feel everything he felt through his emotions. As the young man ran to the tree line, Alice felt that he was deeply emotional, with the weight of the world on his shoulders. He was so full of guilt and sorrow, as well as confusion and pain. When the young man turned on the flashlight, both he and Alice saw what was hanging in the tree. A horrific wave of grief and misery emanated from him.

The ghost girl felt it all: the pain of his pain in his chest, the trauma when he turned on the flashlight at the tree branch, and—*He's leaving.* Alice sensed the terrifying notion of stepping on a bear trap, for that was now on the man's mind as he ran toward the cabin.

Alice followed along with him, and close to the front of the cabin, the man almost tripped. *A hole in the ground! That's where the woman with the gray putty went!* As the man took the rifle and ran away, Alice tried jumping down the hole and only floated over it. The ghost girl was not able to go underground no matter how hard she tried.

So instead, Alice followed the man into the cabin, where the woman who could see her was standing with the woman who fell in the water. All around the cabin's open room stood dozens of violent, rampant poltergeists. Their emotions overpowered the three living people like a tsunami wave over a tiny island. When Alice floated into the cabin, all the ghosts disappeared.

15

The moment the presence of the ghost of the little girl was gone, the creatures, who had been drooling at the smell of the exposed flesh nearby and grumbling at their starving hunger pains, seized the prize. The two male monsters ravaged their charge toward the smell of fresh blood and meaty flesh. Behind them, the third of the pack, the female, followed close by, but once the two males reached the flimsy cut skin hanging nearby, the female stopped in the middle of the high grass in the backyard.

The two gangly male monstrosities latched onto the human skin and fought a tug-of-war until it ripped into two uneven pieces, like dogs fighting over a stuffed animal toy. The purest essence of starvation and raw hunger overpowered the creature's ability to share amongst the pack. The female stopped beside the family truck and was fixated on something else. There was another smell, nowhere near as strong and as inviting as the flesh the males dominated, but still the scent of sweat, flesh, and living odor.

With her flat nose in the high grass, the beast stalked the scent and tipped its ear to the finest of sounds. *The scent's luring and fresh. It was…just here.* The monster silently stepped slowly through the yard, following the scent around the cabin. Among the smell of the ripe meal, there was a foul, bitter smell that was weak and scattered. *Metal.* With ease, the creature batted away each rusty metal bear trap it found, causing them to snap when it impacted the ground.

The female Gray continued its shark-like hunt for the mysterious scent as the two male Grays bolted from the tree line back toward the east side of the cabin. The single micro snack satisfied their mouths, but the taste only made them more ravenous for more.

16

It was Candy who almost jumped out of her skin when Jackson burst into the cabin through the front door. Her scream pierced into Kim's ear, causing a high-pitched ring to start deep in her ear canal. Kim also jumped, but her gasp was overpowered by Candy's scream. Candy screamed due to the forcefulness that Jackson used to open the door, and Kim screamed at the sight of what Jackson found.

"Where In The Hell Did You Get That Rifle!?" Kim shouted in surprise. "Goddamn, Jay, I thought you were someone else!" Jackson didn't answer, but instead, he placed the rifle against the wall, stormed over toward the two girls, and hugged them both as hard as he could. They all had the idea of Thomas being dead in their head, but each one had a hopeful slice of optimism that they were wrong. Only Jackson knew the real truth, at the moment. Jackson was just simply overjoyed to see Kim awake and Candy functional, despite her injury.

When Candy let go of the embrace, which she happily welcomed, Jackson allowed her to let go, turned, faced Kim, and planted a heavy kiss that told Kim everything the woman in her head told her. The sixties woman's voice *'Oh, my dear, how he loves you!'* replayed in her head. Kim opened her eyes after their lips separated, and for the first real time in her life, Kim saw Jackson no longer as a college graduate or just a lover. Jackson, in her eyes, was officially hers.

"I love you," Jackson said to Kim in a deep, low, meaningful whisper. As genuine as he and his words were, Kim heard it differently.

"What's wrong, Jay?" Kim asked, beating around the bullshit. Jackson didn't answer verbally. In his eyes, Kim knew he meant it, more than he ever had before, but his eyes told her something was very wrong…and he might not get the chance to say it again.

"Jackson, what happ—WHO THE *FUCK IS THAT?!*" Candy began to ask and screamed when something walked into view from behind Jackson. From nowhere, a little girl in a summer dress and flat red shoes with tiny buckles appeared. Jackson turned around and jumped back at the sight of the little girl, too. The only one who didn't jump in surprise or shock was Kim. Right away, Kim slowly let go of Jackson and knelt on one knee.

"A-Alice?" Kim asked cautiously.

"I didn't mean to scare you," the little girl said. Alice summoned all her will and appeared in full view, in colorful clothes, so all three of them could see her. The little girl smiled nicely and bowed her dress as Shirley Temple did in 'Baby, Take A Bow'. Alice looked up at Jackson. "Are you still hurt?"

"N-No, I'm okay," Jackson lied and immediately placed a hand on his sore chest.

"Why do adults always lie? I'll never understand," Alice asked rhetorically.

"Jay?" Candy asked concerningly. "What happened?"

"It's nothing, just the punishment of…stupidity," Jackson answered.

"Alice…I…I think I met your mom," Kim said, trying to be cautious but open to the girl.

"What?!" both Candy and Jackson asked in unison.

"I-I don't know how to—" Kim tried to say as Alice walked toward her. As Alice took a step, the three watched Alice's body physically glitch, as if she were just a projector illusion.

"What the—" Candy started to say, but Kim cut her off.

"No, it's okay," Kim said and raised a hand to Candy to stop her from talking. Kim kept her eyes on Alice's gaze. "Alice, I was told to find you, but I-I didn't—" Alice reached out to Kim and extended a handout. Alice caressed Kim's cheek, which caused Kim to shiver. Alice's touch was ice-cold. Alice's face looked curious as soon as Kim and Alice touched, but then after a second, Alice's face glowed with delight, and she smiled beautifully and gleefully.

"That *was* my mom," Alice said happily and smiled. "She was so pretty." Kim exhaled a smile as a tear escaped her left eye. Kim sniffed as her nose began to drain. "I almost forgot—"

"She's in trouble, Alice," Kim cut Alice off sternly. "How can we help her?"

"What is happening…?" Jackson asked in a whisper. Candy reached out and clung to Jackson's arm, not in fear exactly, but in confusion and nervousness. Out of nowhere, the atmosphere inside the cabin grew cold as if an industrial air conditioner kicked on, and the tension in the air grew dark and menacing. All four of them felt it. Alice raised one hand in a 'stop' gesture and stared at the ceiling.

"NO!" Alice shouted in a child's most defiant voice. "I SAID…NO!" Slowly, the room warmed up, but the feeling of being watched was thick and heavy. The three watched motionlessly as Alice slowly lowered her hand and continued to stare all around her. "I don't have long to explain, but you three need to leave. Now! I'll help as much as I can. So many others have died here, and I couldn't help them, but you three, I can help."

"Thomas!" Candy exclaimed in a high voice. "C-Can you help Thomas?!" Alice looked sadly at Jackson and Jackson closed his eyes tightly. *Not now! It's too soon!* Jackson shook his head slightly, lowered his head, then opened his eyes. He turned to Candy, put his hands on her arms just below the shoulders, and exhaled deeply.

"No…no…no…," Candy started to cry between words after she read Jackson's expression. He didn't even say a word, and Candy knew that Jackson knew officially that Thomas was gone. Jackson pulled Candy close to him and hugged her. Candy erupted into an emotional outburst of loss and woe as her bones turned to water. Kim watched Jackson hold onto Candy, and her heart sank. One lost a lover, the other a best friend. It took a moment for Candy to collect herself. When she did, she asked sobbingly, "Did…did you see him, Jay?"

"I…," Jackson started to answer and found it hard to finish, but he knew he had to, "…I saw enough to know."

"I'm sorry," Alice said sorrowfully. "There's so much pain here. This…is a bad place."

"We know," Kim said solemnly. "We don't know what to do. We can't go outside, we can't—"

"You followed me outside, didn't you?" Jackson asked Alice, cutting off Kim by accident. The thought popped into his head, and the words were out before he could think.

"Why are you here?" Candy asked Alice, almost judgmentally. Candy sniffed her nose strongly. "You're a ghost, aren't you, and you're gonna tell us what we're supposed—"

"Stop!" Kim interrupted and rose to her feet. Kim looked straight at Candy and Jackson. "Listen, there's more going on here than what we know, okay? This girl died here almost sixty years ago, and she's been here all this time!" Jackson and Candy turned to Alice. Their facial expressions were apologetic, and Alice felt them to be genuine.

"I'm…sorry," Candy said and lowered her head. Alice glitched again, and the room filled with pressure, making everyone's ears pop, and then the pressure went away.

"No, please, it's okay," Alice said to all three, "but please listen. I'm losing my control, so I must explain your danger quickly before I fade, and you can't see or hear me."

"Go ahead, hon," Jackson said softly. "We'll listen."

Quickly, Alice began to talk.

"Outside, there are terrible monsters," Alice started. "Some call them Grays. Others call them 'the pack'. I've even heard the word 'Wendigo' once. They were here before I was. They're…old." Alice continued as the three adults listened.

"Inside this cabin, there are more ghosts than you know. Now that they're free, I can see and hear them all. Two of them are my Mommy and Daddy, but they're terribly sad and very angry. One of the ghosts is a very bad man, and he's mean and he's strong. He controls them and keeps all the ghosts close. They make him stronger, and he won't let any of them leave."

"I'm aware of him," Kim said bitterly through clenched teeth. "We've met."

"Somewhere below is the family that lives here. They're hiding. I can't go down there, I've tried. The woman with—" Alice paused, turned around, and pointed, "—that gun, is down there right now. She's been helping you, but you being here interrupted her. Now she's trapped underground." Candy and Kim looked at Jackson.

"I didn't take her rifle from her!" Jackson said in defense. "It was in the grass! Right…oh shit!" Jackson cupped a hand over his forehead as he looked up. "Right beside a hole!"

"The Grays, the creatures, are scared of me. They won't come near me," Alice said. "I don't know why. I've never known why."

"At the truck! It was you who stopped them from getting me!" Jackson said to Alice.

"Yes. I didn't stop them; they just won't approach me."

"So, we can't go outside, we can't stay in here, and we can't go downstairs," Candy stated. "There's nowhere to run…and now, we're gonna die here."

"No!" Alice said strongly. "I don't want anyone else to die anymore."

"What do you think—" Kim started to ask but stopped when Alice glitched several times and even faded once. Kim quickly remembered Alice's mother, remembering her glitching meant she was losing her strength and control. When Alice reclaimed control, she continued and spoke quickly.

"The mirrors. They're all around this cabin. You have to trap the ghosts," Alice said, sounding weary and out of breath, which was odd for a ghost. "You two girls can do that. Just show the mirrors around the room, and when they see their reflection, cover the mirror with a cloth, but you have to be fast!" As Alice spoke, the heaviness of the pressure in the cabin flexed again. The ghosts grew angrier as Alice explained. The three could feel it all around them.

"You…," Alice pointed at Jackson, "…have to save the hunter girl underground. Use her gun, find her, and get her out. The people down there are evil people, but they're still just people. They're protecting themselves." Alice faded again. This time, it was slower for her to regain her composure.

"What do you mean by 'evil'?" Kim asked when Alice returned, mostly solid.

"They hurt and trick people," Alice answered sadly. "They…trap people." Candy's eyes widened at Alice's words, and she slowly raised her right hand to her head. As soon as her fingers felt the bandages that covered her mangled ear, it clicked in her head. *They eat people…!* Like a sinking ship in an ocean, Candy's heart sank at the truth, and her thoughts ran to Thomas. Her stomach knotted, but she was successful when she restrained herself from vomiting.

"They're cannibals…!" Candy whispered harshly as if a tennis ball was lodged in her throat. She had to say it aloud to accept it. Speaking was better than vomiting.

"Yes," Alice said sorrowfully. "And worse."

"Why was the hunter girl here helping us? She doesn't know us," Jackson asked quickly. He didn't want to think of Thomas's fate or create any mental imagery of what could be or could have happened to him. Seeing the blood in the tunnel told him enough, and he didn't want to know what 'and worse' meant.

"She knows this place. She'll lead you all out of the woods. I'll follow you as far as I can to keep them away." Alice stumbled and dropped to her knees. Both of her hands disappeared into the floor. Alice turned completely transparent. "I don't know how much time—" Alice disappeared, and the second she vanished, the cabin's air became almost impossible to breathe in. The pressure returned too heavy; all three felt it in their temples.

All around them, the three heard Alice thunderously burst out, "NO!" one final time, and the heaviness went back to normal. Kim, Candy, and Jackson knew that was Alice's last defense. Alice did not return in visual form. Once again, the three were on their own.

"Did—Did we say something to make her leave?" Candy asked, unsurely, wiping her tears away. As Alice talked, Candy uncontrollably drifted away in thought about Thomas, his demise, and whose hands were on her when they took a bite of her ear in the dark tunnel below.

"No. Ghosts have—never mind. I don't have time to explain, but I'm glad she told us all she could," Kim said, walking toward the wall. Kim grabbed a mirror from the wall and said, "I feel sorry for her and all these people she was talking about, but like she said…," Kim threw a mirror at Candy. Candy caught it, and Kim finished by saying, "…we have work to do!"

"What about Alice?" Jackson asked in a shout, clearly concerned.

"I don't think we have to worry about her," Kim said strongly with a smirk. "She—" Kim chuckled cockily, "She's strong!"

18

Jackson ran over to the wall, grabbed the rifle, and pulled the pin back. There was a single shell in the chamber, and Jackson found three more in the magazine.

"Do you think the people downstairs in the tunnels heard anything of what Alice said?" Jackson asked as he shoved the pin back in position.

"I don't think they can hear through the dirt, and if these ghosts are here because they killed them, I doubt the ghosts are going to tell them," Candy said as a poor attempt at a joke. Her heart hurt enough, and she thought the levity was appropriate. No one laughed, but Jackson and Kim appreciated it.

"Find her, Jackson," Kim said sternly. "Go. We'll handle things up here." Kim looked at Candy. "Right?"

"Right," Candy said, then added to build up confidence, "Sure!" Truthfully, Candy wanted the job of going down in the tunnels to find Thomas, just to debunk some of Alice's words, but Candy also knew she would be killed if she did. For a sliver of a second, Candy honestly welcomed the thought, then dismissed it. She was selfish at times, but never suicidal.

183

Jackson hugged the girls, dashed to the front bedroom door with the rifle, and turned back to look at Kim. His eyes told her, 'I'll be back as soon as I can'. It was almost a look of 'In case I don't see you again' and Kim didn't have time for any more sorrow, pity, or anything that would diminish them sooner.

"GO!" Kim shouted with frustration at Jackson. "Get That Girl And Get Back Here!" Right after Kim shouted 'here', Jackson was physically slammed into the wall that supported the bedroom door as Kim was grabbed by the throat and levitated off the floor. Candy was pulled down to the floor flat on her back, then was dragged around the living room by her hair. The dried blood in her hair pulled at her ear wound, and Candy screamed in pain.

The atmosphere dimmed darkly, and a verbal growl of hatred filled the cabin.

Kim, with one hand, turned the mirror in her hand around and aimed the glass in all directions as she gasped for air. Right away, whatever ghost had a hold of Kim let go and Kim dropped to the floor. All around the cabin, in every room, hung pictures swayed rapidly, all the furniture shook about, and the groans, cries, and moans from dozens of ghosts roared, overlapping one another.

The fire in the fireplace burst to triple its size, in brightness and heat. The entire kitchen cabinet rattled violently, and the whole cabin began to creak as if a human giant outside sat on the roof. Jackson picked himself up off the floor, shook his head, and looked for Kim. Kim was aiming her mirror aimlessly in every direction, blindly fishing for ghosts. All around the cabin, the glass in the picture frames cracked in every room as the air pressure thickened.

"GO! NOW! DO WHAT ALICE SAID!" Kim shouted. Candy gave out a grunt as her body slammed against the writing desk in the corner. Kim ran over to help Candy as Jackson ran into the bedroom. It was do-or-die time.

19

Kim and Candy didn't have time to think about Jackson's well-being. The main floor of the cabin was a supernatural tug-of-war, and at the moment, Kim and Candy were on the losing end. The unknown collective of ghosts was physically abusing the girls as they manipulated the atmosphere and projected anything loose in the cabin at the walls.

Several of the mirrors on the walls were also thrown around, but not all of the glass shattered. The ones that broke were the only arsenal Kim and Candy had. Kim couldn't see a single ghost, so she had no idea where they would be or where they would strike next.

Nonetheless, Kim and Candy did everything they could to dodge thrown objects and step over broken items, all while showing the mirrors around the cabin to capture whatever ghost they could. Candy, against the wall, turned her head away to dodge a thrown oil lamp, when two ghosts in front of her physically appeared directly in front of her in full view. It was Candy who caught the first specter.

One was tall, the other was hunched over. Both were women and very different in age. Their figures were not full, but they looked to be made of a bluish, whitish wispy fog, like an invisible laser light being seen in smoke. The ghosts physically appeared when they looked in the mirror and saw themselves. Their faces were ghastly, and they looked horrified when they saw their reflection. First Candy saw them, then Kim saw them.

"Cover The Mirror! Quick! You Got Them!" Kim shouted. "Use Anything!" Candy quickly took the mirror, cupped it under her blood-

185

stained, sleeveless yellow hoodie, and ran over toward the back bedroom door. Lying on the floor, surprisingly untouched, was a rug. Candy slid partly under the rug, removed the mirror from under her yellow sleeveless hoodie, and left it underneath as she slid out.

"There! W-Will that work!?" Candy shouted out, hoping Kim would say yes.

"The sofa!" Kim burst out. "Put the sofa over the rug!" Kim shouted out, hoping Candy's idea worked. Right away, as more and more loose objects shook and were being tossed around, Candy and Kim grabbed the sofa and lunged it on its side directly onto the motionless rug. Two logs from the fireplace rolled out toward the wall where Candy was pulled, and flames caught some oil spilled from the tossed oil lamp.

"Oh…SHIT!" Candy shouted abruptly, seeing the flames catch the oil immediately. There wasn't much oil from the lantern spilled, but any uncontrolled fire inside the cabin was instantly bad news. "Shit, Kim! The last thing we need is a fire in here!" Right away, Candy dashed for the kitchen area when Kim shouted her response.

"NO! Candy, Wait! That's Exactly What We Need!" Kim yelled in an epiphany-like, gleeful burst. "Quick! The Matching Chair!" Kim directed and pointed at the piece of furniture. It was closer to Candy, and what Kim wanted was just three steps away. Candy ran over, grabbed two of the chairs' footlong wooden legs, and picked them up.

It was either lighter than expected or it was the adrenaline rush, Candy wasn't sure, but either way, she felt really strong. Candy chucked it directly on top of the fire-caught oil spill. It hit the floor with an internal crack, but it landed exactly where Kim hoped for. To Candy, it looked as if the chair had put the fire out.

Kim stepped over, grabbed the cracked oil lamp, and was just about to chuck it at the wall where the sofa-matching chair had landed.

With her right hand raised and the base of the lamp in her grasp, an invisible ghost grabbed her right arm and her face and lifted Kim off the floor.

"THIS…IS-OUR…HOME,…*CU-NT!*" a ghost roared at Kim, erupting all around. If the girls didn't know better, they'd swear the voices were coming from speakers in the ceiling.

A picture frame flew straight past Kim's head, hit the wall, and shattered with chips of glass and wood chunks. When Kim's eyes looked in the direction of the tossed picture frame, the ghost holding her came into view and looked in the same direction.

A male ghost in his late fifties and a spirit of the same height looked at Candy. In Candy's hands was another intact mirror. As if a flick of a light switch illuminated them, both ghosts saw themselves, gnarled at their reflections, and Candy covered the mirror with a towel she found. Kim instantly dropped to the floor like a sack of rocks, turned on her side, and threw the oil lamp base at the wall as hard as she could. The moment it hit the wall, it cracked into four thick pieces and spilled the remaining oil over the lounge chair. It instantly erupted in flames.

"That's two more," Candy said proudly, then ducked to avoid a flying box of salt from the kitchen. "How many more are there!?" Candy wondered how long both of them were going to have to keep shouting to be heard. Both of their throats were growing raw.

"I have no idea," Kim answered. "Do you see any more mirrors anywhere?!"

"They're scattered, some are broken," Candy said, looking around, then popped up straight. "In The Bedrooms!" Both women looked at both bedroom doors, and they were still waving back and forth, slamming shut and open again repeatedly.

"Yeah…I don't think so!" Kim said. "Just keep the fire growing! Grab anything!"

"I think I understand why Alice left so fast," Candy said as she grabbed a pillow and whipped it at the burning chair. "I didn't see her with all the other ghosts. Have you seen her?"

Kim answered, "No, I haven't." Kim found one of their backpacks and was about to throw it across the room at the fire. The smoke was beginning to fill the living room. The structure of the cabin began to warp and bend. To Kim and Candy, it appeared as if they were looking at the cabin from underwater. The shakes and vibrations of the cabin were increasing as if the cabin was throwing a temper tantrum. The bangs and thuds of the doors grew louder.

"*IN-VAD-ERS!*" one ghost voice bellowed with hatred. The cabin's walls shook madly.

"It's Working!" Candy yelled excitedly. "I Think We're Making Them Mad!"

"We're Not Trying To Make Them Mad!" Kim stated. "We're Trying To Distract Them!" Kim tossed the backpack at the fire, not caring whose bag it was. "We Need To Find More Mirrors And Buy Jay More Time!" Then, Kim added with a smirk, "And If They're Getting Mad? Then…GOOD! FUCK'EM!" Candy returned the smirk.

20

Unbeknownst to Jackson, Kim, and Candy, the essence and power of the ghosts had overpowered and drained Alice of her unique ghost ability and strength as she talked to the three living humans. When Alice disappeared the final time, she blanked out, which caused her own essence to collapse. It was a ghost's version of a human passing out.

Upon her collapse, Alice was immediately restrained by the strongest poltergeist, the very bad man. Not only was this the same ghost that manipulated Kim three times, but it was the same ghost that harnessed the other spirits to remain the alpha.

He overpowered every ghost by restraint, and none had dared to oppose him. A small, but loyal, entourage to him attacked Candy, Jackson, and Kim as soon as he had Alice prisoner. Only two ghosts of the cabin's haunted horde had an inkling of deviance to strike against him, but after decades of obedience and fear, the thought of a mutiny was as meek as a single raindrop being called a hurricane. As he dominated the presence of Alice, the spirits discharged their emotional state and ripped the cabin up like toddlers in a toy store with no parental authority to stop them.

When they were alive, they may have been tortured, racked, or maimed in the cabin, before their demise, but after being dead and confined to a place for so long, one's prison became one's home. Now that they were all free to roam, even if temporary, the cabin was theirs and their dictator was in command. That is until something in the cabin happened that none of the ghosts expected: a fire. The burning of their encampment meant the destruction of all they knew: their home. None had passed on, so all they knew was to exist in the plane of the living.

The alpha poltergeist saw the fire as something completely different, and it wasn't something he was going to allow. Not once, not ever! If the cabin were to be destroyed, the spiritual inhabitants would be free, maybe even pass on to the next realm if they left the cabin. If they left, he'd be powerless, and that was a possibility the very bad man would never let happen.

Then the red-haired woman defied the alpha by showing the dead their reflections in the mirrors, trapping them once again! The living family below, descendants upon descendants upon descendants, have known for generations the secret to ghostly incarceration, but these three? No.

It was Alice, the ghost of the woods, who told them what to do. It was Alice, the one ghost who didn't share the curse of the cabin's hell, who told how. It was the daughter of two ghosts under his powerful command that started the onslaught. Now that he had Alice, the dead weren't leaving, and the living weren't living long!

But that goddamn fire; the fire would ruin everything! He commanded every soul that he dominated over to contain the fire or reverse the cabin to its previous state a second time. When the first mirror captured two, he felt his power shift slightly. Then, two more were captured, and the power shifted lower again. Enraged, he ordered half of the ghosts after the fire and the other after the breathing bitches that were entrapping his legion.

As ordered, the ghosts began to throw loose objects around the cabin, causing the red-haired woman and brunette to cower repeatedly, but the brunette was clever. Using the bench from the writing test, she wedged the back bedroom door open, ran inside, and grabbed three more mirrors from the bedroom, capturing seven more. The redhead remembered something Alice said and slid the cellphones under the rug with the mirrors.

Several of his followers tried to move the gigantic rug that covered the prison mirrors, but claimed it was too painful to go near. In all his years of existence, the only thing that harms a spirit is electricity, which the cabin above lacked. Power was underground, which meant the tiny silver-colored blocks were electric and powerful. Even if the ghosts got loose under the rug, they'd be barricaded by the little silver-colored objects. While witnessing the chaos, the very bad man grasped Alice tighter, choking the ghost girl the way smoke choked a living thing.

The brunette used one more mirror to capture three more as the redhead ran into the other bedroom, using the same tactic, but with a barstool from the kitchen area. This was the beginning of the end, and the alpha knew it. The fire in the living room was growing beyond control, a third of his ghosts were captured, and the living bitches were winning. Pretty soon, the cabin would be destroyed, and the uncaptured ghosts would learn they could get free of his tyranny.

If the fire destroyed the cabin, then the creatures outside would enter. They'd ransack the cabin in search of something, someone, to eat. The result would be the same: the ghosts would be free, and he'd lose his dictatorship over the imprisoned dead. The family living below was the cause of their deaths, but they had order and control of their home. The ghost's home.

The redhead grabbed two mirrors off the wall, shouted something at the brunette, and slid the mirrors face up through the bedroom doorway along the floor. Several more ghosts saw themselves, but the woman couldn't cover them fast enough. The fire had grown along the back wall and covered the wall beside the fireplace. The matching sofa and chair were full of blaze as windows had begun to crack. The heat did not affect the ghosts, but the living were sweating.

THE BEASTS! the alpha thought abruptly as clawing sounds began to scrape along the roof and the wall that supported the chimney.

"IN-VAD-ERS!" he roared, shaking the cabin with his malice, hatred, and fear of the monsters who inhabit the woods around his prison. And at that, the redhead found an arsenal. As if his shout gave away his exact position, the redhead bitch ran backward to the kitchen as she pulled a blanket along the floor. The blanket had seven mirrors, all lying flat and face up.

Right away, he saw his very own reflection: a rickety, bony, hunched back of an elderly man with a straw hat, four snaggle teeth, and a powerful chin of skin and bone. His entire living life flashed before his eyes: his birth, his childhood, his parents, his wife, his parents' death, his wife's death, the family from the cabin, the family killing…*NOOOOOO!*

The dictator spun Alice around and placed her in front of himself, causing the ghost girl to see herself for the first time in who-knows-when. Alice and eleven other ghosts gathered to view the living, and right away, the brunette screamed something incoherent.

"CANDY, NO! Candy! It's Her!" the other living girl shouted. "It's Alice!"

The tyrant, who knew what 'candy' was, didn't understand the babble from the brunette. In the confusion, he sacrificed the capture of the ghost girl from the woods to escape incarceration by fleeing. As he attempted to flee, two ghosts of his horde charged at him: a male and a female. Right away, the male seized the overpowering spirit, who was losing his power quickly, and confined him in the same way he held Alice as the female sped fast past.

Unbelieving to his own dead eyes, the dictator was harnessed by the male ghost, whose rage he had never felt before, and the female ghost raced to the ghost girl, grabbed her, and threw the child through the wall of the cabin, causing herself to be snagged by the mirror Alice was looking in.

"CANDY! NOW!" is what the two male ghosts heard the brunette shout. The redhead covered the mirrors on the blanket at once at the same time as the male ghost that grabbed the once-strongest spirit realigned their position. The brunette had something in her hands facing them and they both saw it: a small, apple-sized, compact make-up mirror.

"YYYYOOOOUUUU….BBBBIIIITTTTCCCCHHHH!!!" the poltergeist dictator roared, once again, causing the cabin to shake violently. As soon as both male ghosts were visible to the living, the brunette cockily closed the compact mirror with a single snap. The cabin went silent. Every flying object and floating piece of debris dropped like a rock tossed in the air.

Over thirty ghosts remained in the cabin when the most powerful of all was captured and placed in the pocket of one of the living women.

21

As if thrown through a five-hundred-mile-an-hour wind tunnel, Alice was launched from inside the cabin, where she had no strength, no self-essence, and felt the hollowness of non-existence. The moment Alice's presence appeared under the stars of the heavens, the power of her *own* existence raced back into her, filling her soul with her *own* thoughts, her *own* feelings, and all of her memories that she'd harnessed for decades.

In the shadows of the trees and under the twinkling of the stars above, Alice realized it was her father who grabbed the very bad man, and it was her mother who sacrificed herself to be in Alice's place. Her throw sent Alice back to the woods outside so she would not spend a second trapped in a mirrored prison.

Alice's heart was full, and her eyes shone in the reflections of the glitter of the galaxy above. Her parents remembered her and gave themselves up to free her.

"Thank you, Mommy," Alice whispered as she sat on the earthy ground and embraced the lasting emotions her parents emanated to her when they came to her rescue. "Thank you, too, Daddy."

Alice didn't think about the two women inside, nor the man who walked to the river. She thought about her once-loving family and her baby brother, who was still alive. Regardless of how long they've been separated, Alice collected love from her parents and learned that even in death, they still protect her. As for her brother…

22

Below the cabin, Jackson ran through the tunnels as fast as he could, trying to remember which direction went here or there. When he arrived at the first barricade with the unmatching wooden doors, the door was now locked.

"Hey, Alice-ghost, I could use you right now!" Jackson said lowly in the dark tunnel. A second later, Jackson tried the doorknob again, and it was still locked. "Damn it!" Jackson punched the door, instantly retracting his hand in pain. "Well…that was *really* stupid!"

While shaking his hands, wriggling out the pain, a second thought struck Jackson. *What would Thomas do?* went through his mind, and the answer came easy: *Force!* Jackson put the flashlight down on its side and shone the light at the door. Like a man infused with an injection of testosterone, Jackson grabbed the rifle with his strongest grip and began beating the wooden wall with the butt of the rifle. Right away, the boards began to break free. The squealing of tight nails pinched Jackson's eardrum as they were forced free.

"If I —*BAM!*— can't go —*BAM!*— through the —*BAM!*— fucking door, I'll go —*BAM!*— through the —*BAM!*— fucking wall!"

194

Jackson shouted, repeatedly bashing the boards free. Once a few boards had loosened, Jackson began to kick the bottom boards to make just enough room to physically crouch through. Once the area was big enough, Jackson knelt in, crossed through, stood up, unlocked the door, and opened it so his retreat would be significantly easier. Once the barrier door was open, Jackson began down the next set of stone tunnels.

It took less than a minute, but Jackson found the 'Y' again, and knew if he went left, he'd see Thomas's blood puddle again. *Going to the right, though...*, he didn't know what went to the right. *Thomas' body went left because someone dragged his body that way. If I go right, I might end up—* "OH, FUCKING HELL!!! IT WOULD SERIOUSLY FUCKING HELP IF I KNEW WHERE THE GIRL FELL THROUGH!" Jackson shouted angrily at the top of his lungs.

"...h-he...hello?" an echoed, weak voice spoke. "...w-who– who's...t-there!?"

"Where Are You!?" Jackson shouted and looked down at the two directions of the 'Y' in the tunneling. An odd tremble went up Jackson's spine. "A-Alice!? Is That You?! Hey, Now, I Know You're A Good Ghosty Girl, But Don't You Fucking Jump Out At Me! Okay?!"

"...stop sh-shouting...!" the weak and distant voice spoke again, and Jackson took a big sigh of relief. The voice was coming from the right tunnel of the 'Y' split. With his flashlight in one hand and the rifle in the other, Jackson dashed down the right tunnel. The flashlight was along the handle of the weapon, and it showed its light beam straight ahead. The barrel of the rifle was shiny in the light and poked out nicely. If anyone was going to appear in front of him, they'd see the barrel before seeing him. Jackson was through with taking chances.

"I'm coming! Just…stay where you are," Jackson spoke normally and huffed a few words. Running underground was not on his list of everyday activities.

"…w-who are you?" the voice spoke again, dreaded, defiant, and much closer this time. It was undeniably a woman's voice: shaky, but direct. "I'm…I'm armed!"

"So am I," Jackson warned. "You'll see my rifle before you see me, but please, don't be alarmed. I was sent down here to find you, so don't shoot! Alright?" The moment Jackson asked 'Alright?', the girl came to view, and things went from bad to worse.

Firstly, the girl wasn't lying, because the first thing Jackson saw was a handgun pointing directly at him. The light of the flashlight shone nicely on the handgun. Just past the gun, Jackson followed his eyes up her arms and straight to her face. She wore a dirty red flannel shirt, and her hair was straight and dark.

"Don't shoot!" Jackson said quickly.

"Says the man pointing a rifle at—Hey! That's My Rifle!" the woman abruptly stated, then expelled a painful hiss and groan from her throat. The handgun quickly went down and out of view as the woman grabbed at her right leg.

"I found this by a hole in the grass, and I almost fell in, too," Jackson reported as he put the rifle down against the tunnel wall. While Jackson reached down, the flashlight whipped around the tunnel, disorienting him a bit. It was so dark and focusing on the beam of light messed with his head. "Again, I was sent—"

"No one…knows I'm here," the woman said as she hissed in pain. "I'm…alone on this mountain." Her grunts sounded more painful.

"Oh yes, they do," Jackson said matter-of-factly. "And those 'no ones' know more about you than you know." Jackson watched her try to reposition herself, but the high wince of pain that slipped her voice told Jackson things were worse.

"Who 'no ones' are you talking about?" the injured woman asked defensively.

To try and calm her, Jackson reassured, "Believe me when I tell you: you're not alone. You have a…guardian angel on your shoulder named—"

"Ahhh, fuck! Ahh, my fucking leg!" the woman cried out, still trying to move.

"Stop Fucking Moving!" Jackson barked cautiously, and he aimed the flashlight on the ground directly at the woman. The flashlight showed the entire problem: the woman's right foot, ankle, and shin were snared in a sprung bear trap. The metal teeth had sunk into the fabric of her jeans, and seeps of blood had darkened where the teeth bit. Thanks to her black boot, her ankle could be spared. "Holy fuck, that looks bad."

"Wow…you're—OW!—intelligent," she said, attempting to stretch out her left leg.

"Goddamnit! Stop Moving, Will You?!" Jackson shouted firmly. "Stop!" She did, but looked at him harshly. "Every movement you're making is causing the trap to bite harder! The reason why you're not screaming in pain is because of either an adrenaline rush, you have a high tolerance of pain, or you're on fucking crack…So…Stop…Moving!" Both Jackson and the hunter woman froze, locked in a stare-down. After a moment, the woman nodded slightly.

"Yeah…falling through the grassy knoll up there probably didn't help any either," the woman said while still looking at Jackson. Jackson put his hands out at her, palms up, inhaled deeply, and exhaled calmly through his nose. "Are you gonna help me or do yoga?" she snarked.

"Listen…my name is Jackson and today…today has been a
REALLY BAD DAY, okay? Someone knows you're down here, and I'm
here to get you out! So, please, lower your fucking defensive 'I-Am-
Woman, Hear-Me-Roar' bullshit wall and let me help you!" Jackson
boldly stated directly at her. "And besides," Jackson lowered his voice,
"we're not alone down here!"

Both stared at one another for a moment.

"Jackie," the woman stated.

"What?" Jackson asked, confused.

"God, you really are dumb," the woman snarked with a smirk.
"Jackie, it's my name. Jackie Shane."

"Jackson Chad, or call me 'Jay.' Most people do…and now, let's
get you out of that trap."

23

Sunrise was not far away, and the pack knew it.

Nine feet above Jackson and Jackie, in the backyard of the cabin,
silently and slowly stalked the only female of the three Grays. The
creature sniffed the grass with her bony muzzle into the high grass. The
smell of sweat and blood was so fresh, it could taste it, and the voices
were deep and muffled, but they were there. How they were underground
was the first mystery it tried to solve. The second mystery was how to
get down there.

Its steps were so soft and so slow in the grass, like a crane in a
river. It could hear the other two male creatures clawing and tapping
their claws on the wood of the cabin with ease. The smell of the blood
underground was more powerful than the toxic smell of the smoke that
emanated from the cabin. The two male Grays were on a stalking quest

of their own, waiting for their meals to exit. The monsters didn't like the toxicity of the smoke, so neither could the living things inside.

None of the three dared to enter the cabin. The essences of the dead were an entity that they didn't physically fear, but the knowledge and proof of death was a fact the Grays didn't accept. The pack of three had been alive for almost two hundred years. It was never their intention to ever die either.

They've lived on pure survival. They've lived on pure instinct. The wilderness made them what they are from what they originally were: man into creature. Predators of nature, the beasts of all predators. Nothing has, can, nor will kill them.

From the roof of the cabin, one of the male Grays called out in a mixture of hisses, clicks, and gnarled throat babble. The female in the backyard whipped its head up at the call, gripped the ground with all four of its metacarpal paws, released, and dashed for the chimney side of the cabin. *Fuck...something's wrong!*

With the two males on the cabin's roof like spiders on a mushroom head and the female climbing the cement fixture of the chimney, the pack stared at the front yard and watched the ghost of the woods spontaneously appear. All three hissed in hatred at the child spirit and leaped off the cabin with barely a sound. They would only travel into the woods a short distance until the time was right to strike the meals in the cabin.

Their bellies grumbled and their mouths watered at the smells of the blood and flesh. The Grays were beyond starved, and hibernation was months away. The forests of the mountain were scarce of animals and other wildlife, due to their hunts. The traps the cabin family had created were all picked clean, and the meal in the tent only lasted a few days.

There wasn't much to gnaw on when its inhabitants were one thin human and two others a third the size.

Time was running out for their kill, and they knew it. In an hour, the sun would rise, and their belly pains would continue. This was not in their interest as food was right there, ready to be taken to their nesting cave. For only a moment, the three Grays waited for the perfect time.

24

"Okay, listen…this is what we're going to do, okay, Jackie?" Jackson said to Jackie. "I'm going to wedge the butt of your rifle—"

"Scratch It And Die, Jackson!" Jackie snapped harshly, cutting Jackson off.

"I'm GOING to wedge the butt of your rifle," Jackson firmly repeated, "and use the leverage to open the trap, releasing the pressure off your leg. I don't give a fuck about the condition of your rifle—Just You!" Again, both stared at one another, awaiting the other to either argue or acknowledge.

"That's…my father's rifle!" Jackie sternly barked matter-of-factly with a grunt of pain.

"Did you steal it?" Jackson asked as if it would make a difference.

"Family heirloom," Jackie said strongly. "The only one I got."

"So…," Jackson put up both his hands, palms up. "Take your pick: scratched family heirloom that will still fire and you'll be able to keep it, OR lose your leg, get rust in your blood, die from a stupid infection, and never shoot again, all because you're A Pain In The Ass!" A pause between the two. "Which is it going to be?" Another pause.

"So, I'm a pain in the ass?" Jackie asked straightforwardly.

200

"I said all that, and all you heard was me calling you a 'pain in the ass'?" Jackson said, completely beside himself. *Jesus Christ, all I'm trying to do is save this woman, and she's giving me shit about her goddamn father's gun! Maybe she's better off—NO! Stop that, Jackson. Just stop asking her permission and do it!* At that, his mind was made up.

Jackson immediately sat down at Jackie's feet and pulled her left ankle toward him. Jackie shouted a yelp of pain as the weight of the bear trap hit the ground. Jackie instantly wanted to punch Jackson right in the jaw as hard as she could. Jackson reached over, grabbed the rifle, and put it behind him.

"Your sleeve: rip it off. Quick! We're out of time," Jackson ordered her.

"W-What?" Jackie asked, confused.

"No More Bullshit! Your sleeve, I don't care which! Rip One Off, Now!" Jackson was now mad and ready to get her out of the tunnel so *he* could get out of the tunnel. Shocked, Jackson watched Jackie do something he didn't expect: she pulled a small knife from her pocket and handed it to Jackson.

Only for a second, Jackson hesitated, then took the knife, opened the blade out, and told her, "Please, don't move. I don't want to cut you, especially if this flannel is a family heirloom, too!" Without looking at her facial expression, Jackson cut into the fabric all around her—*Damn, she has some skinny arms!*—shoulder, and he unbuttoned the sleeve.

Jackie pulled her arm out, and to her surprise, Jackson held out the cut sleeve in one hand and the knife in the other. Confused, Jackie hesitated but then took both items.

"What am—"

"Gag yourself with the sleeve. Wrap it around your mouth and tie the back tight. Bite down," Jackson instructed. "This is going to *really* hurt, especially if it slips…!" *Christ, this is the second person tonight I've watched bite down on something to grit through pain…!*

At that, Jackie's eyes widened at the possibility, but she knew two things were true. One, this demanding attitude was something she was starting to like about him, and two, the trap very well could slip.

Jackie exhaled deeply and did as instructed. As she tied the fabric, Jackson positioned her right leg as carefully as he could between his legs, and then he removed his green flannel. He was sweaty and smelly, and yet she oddly enjoyed what she watched until Jackson grabbed the bear trap itself. A sharp pain from each metal tooth caused her to shriek through the mouth gag.

Jackson wove his flannel through the gaps in the teeth and placed one of his boots along the side of the trap. Jackie squelched again in pain and Jackson's heart sank, but he didn't let his face display it. Jackson clenched his teeth together to keep a determined face and mindset. Being a dick meant pain, but also meant progress, and progress was getting the hell out of this tunnel.

"Ready?" Jackson asked directly, and Jackie nodded quickly. "I'm going to pull my flannel up to open the upper jaw and push down with my boot on the lower jaw." Jackie nodded. "The *INSTANT* there's a gap, take the butt of the rifle, and shove it in! Got it?" Again, Jackie nodded, then reached over and grabbed the rifle as Jackson handed it to her. "One more thing."

"Mhat?" Jackie asked muffled.

"When we get your foot out, DO NOT SHOOT ME!" Jackson demanded. Jackson watched Jackie chuckle, and then she nodded. Some drool came out of the side of her mouth.

"Mo Pomises," Jackie said, and her eyes smiled. At that exact second of distraction, Jackson yanked as hard as he could on his flannel and pressed down with his right boot on the edge of the bear trap where two teeth were exposed. Jackie screamed painfully through her mouth gag as the pressure of the double dozen-toothed jaws released. Still screaming in pain, Jackie shoved the rifle into the mouth of the trap, and the butt hit the trap!

Jackson, still pulling, saw the fearful look on Jackie's face, and with that, Jackson pulled so hard that he roared in determination as he pushed down and pulled up harder to open the jaw wider. Jackson heard a tear of fabric as the butt of the rifle slid between the teeth, causing the metal teeth to scratch the wood finish of the rifle. Slowly, Jackson set down the trap.

Within a minute, after twisting the butt of the rifle to open the trap more, Jackie was free.

"I Weely Wand Ro Sroot Yu," Jackie exclaimed through her gag. "Bably!" Jackson chuckled, knowing what she meant, and a part of Jackson knew she wasn't kidding. Jackson adjusted himself, then knelt to cup his arms under Jackie and picked her up the way an adult would carry a sleeping child.

"Ileee—" Jackie untied the flannel sleeve, "I-I can walk!"

"Yeah," Jackson responded. "And you can talk, too. Congratulations." Jackson bent down, grabbed the flashlight with one quick hand, and felt Jackie's arms wrap around his neck for support. From under her back, Jackson proposed the flashlight to Jackie, and with one free hand, she took it and aimed it down the tunnel where he had appeared.

Jackson took one step forward, and Jackie coughed harshly in her throat, the way a person does when they're trying to get attention. Jackson stopped and looked at Jackie. Their faces were only a foot apart.

"Don't kiss me," Jackson stated. "My girlfriend upstairs won't approve."

"Umm…my rifle?" Jackie asked in a tone, 'Are you forgetting something?'.

"Consider it a trade," Jackson forced himself to say. "Your father's heirloom for your life. Which do you think your father would want you to have?" Without another word, Jackson carried Jackie down the tunnel to the cellar. Each one of Jackie's wounds throbbed in pain, and Jackie did her very best not to show it, but Jackson knew she needed medical attention as soon as possible. The entire bear trap was covered in chipped rust, and all but three teeth took a bite.

When Jackson passed the broken wooden barrier, it took Jackie everything she had not to ask what it was when they passed through the door, which Jackson had to open with a free hand.

Neither Jackson nor Jackie expected to see an old man, a middle-aged man, and a teenage boy standing on the other side. It was at this moment that both Jackie and Jackson wished they had Jackie's father's rifle.

"And who do we have here…?" one of the three males asked cockily.

EVERYWHERE

1

Kim Michael and Candy Murray were winning the war against the ghosts but were losing the battlefield. The fire was growing out of control and had already caught the ceiling. All that remained of the sofa was the frame and red-hot glowing coiled springs. The matching chair was also in the same condition, but the fabric was still visible in spots. All along the ceiling, black smoke rolled and stained the wood.

"We Have To Get Out Of Here, Kim!" Candy shouted, then coughed, as she pulled the blanket of covered mirrors toward the kitchen area, opposite side of the fire.

"We Can't Leave Yet!" Kim shouted back, then coughed. It was mind-boggling to Kim just how loud an indoor fire truly was. It had a roar of its own that she never knew existed. "Jackson Isn't Back Yet!"

"There Isn't Anything Going To Be Left For Him To Come Back To If We Don't Get The Fuck Out Of Here!" Candy shouted back, trying to make sense to Kim. Kim had a good point, and they had no way of telling Jackson what they were doing or going to do. As they wasted time debating, the smoke increased per second.

"We Don't Even Know If Jackson Had Found The Girl Or—"

"QUICK STALLING, KIM!" Candy exploded. "The Front Door Or The Kitchen Window; *Take Your Pick!*" Candy's ultimatum was concrete. "We're Leaving Now, Now, No Matter What Ghosts Are Left! They're Not Even Bothering Us Anymore! We Got The Big Bad!"

"And Alice's Mom!" Kim added matter-of-factly.

"We Don't Have Time For Semantics, Damnit!" Candy burst out coldly. "You And I Are Alive! I'd Like To Keep It That Way!" More smoke rolled and began to lower deeper, causing Kim and Candy to kneel on the floor.

"The Bedroom Window!" Kim shouted, making up her mind, but Candy's expression told her she didn't approve.

"There's A Kitchen Window Right Here Beside Us!" Candy exclaimed loudly. Kim began to cough heavily as she shook her head defiantly.

"Jackson Went Down The Cellar Door To Find The Girl, Right? If We Go Out The Front Door, He Won't Know We Left! He'll Come Back In Here And It'll Be An Inferno Worse Than This!" Kim yelled angrily and coughed heavily. "We Break The Bedroom Window And Go Out That Way; That Way He'll Know It Was Us!"

"That's The Stupidest Plan I Ha—" and that was when the cabin's roof caved in over the fire along the back wall. Two roof logs landed directly onto the sofa and chair bonfire as shingles and other woodland debris fell inside, and so did a muscularly thin, hairless guest. The moment the Gray hit the cabin floor, it snarled in pain and screeched at the intensity of the fire's heat.

"THE BEDROOM WINDOW!" Both Candy and Kim shouted in unison and fled the kitchen area without hesitation. Candy slipped on the blanket under her that harnessed the seven mirrors and heard one of the mirrors' glass crack. Candy paid no other interest as she scrambled to regain balance. Kim ran one step ahead of her, passed the front door, and slammed against the front bedroom door.

The male Gray snarled and roared at the meals-on-legs, but also cried out with hisses, snarls, and barks as its hairless skin burned due to being too close to the heat. The second male Gray crawled and scampered down the hole in the roof like a scorpion on the side of a rock.

Kim grabbed the door handle, pulled open the bedroom door, and was forcefully shoved in as Candy pushed Kim inside. Quickly, Candy turned around, grabbed the door, and slammed it shut as she made eye contact with both creatures. *Goddamn door opens from the outside!! Shit!!*

"Candy! Move!" Kim shouted frantically. Kim used all her might to shove the dresser along the floor to barricade the door. Candy looked up at the door and saw something she hadn't noticed before: a hook latch. As Candy locked the latch, Kim pushed the heavy dresser. Once the dresser hit Candy's hip, she moved back. Quickly, Candy helped pull the dresser so they could ram it against the bedroom door.

Both Kim and Candy looked around to find anything else to pile on top of the dresser, but it was Candy who had had enough of the entire situation. As Kim ran toward the bed, Candy ran to the bedroom window and opened the wooden inner shutters. Candy turned her head, saw Kim pushing the bed, and saw her answer. Just beside the bed was a small antique-looking hope chest.

Candy pushed away from the window, shoved Kim out of the way, grabbed the small chest, and felt something heavy inside shift to the left. The chest caused her to topple to the left and lose her balance. Kim saw what Candy was doing and grabbed the left handle with both hands.

"Something inside is loose and heavy!" Kim stated as Candy regained her balance.

"Good!" Candy shouted and took the chest away from Kim. "That'll help!" Candy stood fast and surprised Kim by running toward the window. When Candy launched the chest, she gave out a fearsome shout of strength, frustration, and pure rage that competed with the shattering of the glass as the chest crashed through the windowpane. When the chest hit the ground outside, Candy could hear the chest break apart, and whatever was inside that was loose and heavy rolled on the ground. It was so heavy that Candy heard it make thumps.

"Candy, move! Quick!" Kim yelled in caution from behind. Candy turned her head and saw Kim holding a drawer from the dresser. Kim used the drawer to knock away all the remaining window glass and splintered glass framing. Once the additional debris was cleared, Kim extended her hand as if to say, 'After you!', which Candy didn't hesitate.

Just as Candy's feet were propped on the window ledge, a thump hit the bedroom door.

"GO!" Kim roared and shoved Candy out the window. The fall was only six feet, this they both knew. A second thump, much harder than the first, hit the bedroom door, and from behind the wooden wall, a Gray screeched loudly and clawed at the wood.

"GET OUT HERE!" Candy shouted from outside the window, which Kim didn't bother to climb up. Kim looked outside, saw Candy, then turned her head to the floor door to the cellar that was still open.

Kim ran away from the window toward the door, bent down, and shouted, "JAY! HURRY! PLEASE! WE're OUTSIDE! THE CABIN IS ON FIRE!" Kim turned her back to the cellar floor door and looked around the floor.

An unwanted thought crossed her mind: *Jackson didn't hear me.* Another unwanted thought struck her: *Jackson isn't going to make it.*

The thought of Jackson's face when he came into the cabin with the rifle struck her. Kim remembered Jackson looked sad, ill, and deeply disturbed. Kim still didn't know what he saw or what he knew, but something was telling her that she had the same face right now, thinking Jackson wasn't returning. *Someone down there got him!* Kim instantly hated the thought, because it was a real possibility.

Just in case... Kim looked around and found the one thing that could either help Jackson or hurt him, given he would return up the cellar stairs. Kim bent down, found the bedroom oil lamp on the floor, and threw it as hard as she could at the bedroom door. Like the living room oil lamp, the glass base broke into two pieces. Oil spread on the door and the dresser, and then ran down the wall. *Let's hope that catches, too.* A third time, this time hard enough to slightly move the dresser, the Gray slammed against the door.

"GET YOUR FUCKING ASS OUT HERE!" Candy screamed so hard she squealed.

Like a professional diver on a diving board, Kim dove out of the bedroom window with her arms out in front of her and her head tucked down. Sadly, Kim didn't land directly on the high grass of the front yard. Kim landed directly on the broken hope chest and the solid object that was loose inside. Candy dropped to her knees beside Kim as Kim howled in pain, for on her back as she tucked and rolled, Kim landed directly onto a car battery on the small of her back.

2

With mouth clicks, long hisses, and irritated grunts, the two male Grays communicated with the female back in the woodland trees. All three knew the sensation of sunrise would soon be upon them, and they would have to retreat to their nest in the cavern close to the property of the cabin. For centuries, the creatures have not attacked the inhabitants of the cabin, or at least the ones they recognize by scent. The human inhabitants have had their peaceful truce of providing when times are dire, but with the wildlife abandoning the mountain over the last few decades, the truce was growing thinner.

Survival is any living thing's most raw instinct—not truces—and definitely not truces lasting decades to centuries. The Grays suffer from severe age and starvation. They've spent decades adjusting to the world's climate changes. They decided before they ran back to the cabin that the mountain used to be theirs, and after this, it would be again.

Like bullets out of a gun, the Grays launched themselves, tossing the truce to obscurity. The Pack grasped the earth under their three-clawed hands and feet as they ran back to the cabin, ready to overthrow all who inhabited it.

Their plan was for the males to break their way in through the weakest entry: the roof, as the female creature awaited the arrival of one to exit onto the high-grassed yard. Deep in the shadows of the remaining night, the female Gray would wait to attack, like a Venus flytrap would await prey.

The two males, as soon as they crossed the property of the tree line, leaped onto the cabin's walls and clawed their way to the roof, where the roof was much warmer than before. Their claws left grooves in the wood of the cabin and cracked the shingles on the roof. Within no time, the roof gave way unexpectedly and caused one Gray to fall in. The second male climbed into the cabin after it, freshly smelling the sweat and terror of the human inhabitants.

The female, on the other hand, ran from the tree line and, instead of running to the front yard as planned, rerouted to the backyard. The scent from before, and the sounds of voices underground, attracted her attention once again. It made her grow fiercer and more determined to find the way to them, or await their ejection, like a fox out of a hole.

Below her claws, the voices were deep, distant, and continuous, but next to impossible to locate. The smell of human blood was intoxicatingly strong but much weaker than the fleshy strip the males fought over. The scent was the same above ground compared to below ground, but it was coming from below ground, and then there was a way down there.

A muffled scream roared closely nearby, and the female Gray, slowly stalking the high grass, like a spider on the hunt, used all five of her natural senses to find the way down. It was simply a matter of time, which time was her only enemy.

3

"*'Who do we have here?'*" Jackie Shane repeated the man's words in a hillbillyish, mocking tone. "Yaw too dumb ter know!?" Jackson, who still cradled Jackie in his arms, squeezed his arms tightly together in a jerk to get her attention, as if to say, 'Don't! Don't do that!'.

"Watch your mouth, young lady," the middle-aged man in the middle of the three said casually. The light from the cellar was far behind them, making them appear as black silhouettes. Only the flashlight in Jackie's hand showed their faces. None of them held up a hand to block the beam. "I don't think you're in any position to be that cocky."

Jackson did a fast assessment of the situation, by all means not having the confidence his newly found female friend had. Then again, what could be labeled as confidence could very well be simply a natural attitude or a defiance of authority. Either way, Jackson knew they were currently outnumbered, and by the looks of the three shotguns, they were outgunned three to zero.

"I have no intention of 'watchin' my mouth', *fucker*," Jackie snarled.

"They're armed!" Jackson stated in a harsh, low tone to Jackie. "You might want to shut the fuck up this time!"

"Listen to the boy, little miss," the man in the middle said casually. "He's got sense."

"He's a fuckin' idiot who has no idea who you people are, what you people do, what you people have done, and has no idea just who in the fuck *I AM*, you piece of shit," Jackie barked through gritty teeth. The anger in her voice was clear as a symphony triangle's chime.

"And just who might you be?" the man on the right spoke. His voice was aged deeply, but his stature was just as erect as the other two.

"Jackson, put me down," Jackie strongly stated.

Jackson resisted the urge to. *I know she means every syllable of her demand, but just can't do—*

"NOW!" she barked. Jackie's voice echoed down the tunnel behind them.

"I'm not letting you go," Jackson said through a closed throat. The lump had returned. Jackie turned her head and faced Jackson eye-to-eye, and realized he was just as serious as she was. For the second time, Jackie was instantly attracted to his assertive side, but was still angry.

"Fine, then turn so I can face them," Jackie said with a heavy exhale, in which Jackson nodded once slowly. After a few degrees turned to the right, with Jackie's upper body cupped in Jackson's right arm, Jackie turned her gaze back to the three men and faced straight ahead.

"Well?" the youngest of the three said. Jackie simply knew this one either still had the title of 'teen' in their age, or just got rid of it. Nevertheless, there was strength and confidence in his voice, just like the middle-aged man and the much older man.

"Who am I…is a long story," Jackie bluntly said, monotone. "So, I'll cut the bullshit for you." Jackson felt Jackie slightly move her arms in her lap, but didn't pay any mind. "Twenty years ago, on my sixth birthday, my family traveled through here for our yearly vacation. Of all the places to go, my father chose Utah to see a park. Heavy rain detoured us, and he found the road that led to a stone path that housed dozens of campers." Jackie continued. The three men didn't interrupt, but they also didn't lower their shotguns.

"My mother and I went for a nature walk. Of all the paths to walk along, we found yours, which led up the mountain straight to your 'away-from-civilization' cabin. We saw your cabin and instantly retreated down the hill, thanks to my mother. She had the purest heart, and she intended to never oppose people or their property."

"Good instinc—"

"You Shut Your Goddamn Mouth About My Mother!" Jackie roared, interrupting the old man, and choked on the word 'Mother'. Jackson flinched when she barked and hung on each word. Sadly, a part of him knew where the story was going. He guessed that the three in front of them did, too.

Jackie continued, "It was only my mother and I who traveled up the hill. She loved nature, and my father loved people. My father stayed behind with my sister at the RV and mingled with the other RV owners, learning the whos and wheres of the area. I had a sister, just a little younger than me, who loved the Internet." Jackson repositioned his arms, grasping Jackie so she wouldn't slip.

"Just seeing your creepy-ass cabin scared the shit out of me. I knew there was something wrong with it. When we got back, I told my father about the creepy cabin. My sister overheard, and like the nerd she was, she researched it. All of us read what she found: over the ten counties of these mountains, there were over a dozen missing people. All of them were listed as missing; none had been found." Jackie ended that statement with strong authority.

"And?" the middle-aged man asked. "Your point?"

"I'm quite sure that the body count, as well as the number of counties, has expanded in twenty years, seeing as you're still here,"

Jackie said after being permitted to continue. "That afternoon, all the RVs left except two. It wasn't quite sundown, but to shed the worry, my father suggested all four of us go and see the cabin my mother and I saw, saying, 'Just because it's on the Internet doesn't make it real'. My sister got sick and fell asleep, so we left her behind, locked in the RV. We weren't going to be long." Jackson couldn't believe what he was hearing, but he didn't interrupt.

"My mother, my father, and I went up the hill on foot as the sun was going down. I'll never forget his face: he was strong, courageous, and had no worries about the scary Internet reports. That face didn't last long," Jackie choked again, but cleared her throat. Her eyes were straining in the tunnel, watching for their facial reactions to her words. So far, the three were unfazed.

"We passed by a broken tree before we reached the cabin. The trunk was as tall as my dad and was hollow. To make me feel better and not worry, my parents had me climb the broken tree and I fit inside the trunk. I called it 'my home tree' because it was big enough for me to claim as a getaway home," Jackie said, starting to tear up. "Then…you came, asking my parents if they were lost. I heard you while inside the tree stump. You asked if they needed help. You asked if they had a phone. My father whispered to me, 'Don't move, not a sound,' and from inside the tree, a six-year-old birthday girl stayed."

Jackson was losing strength as his arms started to tingle numb, but like a statue, Jackson held Jackie tight, as if he owed her the moment. For all he'd been through today, her story dwarfed his by a thousand.

"I heard something metal being thrown, and it snapped as it hit my father. My father screamed in pain, and I heard my mother scream in horror. I heard the slicing of my father's throat and his gurgles as he bled to death. Then I heard two men rape my mother in front of my dying father. They joked and taunted her about it while defiling her. I heard the slashing of her throat as she pleaded for her and my…fathers…life…," Jackie stopped, feeling her throat squeeze. Jackson swallowed the lump in his own throat. The silence of the tunnel was deafening to Jackson.

"Who Am I?" Jackie choked as she repeated the question, then growled the answer and shouted violently toward the end, "I'm The Girl In The Hollow Log Who Listened To You Kill My Family Twenty… YEARS… AGO… *TO… THE… FUCKING… DAY!*" When Jackie exhaled deeply and stopped talking, Jackson understood her persona and her stature as a person clearly.

From behind Jackson and Jackie came a familiar sound they both knew: a metal pin sliding back, a rifle shell falling to the stone floor and bouncing, and the metal pin sliding back.

"You're also a very loud trespassing bitch," a woman said in the darkness. In front of Jackie and Jackson, two of the three men chuckled cockily and cocked their shotguns.

4

Kim rolled around the ground as she whimpered in pain. The throbbing pain in her lower back from landing on the car battery sent shockwaves of sharp pain through her back, ribs, and spine. Candy was instantly at her side, but was forced to watch her friend struggle.

Flames were emanating from the back of the cabin's roof, but the thin spacing between the roof and the front of the cabin's structure was a solid yellow line of growing fire. The inner roof had already raised the temperature to over a thousand degrees, which would typically start to melt fiberglass insulation. The cabin was insulated, but not up to the standard code.

Candy looked up and saw that the outer rooftop on the south side had escaping smoke vents in the shingles, which meant the roof was going to cave in sooner rather than later. If the roof were to cave in, the Grays would have an easier way out.

"Kim, forgive me!" Candy squealed in a panic and ran toward Kim's head. As Kim withered in pain on the ground with an arm behind her back, Candy reached down, grabbed the crook of both of Kim's elbows, and began to pull Kim down the yard.

Instantly, Kim began to cry and scream in pain as Candy's pulling stretched Kim's back out, but Candy didn't stop pulling, even when her feet stepped into the very edge of the water puddle in the front yard. Kim, feeling every painful strain in her lower back, felt the cold water of the puddle soak her entire back and right leg.

The cold water, the burning cabin, Kim's scream, and knowing the fact that the monsters could appear at any time didn't stop Candy from pulling Kim as fast and far as she could. When they hit the edge of the pool, Candy didn't stop. When they crossed the yard, seeing the cabin in full view, Candy didn't stop. When Candy slipped on the high grass due to her wet boots and her right arm triggered a ready bear trap, Candy stopped instantly.

The metallic snap on Candy's arm was horrific on its own, but the snapping crack of her Radius bone and wrist was gut-wrenching. Candy dropped to the high grass and wailed in tremendous pain, feeling the various metal teeth puncture her skin. The second the jaws snapped on her wrist, her right hand instantly disfigured into a hellacious gnarl. The sensation of several sharp metal teeth pushing their way through her flesh caused Candy to cry, scream, wail, and roar in pain and frustration. It was as if the universe did not want anyone to leave the hell of the cabin or its property.

Kim tried calling out Candy's name as she rolled onto her belly after being flopped down to the ground when Candy slipped, but Candy's ears were mute to anything but her screams. The more Candy writhed on the ground, the tighter the trap clamped down on her arm. Blood was running down her arm and sticking to the grass as a steady stream was escaping from her wrist.

Kim, still trying to call out Candy's name, army-crawled to Candy and saw the metallic attachment on her arm. Each metal tooth was buried in Candy's flesh so deep, the jaw was practically shut. Since shouting for Candy so Kim could help her was useless, Kim began to shout for the only other person she could think of.

"Alice! ALICE! HELP HER, *PLEASE!*" Kim pleaded, not seeing the ghost girl anywhere. Kim had reached Candy and grabbed hold of her left arm, using Candy's body as leverage to pull herself up. The pain in Kim's back ached with muscle spasms, but Kim was not about to compare her back pain to a large bear trap attached to someone's arm. "ALICE, GOD DAMN YOU! WHE—"

Kim's eyes fluttered rapidly for a mini-second.

Kim's pain was gone, and her erratic screaming for help ceased. Kim stared at Candy in bedazzlement, feeling completely numb. Candy's arm pain was also gone, and Candy's torturous sensations of pain were non-existent. Candy felt lightheaded and disoriented. Both women, both in agonizing pain, looked at one another silently as if muted, and neither one was in any kind of pain. If anything, they were…cold.

Ice cold.

And standing between them stood Alice, looking down at them both, smiling pleasantly as if they were enjoying a sunny day at a beach together.

"They'll help you," Alice said calmly and politely.

Without any control of their own, Kim watched her down body sit up straight and reach out with both hands to grab the bear trap attached to Candy's arm. Candy, also under a control not her own, turned to Kim face-to-face and raised her snared arm as if the bear trap was weightless. Candy reached up with her left arm and grabbed the nearly closed jaw, squeezing her fingers through to grab the one end. Candy watched Kim's hands grab the opposite jaw with a powerful grip.

Without any sense of touch or smell, Kim and Candy pulled the bear trap open, and Candy pulled her arm out slowly. Blood pulsated out of each toothless wound, but both women placed the bear trap onto the ground and reset the trap without a single strain of thought or effort. Kim's head was swimming roundly, and Candy's thoughts were null.

Candy's body turned to look at the bear trap, supporting her weight with both arms, feeling no pain of any kind. Not only did Candy not feel pain, but even sitting on the high grass, Candy didn't feel the earth under her body. Candy reached over, saw an inch-thick stick, and stabbed the bear trap in the center dial. The metallic trap clanged loudly and fell over on its side.

When the two spirits who entered Kim and Candy began to eject themselves from their hosts, the sensations of the night's air ruffled the hair on their arms. The swelling pain in Kim returned, and the piercing pains of the metal teeth returned as well. Both of their swimming heads and numbness faded away rather quickly. Candy immediately clutched her arm and huddled it like a football wide receiver would after a catch. Kim arched her back, acknowledging the pain.

Kim saw both spirits leave their bodies and stand beside Alice. They spoke to Alice, but their voices were mute, and the conversation was short. One was a teenage boy, and the other was a middle-aged woman. Then, they faded out of view, and Alice turned to look at Kim.

"They're free," the ghost girl said. "You didn't trap everyone."

"I-I wanna…go…home, Kim," Candy demanded shakily. "N-Now. I-I'm…I'm done…!"

"Don't we all," Alice said and turned her head slowly to the burning cabin. "Don't we all." Candy quickly looked apologetically at Alice and then looked at Kim.

"Jackson…," Kim whispered. "…please hurry!"

Even across the yard, Alice, Kim, and Candy heard two angry roars from the Grays trapped in the burning cabin and the beating of the door against the bedroom dresser. Then they heard the worst possible sound; it was loud, but muffled. It came from underground.

It was gunfire.

5

"That's my rifle," Jackie said slowly and as-a-matter-of-factly.

"Is it?" the unexpected woman from behind Jackie and Jackson responded. "Sounds to me it was your daddy's, and somehow, you gained possession of it."

"You asked who she was. She answered," Jackson said methodically. "She obviously knows more about you all than you expected." Jackson slightly turned his head to the left to speak into the darkness where a woman was with Jackie's rifle. "And it sounds like a justified revenge."

"Ju-Justified?!" the woman stuttered in disbelief. "You and your whores with your meaty friend trespass on our property, take over our home, defile our beds, and disrupt the unholy deviants of the dead that we've kept entrapped for decades, and you say this worthless accuser of lies and deceit gets to receive a justified revenge?!"

221

"You calling me a liar?" Jackie asked, looking at the men, but asking the woman.

"What should we do with them, Dad?" the youngest male asked. "One of us should be with the gi—"

"Shut Your Mouth, Son!" the father barked, cutting him off.

"End this, boy," the oldest spoke calmly. "There be other matters at hand."

6

Not far above them, the female Gray finally found just what she had been looking for…and without any further hesitation…

7

"See, the way I see it," the woman in the darkness said, "you two have no grounds for revenge and have no reason to leave this place. It's punishment for intrusion and a violation of sanctity, which gives our family the right to a justified revenge."

"Then explain Thomas," Jackson jabbed. "He was unconscious and placed under the cot down here just by the cellar door. He was no threat to you, and none of us knew any of you filthy, immoral cannibalistic motherfuckers were even down here!" It was Jackson's turn to get a word in. His arms were locked and completely numb, and yet never moved or shifted while holding Jackie.

"Survival, boy," the oldest man spoke. "What is a loss to one is a gain to another."

222

"Leftover room service, huh?" Jackson coldly stated. "Just leaving the dinner by the door, knocking, and walking away…! 'We'll bill you when you check out'!" Jackson mocked.

"You weren't leaving with him, you know that. He was beyond help," the dad of the youngest male said. "We did what—"

"YOU BUTCHERED HIM!" Jackson exploded, screaming in Jackie's ear. It was Jackson's turn to squeal his voice. "YOU SLICED HIS THROAT IN THE HALL AS WE CHASED YOU DOWN…AND …AND you…you sick bastards sliced his skin off…and hung it outside …to lure…the Grays away…!" Jackson sobbed uncontrollably and slowly lost all feeling in his legs. Jackson collapsed to the tunnel floor and let Jackie fall directly onto him. His arms spasmed and locked around Jackie. "I…saw…it…and—" Jackson's voice had nearly broken. "I…heard one…of you…in the tree line."

One of the three shotguns pointed at them cocked loudly.

"I've done worse, boy," the middle-aged man said. "Your friend saved my family, because you fucked up, and I'd do it again." Another shotgun cocked. The flashlight was no longer shown on the faces of the three men. It was in Jackie's hands and pointed at Jackson's face. Jackie looked at Jackson with a look of 'I'm here with you, and I'm sorry'.

"Aim low, boy," the old man said to the youngest male standing, and the third shotgun cocked. All three weapons were aimed at Jackson and Jackie from just ten feet away.

The wife of the middle-aged man behind them never said another word underground in the tunnels under the cabin, either. Just before the father of the family was going to say, "Now," the wife screamed a one-hundredth of her full scream as she saw the Gray emerge from behind her, and it crushed her skull with one bite in its jaws.

The wife's head popped inside the female Gray's mouth like a stale grape, caking the inside of its mouth with delicious, fresh soup.

8

Jackie instantly directed the flashlight toward the woman who had her rifle, and Jackie's eyes widened as the monstrosity, just mere feet from her, swished the corpse in its mouth side-to-side like a dog with a stuffed animal.

One of the three men shouted her name, but the shotgun blast drowned out all the sound in the tunnel. The blasts were deafening, and every sound after the first shotgun shot had a whomp-whomp muffled in Jackson's ears. The three men each shot one shot from their weapons at the creature, causing the Gray to back into the tunnel it emerged from, taking the body of the woman with it. Jackson couldn't help it: it looked like the spider from 'Lord Of The Rings' when Samwise taunted it with the elves' jewel.

Jackie and Jackson both ducked into the darkness as each one of the three fired another shotgun blast, then just as one attempted to take a step forward, Jackie did something that Jackson had forgotten about.

From under her shirt, Jackie presented her 357 and began firing at the three men, shooting at the group's legs. Not knowing who she shot or who was grazed, Jackie fired from ground level, flinching at the flash of the muzzle, and also hearing the whomp-whomp sound. There was a trickle of fluid seeping from her ears, and it traveled down her cheek.

Jackson let Jackie empty the weapon and found ground at the first click. All three of the males with the shotguns were on the ground, screaming in pain that they'd been shot. Groans and cries were mixed with angry shouts and threats. When Jackson heard the tinkling sounds of the shotguns hitting the ground, Jackson scooped up Jackie to her feet and retreated down the tunnel, opposite the creature.

No! No! No! I Don't—YOU DON'T HAVE A CHOICE, JACKSON! GO LEFT!

Once again, carrying Jackie, Jackson ran blindly down the tunnel to the left. The second barrier door was wide open, and Jackson's eyes were adjusted to the dark, minus a few flashing colors from the muzzle blasts. A few times, Jackie's shoulder hit the sidewall, or Jackson's left arm would graze the stone, but when the moment of truth came, Jackson ran differently.

His runs became stomps.

When the split came to turn left, Jackson stomped his run as hard as he could and felt the puddle under his boots. His stomach wrenched, and his heart sank, but Jackson did not slip on Thomas's blood puddle. It was only two steps in the puddle, but it was two steps too many.

A few feet further, the ground was solid dusty dirt again and the door in the next barrier was also open, and there was light up ahead. Jackson forgot the underground had power because the cellar had a bulb.

The family's area... went through Jackson's mind. If Jackie was saying anything to him, he couldn't hear it. He barely heard his own footsteps hitting the ground. His hearing was next to gone. If another Gray showed up, he wouldn't have heard it. Another left turn in the tunnels, then a small winding right, and lastly, a turn…into an underground living room den, complete with the dim lighting fixture, bookshelves with books, a sofa, a chair, and a dining room table from the early nineteen-seventies.

Jackson stopped running, unable to see a tunnel doorway to continue down. Jackson slowly released his hold on Jackie, who balanced herself quickly on one foot.

9

With the growing heat, spreading fire, and smothering smoke, breaking the door down was more than just following their meal. The interior of the cabin was becoming too congested to be in. Climbing out of the cabin the way the one climbed in was an easy option, but the two humans didn't climb out of the top. They went through the wooden structure and closed a gate.

The wooden gate, or the bedroom door, was loose, and it gave way with each push attempt. One male Gray pushed several times and grew impatient at its lack of success. With a snarl and a clapped bark, the frustrated male Gray called the second to where both shoved on the wall and the wooden gate. The wall didn't give way, but the door did, especially when both shoved with their shoulders.

When the second the door pushed open a foot, a small whoosh of air sucked in some of the scattered flames. Just under the door, a trail of lamp oil had traveled, and a flick of scattered flame ignited the oil, sending half of the bedroom and the door aflame. Both male Grays roared angrily at the direct heat, almost ready to retreat out the cabin's rooftop when…

—BANG!— —BANG!—

…erupted from the black hole in the floor just a few yards ahead of them. There was shouting, screaming, and more loud bangs, but it was the satisfied grunt of the female Gray and the newly fresh smell of searing blood that caused the two males to dash down the cellar stairs.

The first male Gray lost its balance and toppled down the wooden staircase, smacking its head on the bedroom floor. The Gray thudded down the stairs as the second male creature climbed down on all fours and over the other. With a secondary gate already open, the smell of hot flesh, spilled blood, and screaming humans sent all of their senses into overdrive.

Having two arms and two legs, with claws for hands and three talons on each claw, they moved more like spiders in tight areas. And just a few steps forward, on the floor in a cool stone tunnel, there lay their prize: three humans bleeding and in agony.

"DAD! WH—" was all the smallest human could say when the first Gray entered the tunnel. The little human's size was perfect to carry back to the nest: small, light, and stout. The first Gray opened his right front claw and grabbed the smallest human by the head. When the muscular claw gripped its head, there were two cracking sounds that the father and grandfather both heard. It was either the pressure of the monster's grip that caused the skull to crack like an eggshell under a flat palm hand, or it was the teenage boy's neck snapping as the Gray picked the human up.

The two other humans were screaming and scrambling on the floor, reaching for long metal sticks as blood smeared all over the ground. The second Gray pushed itself into the tunnel, shoving the first Gray out of the way. The shove was hard enough that the other Gray shoved back, causing the Gray to fall directly onto one of the humans. The oldest human pushed his arms up to keep the Gray from falling on him, but the weight of the creature was unbelievable. The second the grandfather of the human family raised his arms in instinct, all of the weight of the Gray snapped both of his radius and ulna arm bones, causing his forearms to snap backward.

The old human screamed in agony for just a second, for the weight of the Grays' torso landing on the human's chest caused the human's rib cage to snap and crackle, then cave in. The expulsion of voice, air, and life from the old human was sickening, even to the Gray, but the monstrosity was more concerned about getting to its own feet than caring about the life of its meal. The second Gray used three of its claws to regain balance and used its left upper claw to grasp the corpse. The body was good size, but it was light.

In between the Grays wriggled and crawled the third human. The two male Grays hissed and nicked at one another about which was going back to the nest with two meals. The last of the three humans crawled away from them without using their legs, which they had never seen a live human do, and stared at it. The human crawled on his belly and reached for one of the metal sticks.

When the human pointed the metal stick at the first Gray, the monster that killed his son without thought or sorrow, both creatures heard a very familiar sound: the sound of a shotgun cocking. They didn't know what the metal sticks were, but they knew what came out hurt.

The Gray with the grandfather grabbed one leg of the final human, as the other Gray grabbed the human's opposite leg. With confusion at hand, there was a misunderstanding between the two monsters. They both knew they needed to take their meals to the nest, only one Gray went toward the tunnel, and the other retreated to the cellar stairs.

As flimsy as a piece of paper, the two Grays pulled the last human's legs in opposite directions, ripping the human in two halves, groin-to-torso. An excessive amount of blood, organs, and bile spilled all over the floor of the tunnel. All thought and rationality between the Grays were immediately gone, for the reminder of starvation kicked in.

Without any thought to the female Gray, the two male Grays had a human buffet that they wouldn't have again for quite some time. Like an infant with its first birthday cake, the two male Grays licked, ate, chewed, and immersed themselves in their meal without thought. Neither one ran off to find their female counterpart.

10

Jackson and Jackie both stood in the middle of the underground living arrangement. Neither knew where to go next; it was a dead end.

"I'm not going back that way," Jackson said, more to himself than to Jackie.

"You're not leaving me here!" Jackie threw at him, and Jackson nodded quickly.

"Absolutely not," Jackson reiterated. "I…I just don't—"

"AAAAAAHHHHH!!!" a tiny voice shouted out from their right. In the dimly lit spacious living room, somehow, from behind the sofa, charged a four-foot-tall female child, running at Jackie with two kitchen carving knives, one in each hand.

The little blonde-haired girl ran at them with a facial expression of pure malice and intent to kill them both. Jackie, unable to stand on both legs, immediately hopped backward behind Jackson, grabbing his arms for support. The nine or ten-year-old girl was fast and if it wasn't for the scream, neither of them would have seen her.

"JAY!" Jackie shouted as if she had just seen the world's largest rat, and Jackson did exactly what a person who saw the world's largest rat would do: Jackson extended his right leg out and kicked the child square in the face. He felt the softness of the child's face connected with the bottom of his boot, which caused the child to whip both her arms backward and topple on her back. The sickening thud of her skull striking the hard floor was hollow and wrenching. The child didn't move as both knives tinkled and pinged as they hit the ground.

"Oh shit…!" Jackson exclaimed, not believing what he had just done. Jackson began to kneel to check on the child.

"Just What The Fuck Are You Doing!?" Jackie said, standing on one leg, feeling the pressure points pulse in her leg wounds.

"It's A Fucking Kid, Jackie!" Jackson barked. "I don't want—I didn't want to kill her!"

"You didn't kill her. You just knocked her crazy ass out!" Jackie shouted. "She came at us! With Knives!"

"Because she loves it here," another child's voice said from behind Jackie. This voice was calm, mellow, and sad. Jackie turned around and saw the same girl enter the room from the tunnel that Jackie and Jackson had come from.

"Jesus Fucking Mary…," Jackie choked, not finishing the rest. Jackson rose to his feet and stood in front of Jackie.

"Look, s-she—oh, fuck, t-that's your sister…!" Jackson tried to speak, overlapping his thoughts with his words. "Y-You're twins…! Please say you're twins; I have had enough of ghosts for one lifetime!"

"What!?" Jackie burst out, turning her head at Jackson.

"That's my little sister; I'm her older sister. We're twins, but we're very different," the girl said, still walking toward Jackson and Jackie slowly and steadily. "She loves it here. This is her home, and she never wants to leave."

"Let me help her, ok—"

"No," the girl said. "Leave her be. I'll get her." The twin walked just six feet away from Jackson and Jackie, then turned. The girl heard a deep exhale from the pretty girl with the bloody leg. The twin knelt to her sister, pressed two fingers to her neck, and leaned her ear down to her sister's mouth. "She's alive, and she's breathing." The talking twin slid one arm under her sister's neck and one arm under her legs. With some struggling, the older sister picked up her sister and carried her to the sofa.

Jackson and Jackie stood frozen and watched, not knowing what to do, what to say, or where to run. The older twin repositioned her sister's posture and cradled her neck and head with a pillow. When the sister pulled her hand away, there was blood on her hand that was under her sister's head.

"She needs help!" Jackson said, seeing the blood.

"No, she doesn't," the twin said, still calm and still in tone. "She'll be okay."

"I don—" Jackie started to say when the twin girl pointed at something behind them.

"That way," she said. "That's the North Tunnel. Pull the shelf out. It's a hidden door. It's our escape route to the creek. You need to leave, now."

"What about—" Jackson began to ask.

"YOU NEED TO LEAVE! *NOW!*" the twin girl shouted angrily, still pointing at the way out. "*LEAVE!*"

On command, Jackson ran to the shelf, leaving Jackie temporarily. He pulled on the unit, and as the girl said, the shelf unit pulled out of the wall, exposing a dark stone tunnel. Jackie hobbled over toward Jackson, not wanting to be around either twin. It was at that exact moment that Jackie realized she never wanted kids. Ever. The thought of twins forever creeped her out.

"Let's go," Jackson said, running over to Jackie and once again, picking her up. Jackson turned to the girls. "I-I'm sorry if I hurt your sister. I didn't—"

"Leave," the girl said coldly. "I'll lock it behind you. Get out and don't come back." Without another moment of hesitation, Jackson carried Jackie out of the family's underground living room and dashed down the tunnel. Jackie turned her head and watched the twin walk toward the shelving door. She pushed it to close. Neither Jackie nor Jackson had a flashlight.

11

The twin sister stood at the shelving unit after locking it just for a moment. She hung her head low and heard the patter of boots running away.

"If I can't leave, at least I let someone else leave," the girl solemnly said. The twin turned around and looked at her underground living arrangement that her great-grandfather carved out and deeply exhaled. It was dark, dim, cool, and void of ever having happiness. It was a prison to her, and it was no way to live.

The girl walked to her sister and sat down softly beside her. A small tear trickled down her cheek, and she placed a hand on her sister's chest. Her other hand held her sister's still hand.

"I had to lie to the two people escaping with their lives, or else they wouldn't have left," the girl said to her motionless sister. The chest of her sister didn't rise once, and blood was soaking into the pillow and down the side.

"You love it here, and now, you're here forever," the twin said, sniffed sadly, and kissed her sister's left cheek. The older sister lowered her head and began to sob, but with the second sob came another sound. It was a sound neither twin made. It was a tapping of claws on stone and the hiss of a monster.

The twin sitting on the sofa looked up at a hairless, muscular, four-limbed monster with lopsided breasts. Its hands were like eagle's

232

talons, and dangling from its mouth was her mother, still in her clothes from when she left her and her sister's side fifteen minutes ago.

"I hate it here—" the older twin whimpered…and said no more.

12

"Wait here," Alice suddenly said, then disappeared from the women's view.

"W-Wait Here?!" Candy burst out. "Where The Fuck Does She Think We're Going To Go?!" Candy huffed in disbelief. "Acapulco?!"

"Quiet!" Kim hushed, not wanting to attract any attention. "I don't know! Don't fucking move, okay?!" Kim looked around their bodies. The ground was dry, but felt cold against their legs. "I don't know how many more traps there are, and I don't want to find out!"

"Kim…?" Candy asked, sounding too scared to finish the question, but she knew she had to. "W-What if Jack—"

"SHUT UP!" Kim erupted, choking on the words. "You shut your goddamn—"

"Go…that way," Alice interrupted, causing Candy to almost jump out of her skin. As if someone turned on a switch, Alice appeared in view of them both. Alice was pointing down the yard, almost exactly where they had arrived. "You're safe there."

From ahead of them, a large crack sounded from inside the cabin. Candy and Kim watched the roof of the cabin fall into the structure, wafting a large billow of smoke into the night sky. A burst of flame emerged around where the cave occurred.

"Jackson…Get Your Fucking Ass Out Here!" Kim growled through grinding teeth and tearful eyes. Candy hobbled to her feet, cupped her wounded arm to her chest, grabbed Kim by one arm with her good arm, and again, dragged Kim across the high grass. Immediately, Kim began kicking and clawing the ground. "No! NO! We Have To Stay! We Hav—" and for the first time since they arrived, it wasn't Candy who was smacked.

Kim's eyes grew wide as Candy stood over her friend.

"We…Are…LEAVING!" Candy said forcefully, reached back down, grabbed Kim by the arm, and dragged Kim in the direction Alice pointed. Kim turned her head back to the cabin, watching more rubble and parts of the wall burn and collapse. Candy listened to her friend whisper Jackson's name and sobbed, but Kim didn't fight the retreat.

Just as both women felt the slope of the hill they trekked up when the sun was shining, a voice spoke up behind them, "Let's Get The Fuck Out Of Here." It was Jackson's voice.

13

Without hesitation, thought, or even instinct, Kim whipped her arms free of Candy's grasp, which Candy let go in disbelief, and frantically crawled along the ground directly to Jackson. At his feet was another woman with a curled bloody leg, and she was sitting on the ground of the mountain's slope. With happy and terrified tears and an insane amount of lost hope, Kim clawed the ground, crawling to Jackson, and just as she reached him, Jackson bent down, grabbed her in his arms, and both happily sobbed at their reunion.

Kim squeezed Jackson so tightly that Jackson had a moment where he couldn't breathe, but Jackson didn't fight it or counter it. Once Kim let go, Jackson kissed Kim with the hardest and most passionate kiss he had ever given her. It was a bit awkward as the front of their teeth

234

touched, but neither cared. Both thought the same thing: that they'd never see one another again.

With the rush of emotion spearing through Kim, now that she had Jackson back and he was safe, guilt and sorrow flooded Kim's heart, realizing that Candy would never have this with Thomas ever again. Kim turned around, looked up at Candy, and both read one each other's eyes. Not a word needed to be spoken; Candy knew what Kim knew.

From behind Kim, the girl with the bloody leg said in surprise, "…Damn!" Both the girl and Candy watched Jackson release Kim.

"Where The Fuck Can I Get A Kiss Like That?!" the girl on the ground snarked sarcastically.

"Candy? Kim? Meet Jackie. Jackie Shane," Jackson said with a chuckle and turned in her direction. Jackson looked at Kim and underlined, "And no, I haven't kissed her."

"I almost kissed him!" Jackie stated. "But then he left my rifle behind, and that pissed me off."

Jackson chuckled and asked, "I'm never going to be forgiven for that, am I?"

"Not until you go back in there and get it!" Jackie snarked, then chuckled. Jackson grabbed Candy's hand and pulled her along with him down the hill. Then, Jackson bent down beside Kim and went to help her stand, which Kim winced at her back.

"Why don't you walk your happy ass back up there and go get it?" Jackson asked Jackie sarcastically, then turned his attention to Kim. Kim was arching and rubbing her back with a wince. "You okay?" Jackson asked.

"I-I hurt my back jumping out of the cabin window," Kim answered.

"*DIVING* out of the cabin window," Candy corrected Kim. "Right onto a car battery…now can we *get the fuck outta here?!*" Her voice was cracked, irritated, and impatient.

"A…a car battery?!" Jackson asked in surprise.

"I stepped in a bear trap, fell down a collapsed hole, and survived a shoot-out," Jackie injected. "In case we're keeping score."

"I've been possessed by ghosts, slapped by my friends, had my ear half bitten off, pulled along by my hair by ghosts, got my arm caught in a bear trap, and my boyfriend was killed," Candy reported to Jackie without tone or emotion. "And I'd Like To Leave!"

Jackie put up her hands in defeat. "You win," Jackie said to Candy, then looked at Jackson. "You must have a fetish for injured girls…Jay." Jackson scoffed and shook his head.

Wait… 'Jay?!' Kim jealously thought, then quickly dismissed it.

"Nope," Jackson said back. "Just the strong-headed ones." At that, Jackson picked up Kim, kissed her again, and stared at her. "Let's go home." Kim smiled and nodded. Candy walked past Jackson and Kim to approach Jackie. Candy knelt, and Jackie saw Candy's mauled arm from the bear trap bite.

"How did you get it off?!" Jackie asked, seriously curious.

"I don't want to talk about it," Candy said. "I've had enough of ghosts for one day." Jackie started to laugh, for that was the second time she'd heard it today. Candy helped Jackie up on her one good leg using her good arm, and both Candy and Jackie led the way down the hill as Jackson carried Kim behind them.

"Oh Fuck!" Jackie burst out. "I almost forgot!"

"Forgot what?" Candy asked, stopping their downward trek. Jackie rummaged her hand into her jeans pocket, pulled out a small black device, and aimed it upward.

From the top of the hill where the cabin slowly burnt to the ground, a thunderous explosion erupted, shaking the ground under their feet. The explosive burst echoed massively through the forest trees and down the valley. The four were showered with dirt and debris from behind for a few seconds but quickly subsided.

"Okay," Jackie said cockily. "Now, we can go."

A thought hit Kim and said worried, "Wait…Alice!"

"No—" Jackson abruptly said. "Don't. Don't look back. Don't you dare look back!"

"But—"

"But NO!" Jackson barked, cutting Kim off. "Alice says, we do. Nothing more." Kim squeezed her lips together to refrain from asking anymore. Deep down, she knew Jackson was right and Jackson knew something about Alice that Kim didn't. Kim didn't pry.

14

When Jackson Chad hobbled along down the hallway with Jackie Shane, both continuously bumped into the stone walls, trying to find their way out. Jackson kept wondering to himself why the twin girl called this 'The North Tunnel' because naming a tunnel meant it had either directional significance or another meaning. Nonetheless, he didn't have a choice but to take the girl at her word.

The three men: one was her dad, and another her brother or cousin. The last was too old to guess; they were as good as gone. Jackie took care of that with her gun. And there was one of those creatures in the tunnel. It was going to have a heyday. I wonder where the other two—No, no, I don't. I don't want to know.

"I-I hear water!" Jackie said, then right after it, "I see light up ahead!" While Jackson was in his own mind having a teeter-totter conversation with himself, he wasn't focused on what was around him. His feet and his body were taking over while his thoughts were busy.

When Jackie and Jackson turned the next corner, the room in front of them was brighter than the living room was, and it was the worst place in all of the mountain to have that amount of bright light. Jackie gasped and instinctively turned her face into Jackson's shoulder. Jackson couldn't divert his eyes, even though every cell in his body wanted to.

On a thick wooden table rested the corpse of Thomas Everlast. His body was flat, his chest was down, he was stripped nude, and his head was turned to where his face stared back at them with open eyes. Thomas's mouth was open, and his tongue sat out like a swollen snail. From the bottom of Thomas's neck, the skin across his broad shoulders, all along and down his sides, and to the top of his buttocks was cut and removed. Thomas's back muscles, spine, and shoulder blades were all exposed to the tunnel's air.

One word escaped from Jackson's throat in a choked whisper, "Thomas…"

Jackie muffled in his shoulder with her head still turned, "You know him?" Jackson looked down the tunnel in the room with Thomas in it and knew he was going to be forced to walk into that room.

"That's our way out," Jackson said in a whisper to Jackie, and to himself. Jackson turned his body, grabbed Jackie, and picked her up. "Don't look until I say." Jackson felt Jackie nod. From the next step, the tunnel, Jackie, the room, the table, and Thomas's body all instantly disappeared.

Deep in Jackson's mind is where his subconscious escaped. It was flooded with memories of Thomas that Jackson had once forgotten.

The day Jackson held onto Thomas's hair as Thomas puked in the girls' bathroom toilet at the college during their freshman year. The time Jackson and Thomas had grocery cart races on the college cross-country track. The day Thomas met Candy—

"Jackson!" Jackie shouted, and it jacked Jackson out of his memories of Thomas. Jackson looked around suddenly, and in front of him was a metal ladder and the end of the tunnel. "Jesus, I thought you were going to run me right into it!" Jackson shook his head.

Thank you! Thank You! THANK YOU! Jackson kept repeating. Being mentally lost gave him the strength to block out the horrors of his friend and subconsciously still get to where they needed to be.

"This must be it," Jackson said, looking up at the ladder. "You're first." Without hesitation, Jackie grabbed the metal ladder made of welded rebar and used one leg to climb. Only eight feet up was the circular door, which easily gave way with little hesitation. Jackie ejected from the tunnel and scooted her body out as Jackson began to climb.

It took Jackson everything not to turn around. Forcefully, Jackson pulled up and was out of the underground tunnels in seconds. What Jackson heard before his head emerged was a burst of shock from Jackie, "You Have GOT To Be Kidding Me!"

Jackson poked his head out of the circular door and found himself emerging from a tree stump. All around the tree stump were a few gym bags, some white boxes, and two other commodities.

"You mean to tell me I hunkered here with all my gear to destroy this goddamn place to get my revenge and all I had to do was climb down a stump!?" Jackie exclaimed. Jackson continued to climb out of the tunnel and closed the fake top of the real tree trunk. Jackson turned around and looked at the burning cabin, which looked to be half a football field away.

"You mean to tell me you shot them bastard for us…from here?!" Jackson asked in shock and surprise.

"I could have, but no, I was at the…holy-fuck-me-sideway! It's YOU!" Jackie exclaimed in realization. "Now that I see you out here…and…Jimmy Fucking Christmas Shit! YOU!!"

"Me What!?" Jackson asked, confused.

"You were the guy at the creek! The river path!" Jackie said. "I watched you through my scope!" Jackson stared at her in disbelief and grew cautious. Before Jackson could respond, someone did it for him.

"So did I," a gentle voice said. Jackson recognized it instantly. Jackson and Jackie both turned around, which caused Jackie to instantly hit the forest floor and pull out her gun. Jackie had had enough of kids, and that was a child's voice. Jackson saw Alice when he turned around, but what he saw next, he never would have expected…ever.

Holding Alice's hand…was Thomas.

No words were spoken, nor needed. Thomas and Jackson saw one another, and Thomas was smiling. Alice looked up at Thomas, and she was smiling too. Jackie's hand shook as she aimed the gun at the two visual ghosts, but she didn't have the muscle control to pull the trigger. Jackson stared at his friend and stared at Alice. Jackson's heart was instantly full of joy, sadness, relief, heartbreak, and an overwhelming satisfaction that no matter what happened, Thomas was okay.

Then, Thomas faded away gracefully, but Alice remained.

"You must leave now," Alice said calmly.

"No Fucking Shit!" Jackie burst out, still shaking her gun in terror. Alice continued.

"Follow the river creek. They're waiting for you," Alice instructed. "And when you find them, don't look back." Jackson nodded. "Don't look back." At that, Alice turned her head and looked at Jackie.

"It's nice seeing you again, Jackie," Alice said with a smirk. "You've gotten bigger since you were in the broken tree," and quietly wisped away. Alone, in the woods, for the first time since they arrived, Jackson heard a cricket.

Jackson looked down at Jackie and asked like a smart-ass, "Well…you coming?"

When I started writing *Wayward*, it was **June 30th, 2022.** It's now **July 8th, 2022.** I've been writing for nine straight days. *Wayward* is over; *Rancor* is next, but you need to know some <u>very important things</u>.

At the start of the Prologue, I said that I had found my sister, Jackie, three weeks prior. To be more specific, it was the exact morning of the [Chapter 1 of Warning] section.

Using the frilly wedding invitation, I found her home, ironically in Utah, in early May. Jackie had left her fiancé in January; house, kids, relationship, job, car, and all…and believe me: those were some fucking ugly toddlers! No goddamn way those were hers!

I pretended to be a door-to-door church donation service, looking to collect. He spilled his guts about Jackie, and I learned so much about my sister since I last saw her, when I held the pocket knife to her throat. I regret that so much! My mind was not—never mind. Moving on…

I tracked her down using GPS tricks I learned online. I used her financial transactions from two debit cards, also online, and learned she rented a Jeep using our mother's name and Jackie's middle name. When I located the Jeep, using the very computer I'm using to write this Prologue, my heart sank. The Jeep was on a mountainside of Utah's Wasatch Mountains, just a mile from where our parents disappeared in 2002. I found Jackie four weeks ago today.

The final section of *Wayward* [Chapter 14 of Everywhere] is where *Wayward*'s ending <u>should</u> have ended. It <u>should</u> be the ending Jackson 'Jay' Chad, Candy Murray, Kim Michael, and my sister Jackie Shane deserve. All four <u>deserved</u> to walk away heroically and victorious, as the sun was just about to rise, and as the cabin burned to ashes. It should have…

…fuck…

Remember when I asked you to forgive me in the Prologue? Well…it's with a heavy, painful heart I ask you to remember [Chapter 5 of Underground.] Remember seeing three *** asterisks instead of words? This was not a misprint, nor an error. This was the notch in the story where I was allowed to give *Wayward* the ending it deserved. The ending THEY deserved.

I gave you the fighting spirit of my sister, her tenacity, her back talk, and her fire. I gave her a hero's ending, which… is… WHICH IS WHAT *SHE DESERVED!*

Excuse me for a minute… *(What is seconds to you is 10 minutes of angry tears for me.)*

My apologies…I'm back. This is not easy to tell; it breaks my heart, but you need to know the truth, about many truths:

1. From [Chapter 5 of Underground] to [Chapter 14 of Everywhere] is 95% fiction. It's what my mind believes would have happened if they got away.

2. Jackie Shane did watch Jackson Chad as he walked alone to the creek after they first arrived.

3. The four really had no idea about anything. They thought they had just found an abandoned cabin where a lookout should have been. (Sadly, Thomas Everlast was off by two miles.)

4. Jackie Shane did get caught in a bear trap and fell into the cavern tunnels below through loose soil. Her rifle remained on the front

lawn. Jackie never came back up. She was never rescued. My sister's body was never recovered. (I've tried.)

5. None of the four came back up from the cellar either. Neither did the family.

6. The family was really there. They were in underground tunnels, and the fake tree stump that led underground is/was real, too. (I'll get to the family in a moment…)

7. Jackson didn't find Thomas's skin. Jackie did and watched 'someone' drape it.

8. Jackie really did plant plastique explosive putty on the cabin, with explosive intent, though they never went off.

9. The Grays *are VERY MOTHERFUCKING REAL!*

10. As for Alice and the multiple ghosts in the cabin…well, there's only one way to explain them, and how it is I know so much…

Please, allow me to explain.

The actual cabin faces south. The stone gravel parking area, where Thomas and his friends parked (and where my dad parked the RV), is at the bottom of the mountain hill. To travel up to the cabin along the path, you have to travel north. Jackie was high north, up over the peak, and way behind the cabin. That's where I found her vehicle, then I followed her boot prints.

She really did camp all of her gear at the fake tree stump/tunnel exit, which did (I want to emphasize the word 'did') have a fake top hatch to the underground tunnels that traveled variously inside the mountain. There are plenty of abandoned mining tunnels and excavation digs throughout Utah's mountains. The Wasatch Mountains are no different.

When I arrived, she almost shot me with our father's rifle. She did aim the rifle at me, mistaking me for either one of the cannibal family members, a lone hitcher, or just a stranger, because, let's face it, it had been how many years since we saw one another. Thanks to the internet, and a few pictures I got to see at her now-former home, I knew what she looked like.

When she almost didn't accept who I said I was, I proved it with the nickname my parents gave her: 'Jackie In The Box'. She finally accepted who I was after a few more convincing details. We didn't hug, but she was clearly on edge and panicky. Deep down, she was *partially* glad to see me; just the 'wrong place, wrong time' for me to create a reunion. Whatever she had planned on the mountain, she thought she was alone and planned on keeping it that way.

You wouldn't believe what she had in that jeep of hers! I have no idea where she was able to collect all that military gear (bugs and receivers, electronic wireless earpieces, ammunition, various weapons, explosive gear, etc.) but let me tell you, it couldn't have been legal. Navy friends and special favors, maybe, but she had enough to take down that mountain and an army. It has taken me a few days to go through it all, but… (Sorry, I'm getting ahead of myself.)

After we had a very brief chat, she gave me a small black earpiece to put in my ear and gave me very explicit instructions:

"The earpiece is one-way; I won't be able to hear you. Follow the small creek down the side of the mountain until it comes to a small, rocky cave. Face left and walk straight until you see high grass with tire indentations. Thirty paces past the high grass, you'll find a tree trunk, just a little higher than us in height. It's hollow; climb inside and stay there! Whatever you see, whatever you hear, whatever happens: Do Not

Come Out! Don't Try And Talk To Me; Don't Make A Sound! No one will know you're there, except me. When it's over, I'll come get you."

I had to tell her four times that I understood, and Jackie was correct: I heard everything. I heard her when she ran or breathed heavily, and when she whispered. I heard every gunshot Jackie made with our father's rifle; in the earpiece and out in nature. Not only did I hear everything about Jackie, but Jackie also bugged the cabin as well.

I heard the inside of the cabin, the family's discussion about the pack, and I heard the four's arrival. I heard the sex, the arguments, and I heard the horrible hauntings and ravings of the ghosts. I heard how they were trapped in mirrors that were covered up by cloths, and I heard the hissing, chittering, and snarls of the Grays.

I also heard when Jackie fell into the tunnels below…and I heard everything the family underground did. Not just to my sister, but to all five of them.

I heard them carry Thomas away. I heard his friends run after them. I heard the family snare them as well. I heard…things that will forever make my cowardly heart cry and skin crawl. When the family was 'stocking the pantry', I heard all the blood-curdling work, because Jackie was down there, too. Everything she was near, I heard it all.

I heard all their last words and their last breaths. Jackie was the last of the five.

While trapped, alone, and surrounded by God-knows-what visuals of a massacre, she told me in a barely understandable whisper everything I've ever wanted to know. I think Jackie knew she was at her doom, and she spilled her heart out to me, knowing I could hear it all.

Jackie whispered what happened to our parents while she was in the tree trunk, the very tree trunk she sent me to. She confessed that she did try to find me, multiple times. My running and delinquent behavior made it impossible. Jackie said that everything I was doing, she wished she would have. She masked her entire upbringing as a model citizen and good person, but her heart was a raging wild motley crew of heartbreak, pain, and torment. Her deal with the judge did keep me from prison, but her end of the bargain was to have zero contact with me. One single letter, phone call, or visit, and I'd be in any prison of his choosing that night. She kept her word.

Not one time did Jackie ask me for help, to go get help, or to even rescue her.

I cried so hard inside that tree stump, but I barely made a sound. I muffled my anger, fear, and pain, all hoping Jackie would find a way out and the Grays wouldn't find us. She was such a brave soldier and courageous person! She died…violently…silently…to save…me.

The family under the cabin didn't see Jackie's earpiece until it was her time to be collected. (I wish I could erase all that I heard…) I heard it all…

(I'm sorry. Another minute, please…)

As for the family and the Grays:

I didn't need to hear the Grays through the earpiece; they were all around the mountainside. There were only three of them, but they were everywhere! They sounded like gigantic wolves, as if they were the size of a heavy-duty truck. But, if there was one single thing I heard before the earpiece finally either lost power or lost connection, it was when the Grays found their way underground. It was the hole my sister made when the ground gave way. I heard the family scream for their very lives, and as horrific as it was hearing the mauling they received, I almost cheered through my tears.

Call it cruelty, but I call it justice!

The ONLY one in that family I remotely felt sorry for was the older twin. She despised everything about where they lived, how they lived, and their family's ancestral behaviors. Her opinion was very loud and very clear. (Little shit reminded me of me in foster care…!) Quinton's research included the genealogy of the family, all the way back to the Oregon Trail. I'm not listing their names.

You're asking yourself: "Did I see anything for myself?" "What proof is there?" "Why didn't you do anything more?" "How did you leave?" "How do you live with yourself?" "How could you write such a story?" I've asked myself the same, and I have answers.

"How did you leave?"

I climbed out of the tree trunk when a voice told me to. It was the voice of a little girl, who said, and I quote, "I watched over your sister so long ago, and when it was safe, I told her to run home. Like your sister, I'm telling you: run home."

There was no little girl when I got out, but I did what I was told because I believed her. I believed the voice.

For one, I was in there for a little over twelve hours, and thanks to my sister's instructions…it's embarrassing to admit that I was forced to piss myself. I ran back to the tiny creek, up through the woods, past the fake trunk, took the remaining gear, found Jackie's Jeep, and drove away. The fact that Jackie left the keys in it…I can't explain why.

I didn't drive far. She had a motel key and paid for three days in cash. I had two days left.

The next morning, I drove back to the cabin, but not up the back like Jackie did. I drove to the stone parking area. It had three RVs in it…and a silver SUV. When I saw the RVs, my heart sank, knowing that if Jackie hadn't done what she did, one of them three could have potentially been next.

With some of Jackie's gear, looking like a hiker, I trekked up the hill straight to the cabin. The sun was bright, and the sky was blue. Not a single cloud. It was a sunny day; sunny for my sister's sacrifice. The cabin was there, of course, looking like a rotted decaying tooth amongst the beauty of the mountain.

There were no birds. No animal rustlings. No crickets. Nothing, like being in a bubble.

I found my father's rifle and over twenty set bear traps. I found the truck in the back without keys or a battery. I saw the putty that Jackie slapped on the cabin in several places. Each putty pack had some kind of black pencil-thick thing in each one. (I removed them.) If they were explosives, they would be useless without a detonator. (I've seen 'Die Hard', okay?)

There was no sign of the Grays, but there were plenty of signs that the Grays were there: thick claw marks in the cabin's walls, ground indentations, and actually a single claw that Jackie either shot off or simply broke off. (A souvenir I still have.)

"Why didn't you do anything more?" and/or *"How do you live with yourself?"*

I ask myself these questions every fucking day. I'm curious and defiant by nature, but for some reason, I did the opposite of what every sister usually does: I listened to my older sister and obeyed. And because of that, I'm alive. If I had interfered in any way, I would have become another statistic of a [missing persons] report.

I have done so much wrong in my life, and then I did absolutely nothing with it. I locked down and just…gave up…until I met Quinton. Then, he died helping me. Then, I found Jackie, and she died, to save me. Both of them… equally…gave me my life back and gave me purpose.

Every day I live, I live because of them and for them, which brings us to the hardest question.

"How could you write such a story?"

I love the internet more today than when I was a kid. You would not believe what you can discover, reveal, and report if you do the work. With Quinton's notes, my natural delinquent personality, and my sister's vengeance, I'm using these books to begin to solve all the [missing persons] reports.

The Grays are just part of those answers. The cannibal family was just another part. Somewhere in those mountains are more family ties to that family. I have no fucking doubt that they have answers, too!

My sister deserved a hero's ending, and so did Jackson/Kim/Candy. Sadly, Thomas was taken before [Chapter 5 of Underground] and that's why I've taken things further. It took a lot of nerves, and guts, to walk into that cabin, but I did. I found and collected all of the four's gear and I took it back to their SUV, where I put everything inside. (The RVs were gone.)

Later that day, an anonymous tip called their silver rental in, and they were added to the many [missing persons] reports. It was the beginning of the end of the unsolved [missing persons] reports.

I plan on joining the authority's "investigation", to gather more information, and to contact the families of Jackson Chad, Kim Michael, and Candy Murray. Their families will discover *Wayward* in their mail soon. Whether they believe it or not is not up to me, but any news is better than no news. Also, by the time all my books are all released, that cabin will not exist.

I will see to that <u>personally</u>, but I need help…and that help is where my next book, *Rancor,* will come into play…

— Naomi Shane, **July 8th, 2022**.

13

The snowmobile pack rides on into the woods, following the path that Jared pointed out. The path was tight but not impossible. For those of you who read *Wayward,* you know the uphill path their on.

Their speed never reaches over ten miles per hour, but they never have a single path blockage. The trees are extremely close on either side of the sleds, and several times, Caleb, Rod, & Garrison look backward to see the circular clearing down the mountain getting smaller and smaller. They didn't know just how high they were from sea level.

Several times, Grimm's sled threw snow at Jared's sled, covering Jared & Gene in fresh white powder. Jared's sled did the same to Rod & Garrison's sled. Jonathan caught the most flying snow while taking the caboose position.

Near what they thought was the top, Garrison slaps Rod's shoulder while traveling up the path. Rod leans his head back and shouts, "What!? What is it?!" over the revving engine. Garrison points to his right, and Rod turns his head to see what Garrison is pointing at. All Rod sees is a hollow tree trunk about eight feet high.

"It's Weird!" Garrison shouts. "It's the only hollow trunk, all by itself!" Rod shakes his head as if he didn't care and disregards Garrison's so-called discovery. Garrison doesn't take his eyes off it as they pass it. *Look away, Garrison…look away…!* I say in my head.

Grimm guns the accelerator on his snowmobile so hard, Caleb clings on to Grimm tightly. Jared sees Grimm take off and delays his acceleration, but then punches the gas, too. Rod & Jonathan soon follow in unison, but Jared quickly realizes why Grimm did this. Grimm was

252

coming to a stop and gave Jared room to pull up beside him. Quickly after, Rod parks to Grimm's right; Jonathan takes the far-right position.

"I'll be g-goddamned," is the first thing spoken by more than just the person who spoke it. It was Caleb's words as he shifted his goggles to his chin. With their engines idling, all seven men stare at a snow-covered, dark-wooded log cabin cottage, with a lone-man porch, front steps, and a chimney stack on the right. For the second time, all four snowmobiles are side-by-side. For a moment, they sit motionless.

"You h-have arrived at y-your destination," Gene jokes, mimicking a GPS voice with shivers.

"Um…n-no thanks," Jonathan says sharply, then faces Gene. "I-I'll be camping outside!"

Jared asks rhetorically, "What in the f-fucking hell was Thomas thinking…?", allowing his verbal thoughts to escape his mouth unfiltered. Jared is staring straight at the cabin.

"Can we go inside and get something to eat now? I'm freezing and I'm starving!" Garrison states with quivering lips. Grimm looks coldly at Garrison, and written on Grimm's angry scowl is '*WILL YOU JUST SHUT THE FUCK UP!?*'

But instead, Grimm coolly looks away and verbally says, "The sky's clouding over. Looks like it might snow again." Grimm kills the engine on his sled. "Get your gear; we have work to do." For another moment, no one moves. The sight of the cabin's creepy and odd existence is still a shock to the seven men. None takes their eyes from it.

"It…it's like it doesn't b-belong here," Caleb says loosely. Rod hasn't spoken a word.

[END]

Were you not satisfied with the ending of *Wayward*? Did you feel Jackson, Thomas, Candy, Kim, & Jackie's fate was unfair? Did Alice not help enough? Well, here's your chance with *Naomi Shane's The Cabin* card game! Play as one of the five characters and see if you can give them a safer ending! For 2-to-5 players; escape the horrors of the mountainside cabin!

Visit **https://www.hexagamesohio.weebly.com**

or

Visit The Game Crafter, LLC® today and get your copy!

(Type **Hexagames LLC** in the search bar.)

Designed and created by Hexagames LLC®

Printed in the U.S.A. by The Game Crafter, LLC®

ACKNOWLEDGEMENTS & ABOUT THE AUTHOR

THANK YOU SO MUCH for taking an interest in *Naomi Shane's The Cabin* trilogy, and I hope you enjoyed reading *Wayward*! Like other authors, I depend on reviews from readers such as yourself. Your interests and opinions help turn our literary worlds into realities!

I ask you to please leave your honest review of this book anywhere you choose to leave reviews, and again...***THANK YOU!*** There's more to come...!

J.D. Brown is an indie author who resides in Ohio with his wife, Melissa, and has five children. A forklift operator of almost 30 years and current head writer of Hexabooks™, J.D. completed his first novel, *Bloodday*, in 2004. His other passions include gaming with his kids, outdoor work, and being artistically creative. He's a diehard fan of Stephen King & Jason Voorhees.

Samantha Noseworthy is a freelance editor and avid ARC, Alpha, & Beta reader of many indie authors' works. Splatterpunk is her book genre of choice. With her husband and son, Samantha resides in Massachusetts.

www.ingramcontent.com/pod-product-compliance
Lightning Source LLC
Chambersburg PA
CBHW071638030726
47592CB00005B/1889